THE LEAGUE OF DARK MEN

THE DEPARTMENT Z SERIES

THE LEAGUE OF DARK MEN

DEPARTMENT Z

JOHN CREASEY

OPEN ROAD

INTEGRATED MEDIA

NEW YORK

ISBN: 978-1-5040-9190-9

This edition published in 2024 by Open Road Integrated Media, Inc.
180 Maiden Lane
New York, NY 10038
www.openroadmedia.com

THE LEAGUE OF DARK MEN

1

THE HALL OF BABEL

The police-sergeant beat his arms about his chest until he drew level with the big, ungainly man whose bare head was being brushed by a pennant fluttering in the icy wind. The sergeant looked at the big man's face, which was as bleak as the weather itself on that January morning. He began to walk on.

To his surprise and gratification, the ungainly man glanced at him and smiled. Bleakness faded.

'A bit chilly, sergeant, isn't it?'

'Perishing, sir! I wouldn't be surprised if it snows.'

'Nor would I.' The big man glanced up at the leaden sky. There was no rift visible, just a heavy greyness threatening snow. The wind was piercing. Even the colourful flags and pennants hanging from poles and windows, posts and doorways along the narrow street of tall, Georgian houses, seemed joyless.

'Will it upset things if it does snow, sir?'

'We certainly don't want any until our visitors have arrived.'

'I don't know. The Russians ought to be used to snow, oughtn't they? I'd better get along, sir,' added the sergeant, and went on his way.

William Loftus watched him until he reached the end of the narrow street, where he stopped to talk to three policemen who were standing by a hastily-erected barricade. Three large oil drums, one by each kerb and one in the middle, and two large poles provided an obstacle to any car coming into the street. There was a gap at each pavement, guarded by a policeman.

There was a similar barricade at the far end of the street, also guarded.

Loftus's heavy overcoat kept out the wind, but his cheeks were tinged with blue and the tip of his nose was red. That made him look not only plain but slightly comical.

A man appeared at the top end of the street, showed a card and was allowed to pass. He came walking briskly towards Loftus, shoulders squared, body erect, a man whom the police instinctively saluted.

He stopped by Loftus's side.

'How are things, Bill?'

'Slow,' said Loftus. 'How's the Hall of Babel?'

'Noisy,' said Bruce Hammond. The whole of his upper lip was covered with a close-clipped, thick brown moustache. His eyes were brown and he was dressed in brown. 'They all listened intently enough to the opening speeches, but they're on pins for Virnov.'

Loftus said thoughtfully: 'They're good, these Russians.'

'Yes,' said Hammond, drily. 'They've certainly worked up suspense this session. Practically every nation of the world represented, practically everyone uttering the highest sentiments ever heard from man. Yet some of them are set for a quarrel. Half a dozen are waiting for Virnov as if they would like to tear him to bits. And there's another odd thing.'

'Go on,' said Loftus.

'Russia can either do no wrong or else can do no right,' Hammond laughed. 'You see what kind of a mood the Hall of Babel's induced in me!'

'I get that way myself,' murmured Loftus. 'Question: Who really knows *Uno*?'

'Shocking pun!' rebuked Hammond, and looked about him. 'I see we're all set.'

'Oh, yes,' said Loftus. 'If anything *is* tried this afternoon, I don't think anyone will get away with it. Like old times, isn't it? But for Gordon Craigie, there wouldn't be a Department Z, we'd be merged in Central Intelligence.'

They looked up and down the street.

Casual observers would have noticed little, but there were men at the windows of the houses opposite, who appeared for a moment, then backed away. Others were standing in the porches, half-frozen but with strict orders not to move.

They were members of Department Z, the counterespionage branch of Intelligence which, during the last few months, had found very little to do in England. The trouble centres had shifted around the world, far from London. Loftus, second-in-command of the Department, was thinking of the efforts which his Chief had made to retain a minimum staff at least until after this London meeting of *Uno*.

'They're late,' Hammond said. 'Better move about, or you'll catch cold.'

'I suppose so.' Loftus walked to the end of the street, limping a little, and Hammond slowed his pace, to allow Loftus to keep up. Loftus had lost a leg in the Department's service, and could not take a fully active part in its operations, so worked in the office with Craigie. Hammond was in charge of the outside branch.

A clock struck.

'Quarter past two,' Loftus remarked. 'I hope nothing's happened on the way.'

'I don't think we need worry about that, we would have heard by now,' Hammond said.

They turned and walked towards the other end of the street.

Loftus felt something brush his cheek, and wiped it away. He saw a few flakes of snow, driven by the wind. They settled on the frosted street and houses, like a peppering of cotton wool. Loftus looked up at the leaden sky.

'The wind's too high for it to be much,' Hammond said.

'I hope so,' grunted Loftus.

Hammond was quickly proved wrong. Snow began to fall heavily, and soon the footsteps of the passers-by and the sounds of traffic in Piccadilly were muffled. The white blanket fell with silent finality, covering roofs and roadway, coating the windows of the houses. The air was thick with the driving flakes.

'Pity,' said Hammond. 'I—ah, here they come!'

Two cars had stopped outside the barricade. The police-sergeant, at the end, hurried towards the driver of the first car. He saluted the men sitting at the back, inspected the driver's credentials, and let the car through. Two men clad in heavy coats with huge fur collars sat at the back. Two more sat in the second car, and again the sergeant saluted, examined cards, and waved the driver on.

The cars pulled up outside the house of flags.

The watching men grew tense.

The occupants of the first car got out, helped by men who

hurried from the house, and went inside. Nothing happened. Loftus and Hammond, standing five yards away from them, exchanged glances. Then the fur-coated men from the second car began to get out. They looked cold, in spite of the fur, and one of them spoke in a clear, high-pitched voice, and in Russian. A man from the house answered in the same language as he helped him down. The man slipped on the snow, then regained his balance. Loftus and Hammond stood quite still. If anything were to happen, this was the moment for it.

Tat-tat-tat-tat-tat-tat.

Sharp, clear, menacing, the stutter of a machine-gun broke the flurrying quiet. Another burst: *Tat-tat-tat-tat-tat.* Bullets sprayed the cars, smashed through the toughened glass of the windows, struck the pavement and sent the snow spurting upwards. Some hit the walls of the house and also the man who had just left the car.

He staggered, but did not fall, then rushed towards the house with his companion.

Tat-tat-tat-tat-tat-tat.

The men at the windows and the porches had sprung to life. Dark shapes appeared against the snow, some of them vanishing again in wild snow flurries as the wind became gusty. Loftus and Hammond were staring upwards. The police-sergeant came rushing along the street.

'Was that M. Virnov? Was it?'

'The roof!' Loftus cried, and his voice rose high above all other sounds. 'The roof!' He was still staring upwards, thinking bitterly that there was nothing he could do against a man on the roof; he could not climb up.

One after the other men climbed up, slipping sometimes on a snowy ledge. One man reached a second floor window, then slipped and fell. For a few moments he lay in the snow where he had fallen, then got up, rubbing his leg ruefully. He began to limp away. Loftus reached him.

'That's enough, Mike.'

'I *would* be the muggins,' said the man named Mike, peering upwards. It was just possible to see the roof. 'The family escutcheon's un-blotted, anyhow. There's Mark, up and over. How many men did we have on the roof?'

'Two.'

'They're probably frozen so stiff they can't tell a trigger from a chimney pot,' remarked Mike Errol.

'*He* could,' said Loftus, grimly.

On the roof, Mark Errol, cousin of the injured Mike, was standing against a chimney stack and peering across the ridge. It was a good roof for a grim game of hide-and-seek. The slope from the top was gentle, chimney stacks were dotted everywhere, rooflights protected by little stone cornices seemed on every hand. Over them piled the driving snow. He kept his right hand in his pocket, about the handle of an automatic.

Mark went forward, slithering on the snow. He reached another chimney stack and held on to it for support. He knew that there were two Department Z men up here; Loftus and Hammond had overlooked nothing. But for the snow, catching the man who had used the machine-gun would have been easy.

A dark figure loomed out of the whirling snow. Mark snatched his gun from his pocket. The snow cleared in a gust of wind, and he recognised the red-faced, blue-nosed, rather ugly little man lost in a great overcoat.

'Seen him, George?' Mark called.

George beckoned.

They slithered along, wary, watchful, fully aware that at any moment a burst of machine-gun fire might mow them down.

Another dark figure appeared and was joined by a second, ten yards or so to their left.

'That's Tim,' George said.

'Yes.'

'We'll keep near the edge,' said George. 'The swine might jump for it and break his neck.'

'That wouldn't do,' said Mark.

'Catch 'em all alive-o,' George gurgled.

'Tim' and his companion were keeping pace with them. They had passed from the roof-tops from which the shooting had come; in fact they had traversed the roofs of three houses. Only two more were between them and the end of the street. Somewhere ahead, still silent and hidden by the snow, was the man with the machine-gun.

'If he jumps...' began George.

Tat-tat-tat-tat-tat-tat.

They flung themselves flat, but the bullets did not come their way. As he went down, Mark glanced towards the left. He saw one of the other two men stagger and fall. Bullets smashed slates and sent snow spouting upwards. The man who had been hit began to roll, over and over towards the edge of the roof. His companion, flat on his face, stretched out a hand to try to save him, but failed. The man kept rolling.

He disappeared over the edge, and they heard a dull thud.

Mark and George got up again and moved forward cautiously. The assassin was still on the roof, probably hiding behind a chimney stack. They pressed on, watching the stack for a glimpse of the ugly snout of a sub-machine gun before it spat at them.

It appeared!

Mark and George fired, two shots barked like one. Chippings flew from the chimney stack, the snout of the gun disappeared, only to reappear lower down. Mark flung himself forward, George darted to the left.

Tat-tat-tat...

The burst broke off abruptly. A bullet tugged at Mark's shoe, slates smashed about him, one piece flew up to his face, but he hardly felt it. He reached the chimney stack, knowing that the wanted man was on the other side, he was not a yard away from him, hugging that machine-gun. At point blank range he could not miss, and it would be point blank range. It...

George, out of sight, gave a tremendous bellow.

'Got him!'

There was a clatter as George and their quarry appeared from behind the chimney stack. The machine-gun fell from the assassin's grasp, and slithered noisily to the edge of the roof, then toppled over.

George had a grip on the man's right arm, another on the back of his neck. George was small, but the gunman was powerless. The captive had a thin, gaunt face, his eyes glittered as he tried to struggle but was beaten by that remorseless pressure.

Mark drew level. In his mind's eye was a picture of the man who had rolled over the edge of the roof, and he felt only hatred for this man with the glittering eyes.

George was shouting in a loud voice:

'Bill, we've got him. Send up a ladder!'

Mark, gripping the prisoner tightly, watched his face and read defiance, read also the hatred which the man felt towards him. Here was a fanatic, dangerous and unrepentant. The prisoner was gasping for breath, but as the last note of George's cry faded, he said venomously:

'*I killed Virnov*! Now you will see how united are the nations!'

'Sonny,' said Mark, 'I don't want to hurt you—much.' He raised his hand threateningly, and the man kept silent, but his wild eyes seemed to gloat.

An hour later, Loftus and Hammond stood in the visitor's gallery of the great Conference Hall, looking down on the assembly delegates, the rostrum, the screen with its simple emblem of world unity and world peace, behind the chairman. The chairman was speaking. Loftus and Hammond listened, but hardly heard what he said; but the last word, the name of a man, came clearly enough.

'... Virnov!'

There was a burst of applause. A tall, thin man left the benches where the Russian delegation were sitting, and approached the rostrum. Babel broke out in the great hall. From many delegations the clapping reached a new high level, there was even cheering. Through it all M. Virnov, Deputy Commissar for Foreign Affairs of Moscow, maintained a remarkable composure. He mounted the rostrum and waited. Slowly, the noise subsided. People who had jumped to their feet were sitting down. It was easier for Loftus and Hammond to see into the body of the hall. They noticed that the delegations from several small countries had kept their seats, taking no part in the demonstrative welcome.

Loftus was making notes.

'Run over them for me, will you?' he asked.

Hammond called out the names of the dissenting countries, Loftus checked them on his pencilled list. There were seven.

Someone, perhaps from one of these countries, had hoped to kill Virnov on his arrival in London.

Loftus felt that Department Z had done a fair job in finding a substitute for Virnov, who had been in the building all the time. The stand-in was not dead, and at least they had a prisoner.

2

GORDON CRAIGIE

George, whose full name was George Henry George, looked shrivelled and frozen in spite of his huge coat. He walked briskly along Whitehall until he came to a corner, where he turned right. The snow was now inches deep. The traffic had thinned remarkably. Some cars and buses were fitted with chains, which clanked along. Headlights shone dazzlingly on whiteness. People hurried with their heads down, coats, hats and feet covered.

Everywhere, everything was white.

George reached a little doorway not far from the corner of the street. Many people went past without noticing the spot, but that was not only because of the snow: it was a doorway which few people noticed, because there seemed no reason for it to be there. No steps led up to it, no doorman stood outside.

George turned into it.

He kicked the snow from his shoes, then took off his coat and shook it free before putting it on again and apparently forgetting that his hat was heavy with snow, walked up a flight of narrow stone steps. Others had passed before him; melted snow lay in pools on every step. George went up to the second landing, and paused. Then he walked deliberately up the next flight of steps—and promptly came down again. At the corner, he peered down, but no one was in sight.

George put his fingers beneath the handrail, and stood staring at a wall. He pressed a hidden button.

One moment the wall was blank; the next, part of it slid open. A gust of warm air came out. He looked into a big room in which were four men, including Loftus and Hammond. Immediately in front of him was a large doormat, and he stepped on to this carefully, and wiped his feet.

The sliding door closed noiselessly behind him.

'Howdy, conspirators,' greeted George, beaming about him. 'I now know what the sixth sense is.' When no one responded, he enlarged. 'The sense of caution. Now a careless man would have trodden the floor close to the wall, and any villain following him would know that his quarry had disappeared into a blank wall. Congratulations, everyone—I didn't see a moist spot.'

'Elementary,' Loftus declared.

George looked pained.

'And I thought I was so clever,' he said sadly, and took off his hat. Snow fell on his hands.

'The sixth sense is a sense of caution, and you ought to have shaken your hat,' Loftus said.

'I did shake my coat. And scraped my shoes. See?' George solemnly held out a foot for their inspection. 'Excuse me,' he added, and hurried across the room to a narrow door which opened into a cloak room. He took off his coat and hung it up on a row of pegs where three other coats were hanging. He returned to the room, and beamed at the blazing log fire.

'You don't know what it is to be cold, Gordon,' he said to

an elderly man who was sitting in front of the fire in a winged armchair.

This man's head rested on the back of the chair, and the bowl of a large meerschaum rested in the palm of his hand. He had a lined, rather humorous face, wispy grey hair and a fair complexion. His lips drooped, almost in the shape of the meerschaum.

'I once went out on a winter's day,' he remarked.

'No,' George said, as if in horror. 'I don't believe it. You *never* go out. Bill can venture forth into the horrors of icebound or fog-bound London, but not you. I've never seen you outside these four walls. Well, not often. And when you leave, I swear, you creep out by dead o'night, to spring upon the unwitting villains and to smite them down. Am I talking too much?'

Mark Errol, the fifth man in the room, said quietly:

'You certainly are. Will our assassin? If he doesn't, once his friends know he didn't get Virnov, there will be another attempt.'

'Bad,' George said.

No one else spoke, because for the moment there was nothing to say. Even George's high spirits were damped by the mood. He sat on the arm of a chair, and lit a cigarette. Almost with a sense of strain, he said:

'Nice place you've got here.'

In fact, the room was remarkable.

The end near the fire was furnished as an ordinary sitting-room, with easy chairs, occasional tables, a small bookcase, a row of shelves where more books reclined lazily, none quite upright. The oak mantelpiece was heavily carved. There was a row of little glass buttons along the centre of it, and beneath them a row of bell-pushes; they were the only unusual things one could see at that end of the room—unless one looked into the cupboard, the door of which was ajar. The inside of that cupboard was certainly unusual. Never, in one cupboard, had there been such a miscellany of oddments. Once, no doubt, each shelf had been reserved for a particular thing, for food perhaps, or for tobacco and smoking requisites, another for spare shirts and collars and ties; and the bottom shelf, undoubtedly, had been reserved for boots and shoes and brushes and pans. Now nothing appeared to be in the right place. Packets of food, some opened, some new, jars and bottles, ties and handkerchiefs, stood cheek-by-jowl. It was the only untidy thing about Gordon Craigie, and his close friends believed that he refused to tidy it now, because it had become traditional.

The other half of the room presented a startling contrast.

Even that blazing fire could not soften its cold austerity. There were two large desks, a host of telephones, some filing cabinets and a dictaphone, as well as some tubular steel chairs. The furniture was all of steel, painted pale green in contrast to the light oak panels of the walls.

Loftus sneezed and grabbed for a handkerchief.

'Open cupboard door, first shelf, round the corner to the right,' said George, getting up. He went nearer to the fire and warmed his hands. 'When I was a little boy...'

'*When?*' echoed Mark Errol.

'I know it isn't so long ago,' George said. 'But we were all little boys once. Even our chief. Weren't you, Gordon? Or did you just come? Someone waved a wand perhaps, and this room was created, someone else said *abracadabra* and in you popped. Same lined Red Indian face, same frightful pipe, hair neither thick nor thin. After all,' he added, looking at the little glass buttons and bell-pushes, 'no one but a magician would have thought of *those*. Sliding panels and secret doors in the sacrosanct precincts of Whitehall—sheer melodrama.'

Hammond remarked: 'They work.'

'Oh, I like 'em. That's what I was about to say. When I was a little boy, I dreamed of secret tunnels, priests' holes and sliding doors and things.' He threw his cigarette into the fire. 'Thanks for letting me thaw out. I can now be sensible.'

'Without granting that,' said Hammond, 'what's new?'

'Not much, I fear. George Henry George wasn't the right man for the job, perhaps. I talked to the killer. His conversation, even under persuasion, is limited. He does not like Russia. He thinks evil things of Russia. That's the lot. He talks English fairly well but rather stiltedly. It wouldn't really surprise me if he's White Russian. Or he could be Trotskyist, both hate the Kremlin today.'

'It's too easy,' said Craigie.

'Complexity so often springs from the mind. Stop me if I burble. I jollied him for an hour. Dusty Miller gave me moral support with deep voice and threatening gesture. It all came back to the same thing. Lips turned back and teeth set in the good old-fashioned snarl. Hate Russia, hate Russia. He wanted to kill Virnov, and still thinks he has succeeded. Miller had a go at him, solo. Routine fashion, you've got to admire it. It ran something like this: Your name is Leo Kolsti. *Yes.* You climbed to the roof of the house last night, and spent the night in an attic which you reached through a rooflight. *Yes.* You carried with you a Thompson sub-machine gun. *Yes.* Where did you get the gun? *Silence.* Thunderously: Where did you get the gun? *Silence.* Miller kept it up like that for half an hour or more,' went on George. 'The fellow admitted that he had been there all night, that he had the gun, that his intention was to shoot Virnov, that he knew—or thought he knew—that Virnov would land at Heath Row about two o'clock and be at Oslam House about three. But where he got the gun, whether he worked for someone else, how he got his information—on these he was dumb.'

'Thing is, what do we do if he stays dumb?' asked Hammond.

'We'll have to try scopolamine,' said Loftus.

'The truth drug isn't infallible,' Hammond remarked.

All of them looked at Craigie.

For many years Craigie had been used to receiving masses of information, sifting it, picking out what was relevant, and saying what it was. All of these men had come to expect him to answer questions for which they had no answer. Only Loftus and Hammond, the Errols and the few remaining agents who had been with the Department for many years understood the patient labour and painstaking zeal with which Craigie worked.

He stretched out a hand for a jar of tobacco, took another meerschaum from a rack which held half a dozen, and began to fill it. He gave no sign that he realised they were watching him so expectantly.

Craigie was recalling the circumstances which had led up to an attempt on 'Virnov'.

Immediately it had been known that assassination might be attempted, Craigie had seen some Foreign Office officials, and learned that the Deputy Commissar was to spend one night in Copenhagen before coming on to London. Told of the likelihood of an attempt on his life, Virnov had agreed to come straight to London, but to keep out of the public eye until he was due to speak at *Uno*.

Two Department Z agents had impersonated him, flying first to Paris and then from Paris to Heath Row. The likeness between one of them and Virnov, after due application of make-up by an expert, had been enough to deceive most people, especially at a distance. Two other Department men had met 'Virnov' at Heath Row, and brought him to Oslam House, where the delegates from Moscow were being entertained.

And Leo Kolsti, hugging his machine-gun, had waited until the false Virnov's arrival, and fired.

Kolsti did not know that Department Z carried melodrama to a fine art. Its agents had worn steel-mesh shirts, only one of them had been slightly wounded.

Craigie had first heard the rumour that the attempt was planned from a White Polish secret agent who was working in Paris. No one knew how he had got the information; no one was ever likely to know now. The Pole had given the information to an English agent, and a meeting had been arranged to discuss details, but the Pole had not kept the appointment. The following day his body had been washed up on the banks of the Seine, near *Notre Dame*. He had given no information beyond the bare details—Virnov was to be attacked.

At last Craigie took his pipe from his lips.

'I don't yet know what we shall do,' he announced.

George widened his great eyes. 'Oh dear,' he said, inanely; 'The master fails us. So everything depends on Kolsti.'

'Too much does,' admitted Craigie.

'Bill had better have a go at him in the morning,' George said. 'He's by far the most terrifying of the lot of us. Er—no new line through Paris and the Polish fellow, I suppose?'

'We're doing what we can about that,' said Craigie, 'but there's nothing known yet. The Pole had his credentials. The Poles in the Conference Room seemed glad enough when Virnov appeared, didn't they?'

'Yes,' said Loftus.

'Did you see any indication of hostility?' Craigie asked.

'No, but after all, guilty men would be careful. There were poker faces, icy reception and evident dislike from some. All were small-country delegations. If I had had to pick one as showing more hostility than the others, it was the Shovian party. There was a tall, grey-bearded man whom I did mark down. Who is he?'

'Pirani,' Craigie said. 'His reputation's good.'

'Well,' said George, 'if he had toothache, it might make him look vicious. I know. Polly's had it for three days.' He grinned. 'How many beavers at *Uno*?' They looked at him curiously, Mark Errol's expression showing impatience, for George behaved as if he were the Court Jester and there were times when Mark was a little more sober than the others.

'Beavers?' echoed Hammond, smoothing his moustache.

George beamed. 'When I was a little boy, we used...'

'You've been a little boy quite often enough today,' Mark said.

'Just once more,' pleaded George. 'We used to play beavers. On top of a bus, two or three giggling infants. A beaver was a man with a beard. Whoever saw him first and dared to say "beaver" scored a mark. Roars of childish laughter and a wild rush for the stairs. The very daring, spotting one, could score two marks by pulling at the beard.' George was grinning inanely, now, but the others showed greater interest. 'And if, as never happened in my experience, a beard proved *false*—ten points, all at one go. Pirani is a beaver, you say?'

'Go on,' said Craigie.

'I mean, he's got a good reputation. But who knows him well in England? Only his own fellow delegates, presumably. How many are there?'

'Two others,' Craigie told him.

'Two *could* be a party to a racket,' George observed. 'As Mark has been so careful to point out, the eternal boy lurks in me. I wouldn't mind playing beaver with Pirani, and trying to score ten points. If the beard *did* come off...' he paused, and looked hopefully at Craigie. 'May I?'

Craigie smiled. 'We'll have to do some spade-work first, but if the beard has to be singed, you can singe it.'

'Eternal thanks,' said George.

'It's worth checking,' Loftus agreed. 'But we want another angle, and it's got to be through Kolsti.'

'Hal-*lo*!' exclaimed George. 'The great man has been doing some brainwork. It's a marvel to me how it ticks over so regularly, Bill. Disgorge.'

Loftus was now the centre of attention, and he laughed somewhat ruefully.

'It's an old, old trick,' he said, 'but when we're so empty of ideas as we are now, an old one might be worth trying. We could let Kolsti go,' he declared, 'and watch him closely. Later, we could pull him in again and try him with scopolamine.'

3

KOLSTI'S GOODBYE

No one scoffed at the suggestion. It was agreed next that the following morning Loftus should question Kolsti, try to get the information, and then take him from Cannon Row Police Station, where he was now in custody. In the street, Loftus would be careless. Agents would be watching, on foot, in cars and in taxis, to follow Kolsti wherever he went.

'Anything else, Gordon?' asked George.

'I don't think so,' said Craigie. 'You go and rest. Office work isn't your long suit. You'd better get some sleep, Mark, too.' He paused. 'Did Mike do much damage to his ankle?'

'Only wrenched it,' Mark answered. 'He'll be all right in a day or two.' He got up. 'What time will you want us again?'

'About midnight,' Craigie told him.

'What's all this?' asked George.

'Action stations,' said Craigie.

George and Mark went for their coats and hats as Craigie leaned forward and pressed one of the buttons. The door slid open. The two men went out, and walked quietly down the stairs. At the foot, a gust of wind struck them, and made

George cannon into Mark. With the wind came swirling snow. There was magic in Whitehall, the magic of white crystals falling and piling up one upon the others, lit brilliantly by the street lights.

'Arctic welcome for Virnov,' murmured George. 'Two ways.'

'I wonder if they will have another shot at him.'

'Bound to. Who's watching him?'

Mark grimaced. 'He's brought his own bodyguard, and there is a gang of Miller's men on duty. We're not due for the silent watches of the night.'

'What are we likely to be wanted for?' asked George.

'Your guess is as good as mine.'

They had not far to walk, however, for both lived in Brook Street, only a few doors from each other. In Mark's flat Mike and his wife would be waiting; and in George's, his wife, Polly. They reached Brook Street, and parted, and George shook the snow off his hat and coat and hurried upstairs.

The door of his flat opened, and a rather anxious-looking, buxom girl appeared on the threshold.

'Is that you, darling?'

'Your ownest own!' declared George, springing forward and hugging her. 'What's Pretty Polly getting worked up about? I've never been lost in the snow yet!'

'Idiot,' said Polly George. 'Darling, you look frozen!'

'Frozen I may look, but it's starved that I am,' declared George, and sniffed. 'It smells good.'

'Just frying onions,' said Polly.

They entered the living-room. In front of a bright coal fire were George's slippers. He squeezed Polly's waist and kissed the nape of her neck.

'I don't deserve it,' he said. 'How long before dinner?'

'Ten minutes,' said Polly. She took his damp shoes to the

kitchen, where the maid was cooking the evening meal. George lit a cigarette and leaned back. A smile not far removed from fatuous was on his face. It was a plain but expressive face; when his eyes were closed it looked extremely ugly, but Polly, coming back from the kitchen, looked upon it with much affection.

George opened one eye.

'Did anything happen?' Polly asked.

'Oh, *every*thing. But the great man is all right. Triumph for D.Z again.' He glanced at the kitchen door, but Polly had closed it. He leaned forward, stretching his hands out towards the fire. 'Really worried, darling?'

'I suppose I am,' said Polly.

She looked more than pretty, with the firelight dancing on her clear blue eyes. There was a healthy, wholesome quality about Polly, who was always worried about her figure, but in all things was extremely difficult to deceive. George made no attempt to deceive her about the seriousness of the task which faced the Department.

They had met at the beginning of such an affair as this, and fallen in love. Polly had become one of the few women actively engaged in Department Z. She did not pretend to enjoy the danger, but accepted and faced it.

'It might fizzle out,' George said. 'We can hope.'

'Do *you* hope so?'

He laughed. 'I do, my poppet! The last thing I want is trouble for *Uno*. I don't particularly want trouble for myself, either. Don't take it to heart, sweet.'

'I'm not the only one who's taking it to heart,' said Polly. 'Christine Loftus has been in this afternoon.'

'Oh,' said George.

'George, didn't Gordon once *refuse* to employ married men?'

'In the happy days before the war, yes.'

'There isn't a war on now.'

George looked at her owlishly. 'Just a cold war hotting up,' he said.

Christine Loftus was in bed long before Loftus reached their flat, in Jermyn Street. He tiptoed about the bedroom, in the hope that he would not wake her, and saw her eyes open.

'Insomnia?' he asked.

'No,' said Christine.

She was very lovely. Her fair hair was tucked into a gossamer thin net, and she looked beautiful lying back on the pillows, one arm over the bedspread. There was the gentle hiss of a gas fire, and the room was pleasantly warm. Loftus put on his dressing-gown and went to brush his teeth. He did not find it hard to guess what his wife was thinking, nor that Polly George and the wives of the other Department Z men were thinking much the same. At heart they resented the sudden impact of danger. Yet, Loftus knew, Christine would never ask him to stop working; nor would the others.

He went back to the bedroom and sat on his bed. He could see a red scar on her right shoulder, where her nightdress fell to one side, it was of a bullet wound which she had received in the course of the case in which George met his Polly.

Christine edged to the side of the bed.

Loftus put an arm about her. 'That's my baby,' he said.

'Bill, how serious is it?'

'We don't yet know,' Loftus told her. 'We're divided between plumping for a wild man with a bee in his bonnet and an organisation planning to smash *Uno*.'

'What do *you* believe?'

'I don't think he's just a wild man,' said Loftus. 'There's a lot of discord, economic and military. Malaysia and Indonesia, India and Pakistan, the U.S.A. and Cuba, little places such as Cyprus...'

'Don't!' Christine actually shuddered.

'I know, the nice way to deal with facts is to blink at them,' Loftus said. 'But with Moscow, Whitehall and Washington getting closer together, someone might want to throw in a hefty spanner. Pekin, for instance, or possibly closer at home. If there's only a chance in a million of it happening, we'd have to snuff out that chance.'

'It *had* to happen when *Uno* has a session in England,' Christine complained.

'The danger spot might shift, you know. And we're confined to work in England. No sudden trips abroad—that's up to the other departments. I shouldn't worry too much.'

Christine fell silent.

Loftus thought of the work which he, Craigie and Hammond had just finished. They had been through the dossiers; as far as was known, of all the delegates at *Uno*. There was no large delegation from any country, but with the secretariats, over five hundred people were concerned. They had marked off all who were wholly reliable, finally coming down to eight states where the delegates *might* be bribable. That was one more than the number of delegations which had shown a lack of enthusiasm for Virnov, the mystery man of Russia, freely tipped by many 'authorities' as the next Premier. The people who concerned Loftus immediately were the delegates from the smaller, unreliable nations, many of them new, or under new regimes. The more he considered the problem, the more he thought that Pirani, of Shovia, had come nearest to showing open hostility.

Was there a possibility that the real Pirani was being impersonated at the Conference?

'You ought to go to sleep,' Christine said.

'Believe it or not,' said Loftus wickedly, 'I don't feel a bit like sleep.'

In his flat, Mark Errol told Mike what had happened, and commiserated with his cousin because he would be off duty for a while. Mike's wife seemed delighted.

Not one of the agents of Department Z spoke of the agent who had been shot and had fallen off the roof. Afterwards, he had been picked up dead.

None of them had any doubt about the gravity of the situation.

At midnight exactly, they were called out. So were a dozen other agents. They began the search for people with whom Kolsti had associated. The police had picked up some information. Kolsti had rented a room in a Bloomsbury boarding house, and had taken all his meals in a nearby café. He was a naturalised Englishman, who had come from Poland as a boy. He had few friends but many acquaintances. Throughout the night these acquaintances were awakened and questioned, but none gave any information.

There must *be* accomplices, George had reasoned as he made his way home on the bitterly cold night. The man could not have guessed when Virnov would arrive; someone had told him.

Sighing, George pulled back the curtains at his bedroom window, let in the grey light of dawn, and crept into the snug warmth of the double bed; Polly just stirred.

* * *

At ten o'clock next morning, Loftus was admitted into a small room at Cannon Row Police Station by a sergeant who seemed to enjoy jingling his keys. With Loftus was a big, fleshy man with a pale face and pale hair, a man who looked as if he had been working in a flour mill. He wore a light grey suit, which helped the illusion. At first sight his full face, heavy jowl and half-closed eyes suggested dullness. This was Superintendent Miller, liaison officer between Scotland Yard and Department Z. Loftus had never known him make a false move.

Kolsti was sitting in a small armchair.

The room had a barred door but was otherwise unlike a cell. It was plainly furnished, with a single bed, a chair, and a hand-basin. The bed was made. Kolsti was unshaven. His eyes were bloodshot, but still sparked. His dark hair was cut very short, although it had not been clipped at Cannon Row. His long, thin face with the pointed chin and high-bridged nose was sensitive.

He stood up, looking small against Loftus and Miller.

'Good morning,' said Loftus.

Kolsti did not speak or move.

'We've been very patient with you so far, Kolsti,' Loftus said. 'We won't be if you don't talk.' He had a newspaper tucked under his arm, and he unfolded this slowly, so deliberately that Kolsti stared at it.

Loftus went on talking.

'I'm not a policeman, and I mean to make you talk. You will get hurt. A lot.' He continued to unfold the paper, and then turned it, so that Kolsti could read the banner headline.

VIRNOV'S CALL FOR WORLD DISARMAMENT.

Kolsti's lips opened. He dropped into his chair, looking as if he had been struck a crushing physical blow, as if this were a horror which he had not conceived possible.

Loftus began to read:

'*M. Virnov, Soviet Deputy Commissar for Foreign Affairs, made an impassioned appeal for disarmament to the delegates at Uno in the Great Hall yesterday afternoon. Arriving by air from Russia, the Deputy Commissar drove straight to the hall and his personal appearance was the signal for a great demonstration. In the course of his speech...*'

Kolsti snatched the paper away, screwed it up and flung it into a corner. He was gasping for breath, his hands were working, he could not keep still.

'It is not true, it is a lie, a lie, a lie!'

'You did not shoot Virnov,' Loftus remarked casually.

'With my own eyes I saw him, I saw him fall!'

'You didn't see Virnov,' Loftus said. 'We knew that the attack was going to be made. Virnov had been in the country for twenty-four hours. He was told of what was going to happen, and allowed another man to take his place.'

'You are—*lying* to me!'

'We aren't fools, Kolsti. We know what is going on, we know what plans are being made. You shot at a man who was not Virnov, and you didn't murder even him. A few years in prison for your part in the plot, that's the most you have to fear. That is, if you talk.'

Kolsti stood up, turned slowly away from him, went to the corner and picked up the newspaper. His hands were trembling as he smoothed it out. Loftus let him finish reading, watching closely.

Kolsti dropped the paper.

'We know where your Paris headquarters are,' Loftus went on. He saw Kolsti's eyes narrow in alarm; the man was now fighting to regain his composure. 'We shall soon know where the London headquarters are. But you can help us to find them more quickly, and to save lives. That's all you can do.'

'*No* one can find them!' Kolsti cried.

He stopped, abruptly. Perhaps he realised what he had done; perhaps the narrowing of Loftus's eyes had warned him that he had admitted that there were accomplices. His lips tightened. He clutched at a chair. He did not say another word.

Loftus tried blandishments, then harshness, followed by threats, but nothing had any effect on the prisoner. At the end of an hour Loftus himself was feeling limp and Kolsti seemed to have shrunk.

Loftus turned to Miller.

'I'll take him where I can rough him up,' he said.

Kolsti did not flinch; he seemed not to have heard the threat. He followed Loftus, and Miller brought up the rear. He stepped into the courtyard of the police station, and stared blankly towards the snow-decked edifice of Scotland Yard. Policemen on duty at the gates regarded the three men curiously. Mark Errol and George were in sight, and there were others of the Department, some on the Embankment and some in Whitehall, most of them hidden but watching closely.

The snow had stopped. Great piles were at the kerbs, only the centre of the road was clear. The pavement was slippery and dangerous, and Loftus walked with great care towards Whitehall. Kolsti did not look right or left, and certainly did not look like a man who would seize any chance of escape. He walked dully, apparently unaware of Loftus's light grip on his arm.

Traffic was moving along Whitehall, all the cars with

chains. Buses lumbered by, crunching through the snow when they drew near to the pavement.

Suddenly Kolsti tugged his arm away from Loftus, sprang to the top of a mound of snow, and ran. He ran neither right nor left along the road but *into* the road.

A bus was coming; the driver could not stop in time.

4

DELAYING ACTION?

Craigie looked through report after report, all from the agents who had been at work during the night, talking to Kolsti's acquaintances. Nothing offered any help. He passed them over to Loftus to check.

The big man sat at his desk, smoking a pipe, seldom looking up. He was still suffering from the shock of Kolsti's suicide. He realised now that he should have been prepared for the move, but he had been so intent on following up an escape that the simple solution to Kolsti's troubles had not occurred to him.

He finished his check, and straightened up.

'I can't see a thing. Are all the reports in yet?'

'Tim Kemble telephoned at half-past six, and said he thought he had spotted a hare, and would chase it. He's to come through by three o'clock, whether he's found anything or not.'

'Tim's rather fond of hares,' Loftus reflected.

'We trained him to look for them,' Craigie said, drily. 'What's the latest from the *Uno* session?'

'They're like doves in a dovecote.'

'Which makes it more than every necessary to keep the spanners out of the works.'

'What's the reaction from Number 10?' asked Loftus.

'Hadley doesn't let himself go so freely as Hershall did,' said Craigie. 'I haven't heard from him since he telephoned to tell us to go ahead. With one thing and another, he's got his hands full.'

Loftus said: 'I have wondered whether he's as keen about us as Hershall was. There was that touch of buccaneer about Hershall which made us appeal to him, but...'

'I shouldn't worry. Hadley's was the final word on whether we should close down or not, and we're still open. I...' Craigie broke off, for a telephone bell rang. As he stretched out his hand to lift a receiver, a pink light glowed in one of the many instruments. 'Talk of the Prime Minister!' he said, 'and here he is.'

'I should like to come and see you, Craigie,' Hadley said. 'Can you spare me half an hour?'

'Of course, sir.'

'Then I will come over at once,' said Hadley.

Craigie put down the receiver.

'Hershall would have crashed in, Hadley wonders if I can spare him half an hour! That sums up the difference between them. I wonder if he remembers how to get in? He's only been here once before.'

'I'll go down,' offered Loftus.

He let himself out by pressing the control button. As he went downstairs, the door closing silently behind him, an icy blast from the street swept up. At the street he paused and looked towards the left. Downing Street was just out of sight, but he could see a man crossing the road from that direction; a short, rather slender man. Behind him were two Special

Branch officers. The Prime Minister had on a big overcoat, and walked firmly.

Loftus went to greet him, and he gave a further grave smile.

'Hallo, Loftus. Nice to see you again.'

'Thank you, sir.'

'And I have to thank you for the way yesterday's nasty affair was handled,' said Hadley. He had never taken long to get to the point. 'You took a load off a lot of shoulders.' And put another on when I let Kolsti kill himself, thought Loftus. Hadley led the way up the stairs, and the detectives waited outside. On the landing, he ran his hand over the rail; so he remembered.

Craigie came forward to welcome him.

'I'll take your coat,' said Loftus.

'Thanks.' Hadley shrugged himself out of the coat, and warmed his hands in front of the fire. 'I'd like to know how the situation is developing. I've heard of Kolsti's suicide, of course.'

He sat down rather stiffly at first, accepted a cigarette and settled back. Craigie told him exactly what had happened, what steps they were taking, what casualties they had met, and how slender were their hopes. He reported on the suspect seven delegations, and the possibility of trouble from any one of them.

'We are all worried about that,' Hadley said. 'There are several unknown delegates, all newly appointed. The other Shovian delegates with Pirani are new, as you probably know. There are real possibilities of treachery.'

'What made you mention Shovia?' asked Craigie.

'Pirani has been acting rather strangely,' Hadley said. 'He is hardly the same man who came to the earlier session. He's lost much of his fire, contributes little to the debates and keeps himself to himself.' Hadley broke off.

Craigie told him of George's suspicion that Pirani might not be genuine. Hadley nodded, and was silent for a few minutes. He was continually twisting a plain gold ring round his little finger, as if he found some solace from it.

'The chief danger comes, perhaps, from the possibility of underrating it, I suppose. There are difficulties enough with *Uno* without such an attempt as this to spread discord. Had Virnov been hurt, there would have been very grave repercussions.' He went on deliberately: 'Not only in Moscow, where they would have been outraged had we allowed it to happen. But the assassination itself would have caused less trouble than the suspicion that it was an attempt to prevent any agreement on disarmament—in fact to undo the good done by Mr. Kennedy, and since his death. There are undercurrents of suspicions and of racial enmity, all much nearer the surface than they have been for years. The Conference is *not* single-minded. General conditions are partly responsible, but is that why delegations from some of the newly independent nations are being difficult on matters of procedure? The impression I have...' he paused again, as if to consider his words carefully, then continued with equal deliberation—'is that an attempt is being made to delay progress. The Conference is due to last for another week, but it is already a day behind on the agenda. Any sensational interference might make Russia and possibly other nations walk out. Nothing would be worse. You see that, of course.'

'Only too well,' said Craigie.

'Have you any indications that there is any attempt to slow down the debates?' asked Hadley.

'Not yet,' said Craigie. 'We've told you everything we know.

I've a man following a trail which led from Kolsti. He should telephone me during the next quarter of an hour.'

'I'll wait,' said Hadley.

The interruption came not from the telephone but from the door. A green light showed in the mantelpiece, and Craigie leaned forward and pressed a button. Outside the Department only Miller, Hadley and half a dozen other trusted men knew how to switch on that green light.

George George came bustling in.

'Hallo, hallo!' he said, and glanced at Hadley's head, the top of which appeared just above an armchair. He waved a newspaper and cried: 'I spy "strangers". New recruit? I don't recognise that particular bald patch.'

Loftus waved at him, but George Henry George preferred not to take heed.

'Whoever it is, this will startle him.' He waved the newspaper again; it was an *Evening Cry*. 'Shades of the censor and the M.O.I.! The whole story!' He walked round the chair, stretched out his hand and took from Hadley's ear a cigarette. 'Cigarette?' he asked, blandly—and then recognised the visitor.

He stood stock still, and gulped, twice. Slowly, he lowered the cigarette. Next he shot a glance of infinite reproach at Loftus and Craigie.

'That,' he declared, 'was my foot, going right in. I'm sorry, sir.'

Hadley smiled, and stretched up for the cigarette.

'Where do you get the light from?' he asked.

'I produce that in the conventional fashion,' said George. He took out a lighter. 'Kind friends are always warning me that I'll make a fool of myself one day. The truth is, I'm excited. There is the headline story for one thing, and a five-line par which worked on my risible faculties for another. Have you seen the *Cry*, sir?'

36

'No.'

'Steel yourself for a shock,' warned George, who was never in low spirits for long.

Craigie handed Hadley the paper, and he and Loftus read it over the Prime Minister's shoulder. George had warned them what to expect, but seeing it in black and white reduced them to silence. There was a great headline across the page: ATTEMPTED ASSASSINATION OF M. VIRNOV. There followed a garbled story, close enough to the truth to hurt. Obviously much of it had been supplied by an eye-witness. Then the editor had let himself go.

'What will they think in Moscow if such a vile attempt to kill one of the most influential delegates is hushed up? Is secrecy not an inducement to further fears, suspicions and distrust? Is the evil of censorship to fall upon us again? For the sake of future relations with the U.S.S.R. we demand the full story from Whitehall.'

When they had finished reading, George said brightly:

'Not a bad bit of purple, that. After all, why shouldn't the *Cry* demand this and that? I'm more pepped up by the five-line paragraph. Same page, fourth column, just beneath the cartoon about the plumber's mate.' He pointed, and Hadley read aloud that Senor Pirani, the chief delegate from Shovia, was shortly to hold a reception at the Shovian Embassy, where two famous members of the Massino family of illusionists would perform; for S. Pirani, it said, had a fondness for magic.

Hadley looked puzzled.

'I don't see the significance of that.'

George leaned forward, and produced a half-crown from Hadley's knee. 'I'm not exactly a blood brother of the Massinos but I do hold my certificates of competence and all that kind of thing. Performed before Royalty, Dukes and Duchesses and—oh, confound it!' he added, in self-disgust, 'why *can't* I keep quiet?'

Loftus said thoughtfully: 'You could take the place of one of the Massinos. Is that the idea?'

'Bang on the nose. Get a proper close up. See the Senor when His Excellency is all tuckered up and waiting to be awestruck. I could even have a hearty tug at his beard.'

Craigie looked at Hadley. 'Have you any objection, sir?'

'I have no objection of any kind to anything you think might help.'

'Shall we forget about your sleight of hand for a moment.' There was a note in Craigie's voice which surprised the others. He tapped the headline. 'This is much more important than anything else. Who gave the *Cry* that story? Who embroidered it with eye-witness accounts? It's obviously possible that this is part of the attempt to split *Uno* right down the middle. Not a word was said to the Press, all the police on duty were worn to secrecy, yet...'

Loftus was already on his feet.

'Come on, George,' he said. 'We're going to see an Editor.'

When they had gone, the office was quiet for a few minutes, and Hadley seemed content to sit there, his eyes half-closed against the heat of the fire.

Craigie could imagine his thoughts; fear that the cold war, which had so nearly thawed, could become as bad as ever. If it did then there could be disaster for a dozen countries, and the awful threat of a nuclear war would be much nearer.

The telephone rang.

Hadley looked towards it, and got up. 'I must go.' He watched Craigie walk towards the desk and pick up a telephone with a white disc glowing. The call was local, not on any special line.

A man with a deep, pleasant voice said:

'Is that Craigie? This is E L B M...'

'Carry on, Kemble,' said Craigie.

There was an eager note in Kemble's voice.

'Sorry I'm late,' he said, 'but it's not without cause. The hare, I think, is a big bad wolf.'

'Have you really got something?' Craigie pointed to another telephone, and Hadley picked it up, in time to hear Kemble say:

'I found a man who came from France yesterday morning, at least he says it was yesterday morning. He was in Paris the morning before yesterday. I think we'll find that he spent most of the evening before with Kolsti. Kolsti went straight from him to Oslam House, I got the dope from a porter. Hopeful?'

'*Very*,' said Craigie.

'I need help,' said Kemble. 'There are two or three people concerned. Are you ready to take notes?'

Craigie had paper in front of him and a pencil in his hand.

'My man's name is Parmitter. Middle-aged, fairly wealthy, concerned with iron and steel—top salesman type. He covers France and other parts of Europe for *Super-Steel*. He had permission to go to Paris at the beginning of last week. When I asked him when he came back, he hedged nervously. With him are two other men whose names I don't yet know, and a girl.'

'What's her name?' asked Craigie.

There was a chuckle in Kemble's voice. 'Clarissa,' he said. 'It's got a nice ring about it. Clarissa Kaye.'

'What is she doing with the others?'

'Working, I think. Secretary. There are all the signs of a meeting of conspirators at the Haymart Hotel. Curious fact, that's where the San Patino delegation is staying. I'm speaking from a telephone booth near the hall, but I'm anxious to get back upstairs. None of our other chaps had better recognise me in public, by the way. I'm making remarkable progress with Clarissa.'

'I'll have someone over in ten minutes,' Craigie said. 'This looks the thing we've been waiting for.'

'Always glad to help,' said Kemble. 'Oh, I don't think I would be too heavy-handed with Parmitter yet. He's quite a man of steel. He thinks a lot of himself, and the other two men do the kow-towing. I told him I was from the *Gazette*—you know the Editor well enough to see me through, don't you?'

'Yes.' Craigie stretched out his hand for another telephone, and began to dial.

'Thanks. I told Parmitter we'd heard a rumour that he had done a great deal in Paris for *Super-Steel*. He hasn't committed himself. As a matter of fact,' went on Kemble, 'he doesn't quite know what line to take with me. He doesn't want to upset the Press, but would like to kick me out. He might be talking to the *Gazette* at any minute—I know he isn't doing so just yet, there was a little accident to his telephone. An engineer's up here putting it right now.'

'Off you go,' said Craigie.

As Kemble said: 'Cheerio!' Bruce Hammond spoke on the other telephone.

'The Haymart Hotel, Bruce, to keep an eye on Parmitter of *Super-Steel* and the people with him,' Craigie said crisply. 'The only other name we've got is Clarissa Kaye. Tim is there, as a *Gazette* reporter, not as one of us. Just watch them for the time being. Take two men with you.'

'Right,' said Hammond. 'Aren't the San Patino crowd staying there?'

'Yes,' said Craigie.

He replaced the receiver and looked up, to find Hadley smiling with that rather shy expression; there was a hint of admiration in the Prime Minister's eyes. Craigie made a few rapid notes in a shorthand of his own invention, and pushed the writing-pad away.

'It may lead nowhere,' he pointed out.

'I find you and your men fascinating,' Hadley remarked. 'This over-hearty boisterousness...'

'Just a defensive shield,' Craigie said. 'An affectation of facetiousness which comes almost naturally. They developed it quite soon in Department service, and it's become...'

'Traditional?'

'I suppose that's the word,' said Craigie. 'Hammond is less hearty than most, Loftus has quietened down a bit.' He spread out his hands. 'I don't often talk about them,' he went on, 'but they are a remarkable group of men. I sometimes wonder if we realise how much we owe to them. Loftus and the Errols, Hammond and many others have been doing this work for over twenty years. Much of the time they are in acute physical danger.'

'I don't think they are under-estimated,' Hadley assured him. 'Certainly not by me. I really must go.' Craigie pressed the bell-push and the door slid open. 'Will you let me know as soon as you hear anything more from Hammond?' asked Hadley.

'The moment I hear,' Craigie assured him.

Loftus had already obtained one piece of information. The news of the outrage at Oslam House had reached Fleet Street from a reliable source, a man named Gregory Wilkinson, who had once been closely watched because of his Fascist tendencies. Department Z were watching Wilkinson. At least there was some hope of results now, hope not only of retrieving his own mistake, but in finding out who wanted Virnov dead and an East and West again split right down the middle.

5

NICE GIRL

Hammond reached the Hotel Haymart just twenty minutes after Craigie had finished speaking to Kemble. Mark Errol entered the other door of the hotel about the same time. A youthful-looking man, exquisitely dressed, walked up and down outside; his name was Graham.

Hammond recognised no one in the hall, and he went towards the stairs, glancing about him and taking in the layout of the ground floor.

The Haymart was an old, well-established hotel, catering largely for the provincial visitor. The lounge hall and the lounges were dark oak panelled, bedecked with palms. The reception desk was little more than a hatch into a cubby hole. Behind it sat an elderly woman on a high stool. A white-haired porter was talking to a spotty-faced lad in page-boy's uniform beneath the shade of one of the palms.

The hall was stuffy, but the warmth was welcome.

The dining-room opened out from the hall, and Hammond glanced towards it as he walked up the stairs.

On the second floor landing, he saw lanky Tim Kemble, who glanced quickly up and down.

'Quick work. Going to beard the lion?'

'Is he fierce?'

'Gently does it.'

'Craigie warned me.'

'Don't forget that Clarissa Kaye is a nice girl,' said Tim. 'Did Craigie fix the *Gazette*?'

'I expect so,' said Hammond, 'if you asked him to.'

Tim saw a door opening along the passage, and his smile faded. He looked disinterested in Hammond, and pointed towards the door.

'I think you'll find it in that direction.'

'Thank you,' said Hammond.

A little, dark man came out of Room 15, on the right of the passage. He had a quick, jerky way of walking, and looked about him with bright, suspicious eyes. Hammond recognised him as one of the San Patino delegates. Parmitter's room was 21, only two doors beyond the delegate's. Hammond reached Room 21 and tapped on the door.

Almost immediately, the door opened.

'That's okay, miss, that's okay now,' said a man in blue overalls. 'You won't have any more trouble with it. Good day, miss.'

He was a good-looking young man, with untidy hair and bright blue eyes, which looked with unfeigned admiration towards the girl who had opened the door. Hammond could understand it. She was not perhaps remarkable at first sight, for she was dressed in a simply cut navy blue frock, and she was rather too slim. Her complexion was remarkable, smooth and without blemish; she had nice fair hair, and her blue eyes were quite lovely. She had an attractive mouth, too, as if she found it easy to smile. As the admiring mechanic walked off, she smiled at Hammond.

'Good afternoon.'

Hammond showed an ordinary visiting card.

'I would like to see Mr. Parmitter,' he said. 'Ask him to spare me a few minutes on extremely important business, will you?'

The girl stood aside to allow him to enter. Room 21 was, in fact, a suite of some size. Three doors led from the lounge hall, which was comfortably furnished, with dark and ornate loose-covers on a three-piece suite, dark flowered wallpaper, a heavy mahogany writing table. In that room the girl was light against shade.

One of the doors was ajar. The sound of dialling came from the room beyond, and as the door opened wider, a man said:

'Is that the *Gazette* office?' There was a pause. 'Ask the News Editor to speak to me... Parmitter, Adam Parmitter of *Super-Steel*... Yes.' Hammond could imagine him looking at the girl as she went in. 'What is it?' he asked. The voice registered clearly on Hammond's ears. It had peculiar harshness, almost metallic, and immediately put Hammond in mind of *Super-Steel* products.

'A Mr. Hammond says he would like to see you.'

'Who is he? Hammond—Hammond—we don't know him, do we?'

'No.'

'Then I'm too busy—I told you that I was busy,' Parmitter said testily. 'Send him away. Hallo?... Is that the News Editor? My name is Parmitter, Parmitter of *Super-Steel*. Did you send a young man to...'

The door closed and shut out the sound of his voice.

Clarissa Kaye came towards Hammond with an apologetic smile.

'I am so sorry,' she said. 'Mr. Parmitter is too busy to see anyone. He is usually available between ten o'clock and eleven o'clock in the mornings. If you care to make an appointment for tomorrow...' she broke off.

Hammond looked almost sombre.

'I really must see him now.'

'I am afraid that is impossible,' Clarissa said firmly.

Hammond startled her in two ways, first with a flashing smile which lit up his whole face, then with a movement towards the door.

Parmitter was still on the telephone, standing with his back towards the door. He kept fiddling with the telephone, and once or twice he drew in his breath sharply. At last he said:

'Yes, yes, I will give you any information I can, of course, of course. Goodbye... Eh?... I don't know. At least a week.... Yes, at the Haymart, good*bye*.' He banged down the receiver.

'Mr. Parmitter,' said Clarissa Kaye, 'this gentleman insists...'

Parmitter swung round. 'I told you to...' and then he saw Hammond. He stood quite still. Hammond studied the handsome, rather florid face, the aggressive stare, the physical power of the man. Parmitter was not particularly tall, but he was broad and massive. His dark hair was flecked with grey; on his fingers and the backs of his hands there was a mat of dark hair.

Hammond saw something else; this man was nervous.

He thought that Parmitter would bellow at him, but the man made a palpable effort to control himself, and looked past Hammond to the girl.

'Didn't you tell this man to go?'

'Yes,' said Clarissa. 'He refused.'

Parmitter turned to Hammond. 'Get out.'

'I am afraid...' began Hammond.

Parmitter clenched his fingers and took a step forward; it was very obvious that he was not only on edge, but close to losing his temper. But the expression in Hammond's eyes seemed to make him realise that violence would do no good.

'*Kindly* have the goodness to leave,' he said, in a high-pitched voice. 'I am extremely busy.'

Hammond took another card from his pocket, and held it out. It was the card of a Special Branch man of the Metropolitan Police, and said nothing about Department Z. He held it so that Parmitter could read it.

'I have nothing to say to the police,' Parmitter said stiffly.

'I won't keep you long, sir, but...'

'I have nothing to say to you! Get out!'

Hammond replaced the card. He glanced at the girl, and saw her bewildered expression. She seemed genuinely surprised, but he did not think that she was in any way alarmed at the discovery that he was a 'policeman'. He stood staring at Parmitter, as if willing the man to change his mind; unexpectedly, Parmitter gave way.

'It is an impertinence,' he said. 'You've no right to force your way into my room. What do you want?'

'I believe that you were in Paris early this week.'

'Supposing I was? All right, Clarissa.' As the girl left the room, Parmitter went on: 'There is no reason why I should not go to Paris on business, is there?'

'None at all,' said Hammond. 'When did you return to London, Mr. Parmitter?'

'Yesterday morning.'

'By air?'

'I flew to Paris on Friday, I flew back yesterday. I have

extremely important business to attend to and I have no time to waste.'

'What aircraft did you catch from Le Bourget, Mr. Parmitter?'

'The ten o'clock flight. But...'

'Did you land at London Airport?'

'What the devil does it matter to you *where* I landed?'

'That is the only way that I can check on your story, Mr. Parmitter.' Hammond went to a chair and sat on the arm.

Parmitter repressed an angry comment and watched him. Hammond's manner had changed subtly; he remembered Tim Kemble's warning clearly. He had shaken the man, and had now reached the moment to soft pedal.

'I'm sorry I forced my way in,' he said, 'but I am carrying out important inquiries, and you may be able to help. Have you a copy of the *Evening Cry*?'

'No. I don't read it.'

'If you did, you would have read the story of an attack on one of the delegates of *Uno*,' Hammond said. His manner now suggested that he was taking Parmitter into his confidence. 'The attempt was not officially known until this morning. I am making inquiries about the man who carried out the attack—a man named Leo Kolsti. You know him, don't you?'

Parmitter backed to the table and leaned against it.

'Kolsti,' he repeated. 'Kolsti? I don't recall—oh, *Kol*-sti!' he exclaimed, as if he had suddenly remembered. 'A little dark fellow, a Pole or something? Yes, I know him slightly. You don't mean to tell me that *Kolsti* shot at anyone?' When Hammond nodded, Parmitter burst out laughing. 'It doesn't make sense!'

'Why not?' asked Hammond.

'He's such a mild little man.' Parmitter had quite recovered his composure. He moved towards the window and stood with his back towards it, his hands clasped behind him. 'He claimed acquaintance with me because he was once in the same business—you know I'm Parmitter of *Super-Steel*, don't you?'

'I didn't,' lied Hammond.

'Well, I am. How did you get on to me?'

'By making inquiries among Kolsti's friends. One of them told me that your name had been mentioned.'

'Oh, I see. Well, Chief Inspector, this man was out of a job. I felt sorry for him. He's a naturalised Englishman, I believe, but has the mid-European mentality. Not the kind of man we can employ. These days people who want jobs seem to think I can distribute them with the prodigality of a magician!'

Hammond nodded, understandingly.

'Kolsti came to me several times,' Parmitter went on. 'He once travelled for Kruber's, the Polish steel firm. I don't doubt that he knows his job, but our European representatives are all doing an excellent job. I gave him one or two meals,' went on Parmitter. 'Didn't altogether trust the fellow, but I can't believe he would attempt murder.'

'Well, he did.'

Parmitter turned to the desk, picked up a box of small cigars, and proffered them. Hammond took one. Parmitter struck a match.

'He had a grudge against life, you know, because he couldn't get a job. Now if you told me that he had committed suicide, I could have understood it. But you know what these mid-Europeans are like. May have had a personal grudge against the man he shot. Who was it?'

'Virnov, of Russia,' answered Hammond.

Parmitter gaped.

His gape was rather overdone. A start of surprise, followed by a word or two of astonishment, would have been enough, but his thunderstruck air convinced Hammond that he had known about the attack.

'*Vir*-nov!' gasped Parmitter.

'And I don't think Kolsti had any acquaintance with him,' Hammond said drily.

Parmitter waved his cigar in the air.

'No. No doubt you're right. I've no time for politicians. They're always grabbing something that belongs to someone else. All they want is a ready tongue, a specious pretence at being knowledgeable, and cast-iron conscience. As for this conference...' Parmitter waved his hand again. '*Uno* won't get anywhere if it relies on politicians. They say they want to keep the peace, but in my view, and I don't mind who knows it, there's only one way of keeping this country out of war, and that's to have armaments piled up so high that no one will ever dare attack us. I'm all for our own nuclear deterrent, and a big standing Army, Navy and Air Force.' He broke off, and glanced at his watch. Then he went on: 'But I've given you more time than I can spare.'

'You've been very helpful.'

'I'm glad to help. The truth is, I thought you had gate-crashed for a job.' Parmitter moved towards the door, and rested a hand on Hammond's arm. 'There's one little thing.'

'Yes?'

'Actually, I returned from Paris the day before yesterday,' said Parmitter. 'The truth is that—er—a certain attractive young lady...' he smiled knowingly. 'I don't want my wife to know. I had a feeling that you might be pretending that you were a C.I.D. man. One can't be too careful. You do understand, don't you?'

'Perfectly,' said Hammond. 'When did Kolsti last see you?'

'Let me see now, it would be three—no, four days before I left for Paris. Last Monday. Just a moment, Miss Kaye will be able to confirm that. I'm blessed with a wonderful secretary, Hammond, she is really first-class.' Parmitter opened the door, and called: 'Miss Kaye—oh, there you are. What day last week did I give that fellow Kolsti lunch?'

'Monday,' said Clarissa.

'There you are, Chief Inspector—Monday. I hope you find the fellow.'

'Oh, we've got him,' Hammond said.

He left Parmitter gaping, and walked along the passage. If Tim were right, then Parmitter had lied about the last time he had seen Kolsti. It should be easy to check Parmitter's movements since he had returned to London.

Tim was waiting in the hall. He was much taller than Hammond, a fluffy-haired beanstalk of a man with a cheerful smile and, judging from his appearance, no great strength of character. He was reading the *Evening Cry*. He glanced up at Hammond, and tapped the arm of an empty chair next to him, but did not put his paper down. Hammond walked to the door and looked out, then went to the desk and bought some cigarettes.

'I see it's beginning to snow again,' he said.

'It's wicked cold weather, sir, isn't it?' remarked the faded woman at the desk.

Hammond sauntered to the vacant chair, and sat down. Tim continued to read the newspaper, and spoke with hardly any movement of his lips. 'How'd it go?'

'Nicely.' Hammond was still smoking the cigar which Parmitter had given him. 'Keep at the girl. Try to find out for certain where P. was on Wednesday evening.'

'Was he in London?'

'Yes.'

'So my porter wasn't wrong. Anything else?'

'Not of importance.'

'Oke,' said Tim. He tapped the front of the paper, as if to straighten it out. 'Seen that?'

'Dirty work.'

'*I'll* say!'

Hammond waited long enough to finish his cigar. He looked up as the little dark man who was a delegate from San Patino came in at the revolving doors. He was dressed in an astrakhan coat, which dwarfed him, but in spite of that he looked frozen. A powdering of snow covered him, and his absurdly large Homburg hat. He hurried to the stairs and went up quickly.

Tim got up and followed him.

Hammond left the hotel.

Tim sauntered up the stairs, yet moved much more quickly than he appeared to. He was on the landing when the man from San Patino entered Parmitter's room, not his own. He did not tap, but opened the door with a key. Tim's eyes widened as he strolled a little way along another passage, knowing that it would be difficult to overhear what was said, for Parmitter and the delegate would talk in the inner room.

Clarissa Kaye might hear what passed between them.

Tim, who was of a romantic turn of mind, had already decided that whatever tricks Parmitter got up to, Clarissa Kaye was innocent of them.

He heard her cry out.

The cry came so unexpectedly through the quiet of the hotel that he stood still, the noise startling him. He listened for a repetition. He did not hear one, but he heard the bark of a shot.

He turned and raced towards Room 21.

6

BULLETS FOR PARMITTER

The door was wide open.

Keeping his right hand in his pocket, about the handle of an automatic, Tim crept along by the wall and peered inside, thus, he was safe if anyone took a potshot at the doorway. There had only been that single shot and then silence. No one else seemed disturbed.

The inner door was wide open.

Tim saw a pair of slender nylon-clad legs on the floor and neatly-shod feet at an odd angle. He could just see Clarissa's knees, the skirt inches above them.

He went into the room. Clarissa was lying flat on her back, her head towards the wall. He could not see any sign of blood.

Parmitter was saying in a voice shrill with fear:

'Nothing, I tell you, nothing, I...'

There were three shots; three bullets for Parmitter.

Tim leapt towards the door as he heard the first. In one swift glance he took in the whole scene. Parmitter was leaning against the desk, his hands clutching his chest. There was a trickle of blood through his widespread fingers, and his mouth sagged open. The delegate from San Patino was on his knees behind the desk; a third man was standing just behind the door, with a smoking automatic in his hand. It seemed to Tim that Kolsti had cropped up again. The gunman had dark, close-cropped hair, and very thin features. He seemed unaware of danger from outside. He was pointing the gun towards the San Patino delegate, without speaking.

'Why, hallo,' said Tim, brightly. 'This won't do.'

The man spun round, and Tim shot the gun from his hand. It fell to the floor and slithered towards the desk. The man seemed petrified. He stared at Tim, as the little delegate from San Patino jumped to his feet.

'That iss a murderer!'

'Yes,' said Tim. 'Telephone for a doctor.'

'He iss a murderer! He...'

'Telephone!' snapped Tim.

The little delegate gulped, then plucked up the telephone. As he did so someone came hurrying into the outer room. Tim caught a glimpse of a plump man who stopped in his tracks at sight of Clarissa. Perhaps that was because he also saw a gun in Tim's hand.

Tim said: 'Danger all over. Come in.'

The man came forward hesitatingly. 'What...' he began.

The delegate from San Patino was speaking into the telephone.

'A doctor iss wanted, pliss, quickly, pliss.' He kept repeating the words over and over again, while Tim took a good look at the man who had entered, and recognised him as one of the hotel staff. Tim held the gun towards him, but still pointed it towards the assailant.

'Cover him,' he said.

The man took the gun without protesting. Two or three other people had entered the outer room, a waiter, a maid and a portly old man in pepper-and-salt plus-fours. The maid looked at Clarissa and exclaimed: 'She's dead!'

'Now, don't be silly, don't be silly,' said the old man. 'She isn't dead. Come and help her to sit up. Look, she's opening her eyes!'

Something seemed to click in Tim's mind: or, he asked himself absurdly as he went towards Parmitter, was it in his heart? In any event, his relief at the words: 'Look, she's opening her eyes,' was real indeed. He reached Parmitter, who was slumped down against the desk. He did not think that he or anyone could do anything for the man. He kept a wary eye on the assassin, who still seemed petrified, as if he could not realise that such a thing as this could have happened.

Tim and the delegate from San Patino straightened Parmitter up, and put him in a large armchair. Tim felt for his pulse. It was a futile thing to do, for Parmitter's lips had dropped open and his eyes were closed; there was no sign of life. One hand was still pressed against his chest, and the blood seeped through.

The man holding the gun glanced at Tim.

'This is shocking,' he said, absurdly.

'You'll get a shock if you don't watch that customer,' said Tim. As there was nothing he could do for Parmitter, and as Clarissa was presumably in good hands, he went forward and held out his hand for the gun. The man moved away from him, and Tim widened his eyes.

'*I'll* keep this, thank you.'

Tim looked at the man who was so much like Kolsti at first sight. The resemblance was largely superficial, and was chiefly due to the dark, cropped hair—cropped in monkish fashion. It made his round head look like a ball which was spouting hairs. His eyes had the same wild gleam as Kolsti's.

The man jumped forward.

One move, one sweeping blow with his arm, sent the gun and the man holding it away from him, and he leapt for the door. Tim was a couple of yards away from him. He dived forward and shot out his foot, but failed to trip the man up. He shouted a warning and raced after him. The maid was still in the doorway. The man with the cropped hair swept her aside with a violent blow, and she thudded against the door.

The man turned right, towards the end of the passage and the windows, not towards the stairs.

Tim went after him.

The man was running so fast that if he went on at that pace he would crash into the window at the far end of the passage. There seemed no way for him to avoid it. Tim slowed down, so that the impetus of his rush should not bring him up against the window with a crash; probably the man would twist round at the last moment, and make for the stairs.

Two yards from the window, *the man jumped*.

Tim stopped in his tracks.

It was happening in front of his eyes, and yet he could not believe it. A running jump, *at the window*. The man made no attempt to protect his head. His shoulders were hunched, and he went through the window head first. The crash of glass and the sickening crunching sound seemed to come at the same time; and then the man disappeared.

He had uttered no sound.

Slowly, his lips stiff with tension, Tim went to the window. His feet crunched on the broken glass, but he did not notice it. He put out a hand, held the broken pane to steady himself, and looked outside. It was a sheer but not a long drop, into a narrow side street. There, spread-eagled on the ground cleared of snow, was the little man with the cropped hair. He had met the ground head first.

* * *

Tim turned slowly from the window as he saw a policeman and several passers-by hurrying towards the broken body on the pavement. Because he had been out of touch with the office, he did not know that Kolsti had killed himself, throwing himself in front of the bus with the same suicidal compulsion as this man had flung himself out of the window. Tim felt sick. He looked into the outer room of Parmitter's suite, which was now crowded with people, including a policeman. Clarissa was sitting in an easy chair and someone was holding smelling salts to her nose. She strained her head away from them, and he heard her say that she was all right. He walked down the stairs.

People were gossiping in the halls. 'But I heard shooting, my dear.' 'It couldn't have been.' 'Well, a policeman has just gone upstairs.' 'And I think the doctor has, too.'

Tim walked past them, and only the white-haired porter took any notice of his strained face or his narrowed eyes.

'Aren't you well, sir?'

'Er—yes, I'm all right,' said Tim, and forced a smile. 'Quite all right,' he said. There was a flurry of footsteps on the stairs, and the man to whom he had entrusted the gun came rushing down, with the policeman in his wake.

'Stop that man!' he cried. 'Stop that man!'

The porter, so frail and old, laid a hand on Tim's arm.

'I think he means you, sir.'

Tim's smile was more natural.

'Probably,' he said.

The man with the gun came up to him breathlessly, with the constable in close support.

'*This* is the man who had the gun!' he cried, and everyone in the hall turned and stared. Tim could see their startled faces turned towards him in accusation. He felt suddenly angry with them all, but more angry with the man in front of him than anyone.

He said: 'I told you to watch that man.'

'You—you *told*...'

'And he has committed suicide,' Tim said. 'May it forever bedevil your conscience.' He turned to the policeman, and said: 'You'll find that the shots were fired from the gun on the floor near the radiator, not from mine.' As he spoke, he took out his wallet and extracted a card; it was one similar to the type which Hammond had shown Parmitter. The policeman glanced at it and raised a hand in surprise.

'*Oh*, that's all right, sir.'

The pompous man snapped: 'What do you mean, that's all right?'

Tim said: 'It means that I am his superior officer. I'll send for your statement soon, constable.' He nodded, the porter released his arm, and he went out into the icy streets.

The snow was falling heavily, now; a fresh white coating had spread over the cleared patches of the road, and a little way along a bus was stuck in a great mass of slush and ice and snow near the kerb. A little crowd had gathered about it.

Tim shivered.

He heard a call from behind him, and turned, prepared to deal ruthlessly with the pompous man, but instead he saw the porter, holding his coat.

'You mustn't go out without this *today*, sir.'

'Oh,' said Tim. 'No. Quite right. Thank you.'

The porter himself was shivering as he helped Tim into the coat. Tim slipped a coin into his hand and hurried towards the side-street. There was a little crowd, shocked by what they had seen, and a woman was leaning against the wall, retching. Two policemen were in the middle of the crowd, and a third was shifting the stragglers along. From somewhere not far off there came the *ting-a-ling* of an ambulance bell.

Tim forced his way through the crowd, and showed his card again. The two policemen saluted, and Tim looked down at the man.

He had known from his glance out of the window that the man was dead, but at close quarters the sight of his head, cracked like an egg-shell with the yolk oozing out and coagulating in the bitter air, made him understand why the woman was sick. He steeled himself, and went down on one knee. The snow bit through the cloth, but he ran his hands through the man's pockets. He found only one thing that might be useful, and that was in a waistcoat pocket, a red, diamond-shaped card with the figure 9 printed on it. The card was rubbed and soiled at the edges.

A policeman was collecting all the other oddments, and the ambulance turned into the street, slowly because of the treacherous road.

'I'll take these, thanks,' said Tim, and thrust the cheap wallet and other oddments into his pocket. The ambulance men forced their way through the crowd with a stretcher. A doctor appeared. The body was loaded into the ambulance, and Tim watched it out of sight. His right knee was frozen; he forgot that it was because he had been kneeling in the snow.

He fingered the card. Number 9.

Now that he was beginning to think clearly, he stopped blaming himself. He had done all that could be reasonably expected of him. He had asked Craigie to send several men to the hotel; they should have been watching Parmitter, too. The Department had slipped up, but he did not see how anyone could properly blame him. He felt resentful towards Craigie. That was a novel feeling which sprang from the fact that Tim, a comparatively new agent, had come to expect Craigie to be infallible.

It was Tim Kemble's first big 'show'.

He had served in the Intelligence Branch (Active) during the war, and his record was good. Craigie had marked him down as a recruit, and he was one of the few really new agents. All who knew him liked him. He was particularly suitable, in Craigie's opinion, because he had no close relatives living, and was fancy-free.

He walked to a telephone kiosk, and dialled Craigie's number. There was a long pause before the call was answered, and then he heard Loftus's voice, not Craigie's.

Kemble began to spell his name backwards, a simple code which had served the Department for many years, and had never been misused. By that system it was possible for Craigie or whoever answered the telephone to know at once that he was talking to a *bona fide* agent.

'All right, Tim,' said Loftus.

'It isn't all right,' said Tim. 'It's very much all wrong. I asked Craigie to send some men. Hammond came and went, I haven't seen any others.'

'They were there,' said Loftus.

'Then they were work-shy!'

There was a slight pause, followed by a sound very much like a chuckle, which momentarily incensed him.

'You sound a bit low, Tim,' Loftus remarked. 'Where are you?'

'Near the Haymart. I can't leave because Parmitter's been shot, and...'

'Come straight round,' said Loftus. 'I'll send someone over to relieve you.'

It was not more than a ten minutes' walk to the office, and there was no hope of getting a cab. The roads were chaotic;

Tim saw several cars and two taxis caught in heaps of snow at the side of the road, and two drivers were saying that they had never known such weather.

It was unusual for him to be invited to the office. He had been there no more than half a dozen times, and it was a general practice for agents to stay away from headquarters during spells of duty. He walked past the entrance to the side-street where Department Z was housed, then turned and looked behind him. That had become almost second nature. No one had followed him from the Haymart, and there was no one on the other side of the road. He passed through the doorway and hurried upstairs, then went through exactly the same process as George had done. The result was the same.

The warm air of the office struck at him as he stepped across the threshold on to the mat.

Craigie was at his desk, Hammond in front of him; Loftus was standing with his back to the fire, smoking a pipe. The scene was quiet and peaceful; and Tim gave a snort of a laugh.

'That sounds better,' said Loftus.

'Does it?' asked Tim. 'Now I'll really cheer you up.' He told them what had happened in brusque, clipped phrases, while watching Craigie, whose face held no expression, and Hammond, whose only reaction was to push a writing-pad away from him and stare at him intently. Once, Loftus took his pipe from his lips, shook it, and put it back. That was all.

Tim felt better when he had finished, and a little rueful when Loftus said:

'Not so good. Let's have your coat, Tim, or we'll be flooded out.' He took Tim's coat and hat into the cloakroom.

Craigie pushed a telephone away from him, and stood up.

'I still think that the others should have been around,' Tim said.

Hammond smiled grimly. 'They were there, at first. Other

things happened, and they couldn't be in two places at once. Pirani of Shovia arrived at the hotel, and went up to the fifth floor. Mark Errol followed him, and Graham waited outside, to follow any one of our possible suspects. He followed Nassi.'

Tim raised his eyebrows. 'Who is Nassi?'

'A San Patino delegate,' said Hammond. 'Nassi went out for twenty minutes, and came rushing back—you know about that. He'd been to the telephone, and apparently preferred to use a street kiosk. Graham was busy telling us to get the call checked, because any man who preferred to telephone from *out*side on a day like this wanted watching.'

Tim was thawing, in more ways than one.

'I see. Sorry. But when I saw that little fellow...'

'You did everything possible,' said Craigie, and glanced at Loftus. 'Bill will tell you that someone else committed suicide on him this morning.'

Loftus said: 'Make a job of it, Gordon. I had much less excuse than Tim. But we'll know in future that hari-kari is a favourite practice among these people.'

'Not *Kolsti*!' exclaimed Tim.

'Yes.' Loftus looked at the little diamond-shaped card which Tim had taken from his pocket. 'What's that?'

'I found it on the dead man,' said Tim. 'I've got the other stuff from his pockets here.' He put everything on a table. 'I don't think there's much. I can't imagine he would carry anything incriminating, if he preferred to kill himself rather than be questioned.'

Loftus was looking curiously at the card.

'I don't think Kolsti had anything like it,' Loftus said. 'It might be a cloakroom ticket.'

Craigie was examining the other contents of the dead man's pockets. They gave little away; not even the man's name. He finished, and watched Tim Kemble.

'Well, that's another clue gone,' Tim said at last. 'I thought we had something on Parmitter.'

'We were getting it.' Hammond outlined the results of his talk with the man. 'It's not according to plan, but we've got to expect them to act like this now. There's no longer any doubt that this business is well-organised. No wild man,' he added, with a smile at Loftus. 'What do you make of it, Bill?'

'I'm wondering whether Tim really closed his mind to everything that happened at the Haymart,' Loftus said, looking at Tim with a mild smile. 'It's almost too cold to think, Tim, isn't it?'

Tim looked startled and annoyed.

'That's right, blame me.'

'Don't be an oaf. Nassi's still alive, isn't he?'

Tim stared at him, trying to see what he was driving at. Loftus was not rubbing salt in the wound, but challenging him to use his wits. They *had* been stultified after that suicide jump. Now he began to see things more clearly. Nassi had gone out, telephoned furtively and hurried back, and judging from his manner he had been going to take an urgent message to Parmitter. So Nassi might be able to tell them something, although he was a San Patino subject and, as a delegate to the Session, would expect more than usual consideration from the police. Yes, Nassi might be a fruitful line of investigation. There was Clarissa Kaye, too.

They could search Parmitter's rooms, question his friends, and check all his movements. A man of Kolsti's brotherhood, presumably, had killed Parmitter; there was now no doubt that Parmitter had been associated, in some way or other, with the attempt on Virnov.

He put his thoughts into words.

'That's better,' said Loftus. 'Yes, we've something to work on. Parmitter's death is a help rather than a hindrance. Obviously he was killed to prevent him from talking. It followed so swiftly on Bruce's visit, that it means that Bruce was seen to go there and known to have interrogated him. So there is someone watching in the hotel. It isn't likely to prove to be Nassi, as he was in danger of losing his life, you say.'

Tim nodded.

Craigie, who often had periods of keeping in the background, suddenly pulled a telephone towards him and dialled George Henry George's number. While waiting for George, he said to Tim:

'Clarissa Kaye—what has she really got, besides charm?'

Tim said: 'Commonsense, I should say. I'll be surprised if we have trouble with her.'

'You see her, Bill,' Craigie said to Loftus.

'Right.'

'Who'll take Nassi?' asked Tim.

Loftus nodded towards the telephone, where Craigie was saying:

'Yes, George, tonight. Don't do much between now and say ten o'clock. You'll want to be fresh for the job. You're not taking notes, are you?... Good. And don't tell Polly. At ten o'clock I'll tell you where Nassi is staying tonight. It will probably be the Haymart. You're to tackle him as if you were a private individual... Take no cards with you... That's right... Because if any officials have a go at Nassi, it would cause international complications. We don't want formal protests, but we want Nassi so frightened that...'

He rang off, to find Tim smiling almost sombrely.

'That's the ticket,' said Tim. 'Er—about Clarissa Kaye,' he added, with a painstaking effort to appear casual, 'it's possible that she'll be in some danger, isn't it? Hadn't she better be watched?'

'We had men among the crowd at the hotel,' Loftus assured him. 'She'll be all right now.'

'I hope so,' said Tim. 'Next orders?'

'Take it easy for a few hours.'

'I'm quite fit and ready for...'

'Try the *Palladium*,' suggested Craigie. 'You can't work at high pressure all the time, and you're probably suspect among Parmitter's friends. There'll be plenty to do before this is over.'

Obediently, Tim went out.

He had not been gone five minutes before a green light showed in the mantelpiece of the office. Loftus pressed the control button, and they looked up to see Superintendent Miller. Miller's dusting of flour had disappeared in a coating of snow, and his cheeks were a fiery red.

They welcomed him warmly, and Loftus said:

'You're quite right, Dusty, things have been happening. And we've been flourishing S.B. cards more than usual. I suppose you've heard of the Haymart affair?'

'Just,' said Miller, in a ponderous way. 'I've given up trying to keep pace with you.' He took off his coat. 'I found a little thing in Kolsti's clothing which I thought you'd like to see,' he added. 'It was inside the lining of his waistcoat, there was a hole in it we didn't notice when we first looked him over. Not that it should have been missed,' he added, with a touch of severity, and drew his hand from his pocket. 'It's stiff enough.'

He held out a small, red, diamond-shaped card, with the numeral 11 on it.

7

SHOCK FOR LOFTUS

Miller had gone, and Hammond, Loftus and Craigie gathered round the fire. Craigie sat down in his armchair, while Loftus looked again at the two diamond-shaped cards. There were finger-prints on them; Miller had already checked those on Kolsti's card and found only Kolsti's prints. His next task was to try to identify the unknown suicide. That was a matter which the police could do much more quickly than Department Z.

'We're making progress, anyhow,' said Loftus. 'I'd better go and see Tim's Clarissa Kaye.' He waited, expectantly.

'Tim seemed anxious that we shouldn't misjudge her,' remarked Hammond.

'I don't think we need worry about him,' Craigie said. 'He had a nasty shock.'

'There are going to be plenty of those,' Loftus said. 'What's your programme, Bruce?'

'Gordon thinks it's time one of us tackled Pirani,' Hammond said. 'I'm not too happy about it, but it might force him into the open. I felt much happier about seeing Parmitter.

He was a British subject, there was no need to feel that the wrong word might precipitate an international crisis. If Pirani starts talking about diplomatic privilege...'

'All the better,' said Loftus. 'The last defence of the guilty. I think Gordon's right, we need to try to find out whether he is really nervous. You say that Parmitter was?'

'So nervous that he lost his head,' said Hammond. 'If I were asked what was the most significant thing that he said I'd say it was his talk about piling up conventional armaments as the only way to secure peace. When that sort of talk comes from a man high up in the steel industry, it's got a nasty ring of more dividends from death.' Hammond spoke with no hint of flippancy. 'I'm not a bit sure that I oughtn't to leave Pirani for a while, and find out what I can about *Super-Steel*. With Parmitter's death, we've every reason for making the inquiries.'

'And just watch Pirani,' mused Craigie.

'George can try his little game,' Hammond said. 'You've fixed it with the Massino act, haven't you?'

'Yes,' said Craigie. 'All right, Bruce! Try it your way.'

'Thanks,' said Hammond gratefully. 'I'll go to the Head Office of *Super-Steel* first.'

'You're biting off something there,' Loftus said.

Hammond laughed. 'The great Marchant. But he's a British national, and can't threaten diplomatic action.'

He let himself out.

Anyone watching the others, unseen, might have thought that when alone, Craigie and Loftus took things very easily. In fact, they were thinking along the same lines, with the same single-mindedness which had helped them to establish the reputation of Department Z. They set themselves a task and carried it through; and though they had had their failures, there had been no catastrophe due to the failure of the Department; and many catastrophes had been averted.

Both were thinking of Sir Hugh Marchant.

They could see his face in their mind's eye, a middle-aged, handsome man, whose photograph often peered up at them from the pages of the daily newspapers.

Loftus thought: 'He isn't far short of being the most popular man in the country.'

Marchant's popularity had begun when, during a period of economic crisis, he had performed prodigies in obtaining export orders. He had a faith: he believed in steel and in Britain. No politician, he had dropped out of the public eye immediately afterwards, only to come back on a wave of popularity when he had declared that, given the facilities, he could overcome the worst difficulties of the housing problem. The Government had supported him; using steel freely in the manufacture of houses, Marchant had been as good as his word. His popularity had reached a new high level.

He always preached the gospel of the peaceful uses of steel, but there were the other uses, and Loftus could not get Parmitter's words out of his mind.

Craigie stirred.

'Well, Bill.'

'Let's ponder a bit longer, until we've heard how Bruce gets on.' Loftus got up. 'It's time I went to see Clarissa Kaye.'

'I wish you hadn't got to go,' said Craigie.

Loftus grinned. 'Staff shortage!' He limped to the cloak-room for his hat and coat and a stout walking stick.

He was glad that the Haymart Hotel was not far away. The snow was still falling and making the ground more treacherous, and he slipped several times before reaching the end of the road. He did not often feel uneasy, but just then he had an uneasy feeling that he was being watched. He did not like to think that anyone knew which door he came from. The driving snow prevented him from making sure, and he walked slowly towards Trafalgar Square. No one approached him and, after twenty minutes, he reached the hotel. Young Graham was still outside.

'Miller's been here, and instructed the policemen on duty not to let anyone in or out of Parmitter's room,' he said. 'The body's been moved. All the stuff of interest to us has been locked in one room.'

'Good.'

'Nassi hasn't been out again,' went on Graham. 'Oh— Mark's following Pirani, who came out a quarter of an hour ago. We could do with more men,' he added, hopefully.

'None to spare,' said Loftus. The shortage of active agents always worried him.

He handed his coat to the white-haired porter, and keeping his stick went upstairs. He knew exactly how to reach Room 21 from Hammond's description of the hotel.

A policeman was on duty at the landing, another outside the door of Room 21.

Loftus showed his card.

'That's all right, sir, thank you.'

'Who's in charge?' asked Loftus.

'There's only the young lady.' The policeman opened the door.

Clarissa Kaye was not in the first room.

It had been tidied up, and there were no signs of the chaos. He remembered Tim's vivid description of the girl lying on the floor, and called out: 'Miss Kaye.'

No one answered.

He went to the door immediately opposite the passage. As he opened the door, he thought of the two men who had been with Parmitter, according to Tim's first story. He had not thought to ask Tim more about them, which was careless. There was a quality about this case which seriously troubled him; he thought that it was perhaps the blind, reckless courage—and courage *was* the word—with which two men had committed suicide. It could only have been to make sure that they did not talk, and so betray...

What?

What was worth such reckless sacrifice?

The room had been partly cleared of furniture but not tidied. There, on the floor by the desk, were dark spots of Parmitter's blood.

There was no sign of the girl.

Loftus fought down his rising alarm, and hurried out of the room to the only other one not supposed to be locked. He tapped on the door, and got no answer. He tried the handle, but the door was locked.

With hardly a second thought, Loftus put his shoulder to the door and exerted all his strength. The wood creaked and groaned, and he felt it sagging. He drew back, perspiring, and tried again. The door still held. There was a call from the policeman, who pushed open the outer door, and asked:

'Is everything all right, sir?'

'No,' said Loftus. 'Come and help me.' As the man hurried to obey, he asked: 'No one has been in here, have they?'

'I'm quite sure they haven't.'

'And Miss Kaye's in here?'

'Well, I *saw* her,' said the policeman.

As they put their shoulders to the door, Loftus had a fleeting vision of Kolsti, jumping in front of the bus. The girl was not in the outer rooms; she must be in this one, and yet his calling and the thudding on the door had brought no response from her. He had felt confident that she was safe from attack, but in spite of what had twice happened in this case, he had not given a thought to suicide.

The door sagged and swung open.

Loftus stumbled forward, and the policeman saved him from falling. The room was a bedroom, heavily furnished like the rest of the hotel. The bed was made, and empty.

The room was empty, too.

Loftus limped towards the massive mahogany wardrobe, catching a glimpse of his own face in the long mirror. The policeman hurried to a corner, where someone might be hiding behind the dressing-table; there was no other hiding place in the room.

The wardrobe contained women's clothes, as far as Loftus could tell, all expensive. There was a faint, attractive perfume.

The policeman, on his knees, was looking under the bed. He straightened up, and grunted.

'Well, that's a caution!'

'It's more than a caution,' Loftus said, coldly. 'If you were on duty all the time, it's a miracle. How long did you leave the passage?'

'But I didn't, sir! It—it's just possible that she's in the locked room, there might have been a spare key.'

The constable had the key, and unlocked the door. He pushed it open, and Loftus went in first.

The room was filled with oddments, many piled on the bed and a small writing table pushed just inside the door. There were suitcases, men's clothes, a small cabin trunk, all the paraphernalia a traveller would have with him.

But Clarissa Kaye was not there.

'I just can't understand it,' said the constable. 'I was outside every minute, sir, I didn't move more than a couple of yards either way. Superintendent Miller spoke to me himself, and told me how important it was to let no one in without a police pass, and to see that the young lady did not leave. She *couldn't* have got out.'

A loud bang startled them both.

'What—what's that, sir?'

A rumbling noise followed, and then a tapping. It was coming from Clarissa Kaye's room. Yet Loftus had seen for himself that the girl was not there.

Another bang followed.

He relaxed. 'It's a window,' he said, and they hurried into the bedroom.

The window had opened in a gust of wind, and snow was already drifting in, spattering the dressing table. It had been open all the time, Loftus realised, but had been closed by the wind, opening when caught by a sudden gust because he had left the door open.

He looked across at a blank wall, for the window overlooked the narrow street where the unknown man had fallen to his death. Immediately beneath this window was a small balcony. Loftus brushed the snow out of his face as he peered down, leaning so far out that the constable called:

'Careful, sir.'

Loftus thought he could see faint impressions in the snow on the floor of the balcony and its front ledge; it was not smooth, as it was on the side ledges and on the balcony of the next room. He withdrew his head and turned round.

'Come on!' he said.

He had not moved so quickly for a long time, but as he half-ran along the passage, thumping with his stick, he counted the doors. Number 21 was the fifth from the corner of the landing. He hurried down the stairs, and turned into the passage which ran immediately beneath the one outside Parmitter's room. As he approached the fifth door, a maid came out, carrying a bundle of linen untidily clasped to her big bosom. She peered over the top of it.

Loftus pushed past her and went inside.

It was a suite exactly like Parmitter's, but rather better

furnished; and it was empty. The beds were stripped, there was no luggage. He hardly needed the indignant maid to tell him that the suite had been vacated.

'When did they leave?' Loftus demanded.

'Half an hour ago, sir,' said the girl, who looked scared now that she had a clear view of his face. 'They didn't say a word to anyone it seems, just paid their bill and went off. I didn't think there'd be a suite to do this afternoon.'

Loftus said: 'Have you taken anything a way yet?'

'No, sir, this is the first lot.'

'Have you emptied the wastepaper basket?'

She protested: 'Give me a *chance*, they haven't been gone more than half an hour.'

Then Loftus beamed upon her, and she was more startled by his smile than by his frown.

'Put that stuff back and leave the rooms just as they are,' he said. 'I'll put it right with the manager.'

'But I've got...'

'Do what the gentleman says, miss, if you please,' chimed in the policeman.

The maid dropped the sheets and pillow cases back on to the bed, and went along the passage, muttering. Loftus sent the policeman for the manager, and looked about. It was easy to understand what had happened. He hardly needed to look at the window immediately below the balcony, and to see the traces of melted snow on polished boards and carpet, to know what 'miracle' had transported Clarissa Kaye out of her room. She had climbed to the balcony, swung over the edge and then entered this room by the window.

He put his stick against the wall and, with some difficulty, got down on his knees. He examined the melted snow closely. There were several little pools, some of them larger than others.

Had the girl come alone? Or had she been forced to climb down?

In the blizzard, and the snowstorm amounted to one, it was easy to understand why she had not been seen from the main road further along. This narrow by-street led to nowhere in particular; it would have been sheer chance had anyone happened to be passing when she had climbed out.

The manager came in, a pompous individual whom Loftus immediately recognised from Tim's description as the man who had let his captive get away.

'What *is* the matter?' demanded the manager, querulously. 'I cannot be continuously at the beck and call of the police.' When Loftus did not immediately answer, he went on: 'Surely there has been enough disturbance here this afternoon.'

'I've had plenty,' said Loftus, 'and I'm not making it. I'd like full particulars of the people who were staying in this suite, please, and their forwarding address.'

'But I haven't one,' said the manager. 'They didn't leave one. They did not intimate that they were leaving until half an hour before they left. But you won't have difficulty in finding them, if you want them,' he went on, 'or you shouldn't have.'

'Why not?' asked Loftus.

'Sir Hugh Marchant should know where his son is,' said the manager, huffily.

8

SIR HUGH MARCHANT

Marchant's photograph, though widely publicised, did not do the man justice. He was impressively hand-some as he stood behind a large, flat-topped pedestal desk, a work of art in walnut. The corner room in his City building was spacious, furnished in excellent taste with unostentatious luxury. The walnut panelled walls shone; there were no pictures. The deep pile of the carpet gave under Loftus's feet as he went to a chair which Marchant indicated, and sat down. Standing by another chair was Bruce Hammond.

Marchant sat down behind the desk.

Concealed lighting made the room bright, but through the wide windows could be seen the darkness of the streets outside, a darkness still filled with the murmuring snow. Marchant's chair creaked a little as he sat down, making the only sound in the room. He looked from Loftus to Hammond with a somewhat puzzled smile, and said:

'Do I understand that you gentlemen know each other?'

Loftus smiled. 'Same department,' he said.

'The Special Branch?' Marchant straightened a silver pen

in a silver holder. 'I understood that your business was urgent, Mr. Loftus, but I did not realise that it was connected with Parmitter's death.'

Loftus had come straight from the Haymart Hotel, entered the great modern building which housed the London offices of *Super-Steel*, been guided through palatial ground floor halls to a secretary of secretaries, and had sent in his name. He had been kept waiting only for ten minutes, and had been surprised to see Hammond still in Marchant's office.

Watching the finely carved features and the steady grey eyes, Loftus wondered if his imagination were playing him tricks. It might be that the calm, mellow manner of the steel magnate was deceptive.

He said: 'It is urgent, I assure you. I have just come from the Haymart...'

'The Inspector has been telling me about the occurrence.' Again Loftus was impressed by Marchant's casual air. Parmitter did not seem to matter, in fact Marchant spoke of his death with some distaste, certainly not with sorrow or horror. 'I understand that Parmitter was in the company of M. Nassi, the San Patino delegate to the United Nations Conference.' The distaste became even more marked. 'I think perhaps I had better tell you what I have already told your colleague. Parmitter was about to leave my organisation. His methods and his activities have not been satisfactory, and I have reason to believe that he has been acting for another Corporation, either English or foreign. May I add further,' went on Marchant grimly, 'that I had twice warned Parmitter that unless I had his undivided loyalty he would have to leave us.'

Hammond looked at Loftus with an eyebrow raised, and Loftus's first feeling was one of disappointment.

'You have no idea which other Corporation?'

'None at all. I can tell you that if he did business with the

San Patino Government, it was not for *Super-Steel*. At one time San Patino did buy a certain amount of heavy armament from us, but we have ruthlessly cut out all such sales, from our British as well as our European and South American plants.'

Loftus nodded, slowly.

Marchant paused, and when neither of the others spoke, he raised his hands.

'Don't hesitate to call on me if there is any other help I can give you. Parmitter's office records are entirely at your disposal.'

'Thank you,' said Loftus, but did not get up. 'There are one or two other things, sir.'

'Yes?'

'Did you know Miss Clarissa Kaye, Parmitter's secretary?'

He put the question out as a feeler, expecting to see Marchant shake his head: his bombshell was intended to burst later. But he was amazed at the astonishing change in Marchant's expression. The pleasant, half-smiling face suddenly clouded, the eyes narrowed and seemed to darken. Marchant's hands, a moment before resting lightly on the table, tightened with tension. Now Loftus could see something of the real strength of the man; and he wondered what was going on behind those narrowed eyes.

Marchant demanded sharply: 'What is that? His *secretary?*'

'Yes.'

'I cannot believe...' began Marchant, and then broke off to add abruptly: 'Be good enough to describe her to me, please.'

'I haven't seen her,' Loftus replied, glancing at Hammond.

'Tall, fair, rather thin, with a remarkably good complexion and most attractive eyes,' Hammond said. 'About twenty-seven. A pleasant, rather husky voice. Does that help?'

Loftus was watching Marchant's face closely. There was

now little change of expression except, perhaps, a slight tightening of the lips.

'Did you say that she was Parmitter's secretary, Mr. Loftus?'

'She gave us to understand that.'

'I think I also see why you came here so hurriedly,' declared Marchant. 'Miss Kaye is, of course, my niece. You had some reason to suspect that she was related to me, I have no doubt. I have not seen her for some months. She did not take kindly to my attitude towards her recent behaviour. Please don't misunderstand me. She resented the discipline that a member of my family found it necessary to accept. But I had no idea at all that she had gone to Parmitter. I did understand that she had accepted a commercial post.'

'Exactly when did she leave your house?'

'It was at the end of August. We were at St. Ives. I needed a rest after a strenuous winter and spring.'

'Did you quarrel with her?' asked Loftus.

'We differed,' Marchant said. 'If you mean, did we brawl or shout at each other—no, Inspector. Why are you asking these questions? My niece is not hurt, is she?'

'She has disappeared, Sir Hugh, and we want to question her in connection with the murder.'

After a long pause, Marchant demanded:

'Is she suspected of complicity?'

'I wouldn't like to commit myself,' said Loftus. He was glad that Hammond had not gone into much detail about Parmitter's murder. He wanted to judge the effect of each disclosure on Marchant, who sat watching him, his manner watchful and wary. It was difficult to guess what he was thinking, but Loftus had an impression that talk of Clarissa had hurt him.

'That is not very reassuring,' said Marchant.

'Nothing in this affair is reassuring,' Loftus said. 'The facts are these: she was in the outer room of the suite at the Haymart Hotel when the attack took place. The assassin entered the room and apparently first thrust her aside, knocking her unconscious, and then fired at Parmitter. Before Parmitter was shot, a single shot was fired—possibly at your niece, but also possibly to give the impression that she too was in danger. She appears to have had the opportunity to warn Parmitter that there was danger. Was she in need of money?' he added, abruptly.

'She was not. I made her an ample allowance.'

'Thank you,' said Loftus. 'After the murder, she went to her room to rest. No one else was in the suite. Parmitter's body had been removed, there was no danger, because a policeman was on duty outside the passage door. He had instructions to stop anyone from entering *or* from coming out. Presumably Miss Kaye was aware of that. She chose to leave by the window, climbed on to a balcony to the floor below and went into a room there.'

Marchant kept a poker face.

'The rooms below Parmitter's suite were occupied at the time of her disappearance from the upper floor,' went on Loftus, 'but the occupants left hurriedly, and, presumably, Miss Kaye went with them. The occupants did not leave a forwarding address.'

He paused again, and Marchant said:

'I shall regard it as a matter of first importance that she is found, Inspector. I refuse to believe that there is any possibility of her having been a party to murder.'

Loftus said gently: 'But she might be to lesser crimes, Sir Hugh?'

Marchant snapped: 'Don't put words into my mouth.'

'I'm sorry,' Loftus said. 'But I hope you will be wholly frank with us, because this murder is concerned with another—had you told Sir Hugh so, Bruce?'

'No,' said Hammond.

'What crime?' demanded Marchant.

'The attempt on Virnov,' murmured Loftus.

Marchant pushed his chair back abruptly, and stood up. He walked to one of the wide windows and stood looking out into the darkness, which was broken only as the light from the room shone on the falling snow. He looked round at Loftus, standing with his hands behind him, and there was now no doubt of the pain in his eyes. Was there also fear?

'Why are you not frank with me, Inspector? Is it necessary to approach this matter in such a roundabout fashion?' Loftus was taken aback by that, expecting Marchant to tell him that he knew his son had been at the Haymart. But Merchant's next words startled him far more. 'Why don't you admit that you know my niece is violently anti-Soviet? Her dislike of Russia as it is amounts almost to mania. Her father was killed in Korea in 1950.'

'I see,' said Loftus. 'I didn't know.'

Marchant raised a hand. 'I thought you were playing with me, Inspector. However, you would have found that out soon enough. That was largely why...' he broke off, then stepped to his desk, picked up a cigarette and lit it; he did not think to offer the box to the others. 'I objected to Clarissa's activities because they were closely allied to a small but active and virulent group of politicians who are Fascists in everything but name. I thought—and I still think—that she was misguided, but she preferred to keep their company rather than my family's. The rupture was inevitable.' He drew on the cigarette, took it from his lips and contemplated the glowing tip. Then he added quietly: 'You see, Inspector, I am being wholly frank.'

'And we appreciate it,' said Loftus.

'And I want to help you find my niece,' Marchant went on. 'My secretary knows as much about her and her friends as I do. I will give him instructions to tell you everything he can. Will that be satisfactory?'

'Very, thanks.'

Marchant stretched out a hand to press a bell.

'Just a moment,' urged Loftus, and Marchant withdrew his hand. 'Were any other members of your family sympathetic towards your niece's activities?'

'They were not.'

'Your son...'

'My son first brought my niece's activities to my notice,' Marchant said, looking at Loftus intently. 'I cannot catch the drift of these remarks.'

'You see, there are indications that Miss Kaye did not leave her suite of her own free will,' Loftus said. 'She was forced out, made to go downstairs and then to leave the hotel. The suite below, if I am to believe the manager, was at the time occupied by your son.'

'My *son*?'

'I checked the information and we saw the registration book at the hotel. It was signed by Lionel H. Marchant.' Loftus took a buff-coloured slip of paper from his pocket and, getting up with an effort, handed it to Marchant. 'He also signed that room service chit. Is it your son's signature?'

Marchant stared down. His lips were pressed tightly together but his jaws were working, as if he were clamping his teeth. The silence lasted for a long time, and the tension was almost unbearable. Loftus and Hammond exchanged meaning glances, then looked watchfully at the steel magnate.

'Yes. I find it—incredible!' Marchant exclaimed. 'Quite incredible, Inspector. I had no idea that my son was in London, I thought he was still in Colston, with his wife.'

'His wife was with him at the Haymart,' said Loftus. 'They had been there for three days.'

'It is most unlike my son to move without telling me.' He went over to a loudspeaker unit box and pressed down a switch. 'Hallo—Carfax, when did you last hear from Lionel?'

The answer came promptly in a quiet, modulated voice: 'Last Friday, sir.'

'Was he at Colston?'

'Yes.'

'Did he say that he was about to leave?'

The disembodied voice was tinged with surprise.

'He gave me no indication of that, Sir Hugh.'

'All right.' Marchant switched the instrument off. He looked at Loftus, and spread his hands out. 'I cannot help you, Inspector. I shall, of course, make immediate inquiries, and find out when my son left Colston...'

'Where is this Colston?' asked Loftus.

'It is my Berkshire house, near Reading. It is just possible that my son discovered that Clarissa was in some kind of difficulty, and was quixotic enough to help her, although that does not explain...' he broke off. 'But guessing will not help you or me, Mr. Loftus. I would like to say, briefly, that I shall afford you every possible assistance. I am as eager as I am sure you are to find out the truth about these rather mystifying movements of members of my family.'

'Thank you,' murmured Loftus.

Marchant switched on the talking-box again. 'Carfax—I am sending two gentlemen from Scotland Yard in to see you. I want you to afford them every assistance. They will want personal information about Clarissa and Lionel. Keep nothing back.'

'Right,' said Carfax.

'And see that they get some refreshment,' Marchant said.

He switched off, then stepped to Loftus with his hand out-stretched. 'If you need to see me personally again, just tell Carfax. I wish you every success in your investigations. I shall be happy when I know the explanation and can be sure that none of my family has become involved in the scandal. Just one request.' He said that to Hammond as he shook hands.

'Yes?' said Hammond.

'If you can, please keep this out of the Press.'

'I will certainly try,' Hammond promised.

Loftus said quickly: 'I think we should warn you, Sir Hugh, that the attack on Virnov was kept from the Press as far as we were concerned, yet the story was published.'

'I can only hope that there won't be another leakage of information,' said Marchant. 'I should not like to think that my niece's name was associated in any way with those reac-tionaries, who might become violent. You will give them close attention, I have no doubt. As Carfax will tell you, the most persistent and probably the most dangerous of them is Gregory Wilkinson. Have you heard of him?'

Loftus nodded, and thought of the leakage over Oslam House.

Marchant took them to the door.

Carfax proved to be an elderly, healthy-looking man, with greying hair and a curiously youthful complexion. He was all courtesy and helpfulness. Throughout the next hour, fortified by sandwiches, and beer, Loftus and Hammond took in every-thing he said, and formed a picture in which Gregory Wilkinson loomed large.

Loftus found it difficult to think of anyone else.

* * *

By seven o'clock that night, a close watch was being kept on *Hatch End*, the Wimbledon home of this man who had suddenly loomed large in the mystery of *Uno*. Every available man of Department Z, except for George Henry George and Mark Errol, who were wanted for other work later in the night, were at Wimbledon. The house was completely surrounded and, because it stood in its own large grounds, was easily isolated. Miller's Special Branch men were also there, held in reserve.

Later in the evening, Hammond was to go to see Wilkinson, who was known to be in the house with his family and with three friends, all of them closely connected with the small but possibly dangerous organisation which Wilkinson led. No one had taken Wilkinson seriously until now.

In Whitehall, Craigie, Loftus and Hammond sat at the desks going over all that they had learned from Carfax and Marchant. Seldom had Scotland Yard and the Department worked with such speed and produced so many items of information so quickly. The history of Clarissa Kaye, of Lionel Marchant and of Wilkinson was now spread out in documents on the desk, and Craigie had summarised them, finding where their lives intersected.

Clarissa had met Wilkinson two years earlier, when Wilkinson had returned, badly wounded, from Brunei. His army record was irreproachable, and he had been decorated after an expedition into the Borneo jungle following the early troubles there. His sudden and vitriolic outburst, condemning China and Soviet Russia and all who were in any way sympathetic towards the countries or the regime, had startled a great many people.

Wilkinson edited a magazine which had a tiny circulation, in which the articles were mostly violent diatribes against the Soviet. Frequently there had been demands that it should be suppressed, but the House of Commons, still able watch-dog of personal liberties, had declared with justification that the articles reflected the opinions of only a few men and women. Wilkinson was a married man, with two young children—both, at the time of the attack on Virnov, were at school. Violet Wilkinson had been on the stage, had travelled widely, had a good reputation and was known to be a lovely woman. Both Wilkinson and his wife were wealthy, and so could afford the costs of their extravagant and perhaps under-rated propaganda. The woman, it was clear, shared all her husband's views.

Their organisation, which had less than fifty members as far as the police knew, and the police had watched it from the first, was called *Warning*. The magazine was called a News-Letter, and had a circulation of less than a thousand.

Clarissa had first met Violet Wilkinson when she had served overseas on work for Oxfam. According to Carfax, she had held strongly anti-Russian views before that, although she had seldom voiced them. The influence of the Wilkinsons had brought them into the open.

As far as was known, Lionel Marchant had never expressed anti-Russian sentiments, was undoubtedly well-disposed towards the Soviet, and was not connected with the *Super-Steel* Corporation or with any other business. He managed his father's private affairs, including the large estate at Colston in Berkshire.

The names of the three men who were with the Wilkinsons at the Wimbledon house were known.

James Mendicott, like Wilkinson, had lived in the Far East. He had not been associated with any political organisation until recently. He was a middle-aged writer of obscure poems and more obscure short stories, and had the reputation of being a dilettante. Whether he believed in his diatribes against

Russia or whether he indulged in them to satisfy a complex combination of aesthetic sensationalism and a superb command of words, no one knew.

Herbert Ferguson was a younger man, slightly crippled from birth, who also had a gift of vituperative language; he was a cousin of Gregory Wilkinson.

William James Abbott was the only one even remotely connected with post-war Fascism, but little was known about him. Unlike the others, he did not come from a 'good' family. He was self-educated and had for some time worked in a car factory. How he had met the others was not known. He was the best-looking of all the men at the house; and, if Carfax had told them the truth, Clarissa had always been attracted by him. Carfax, in fact, believed that Clarissa had joined *Warning* because of him.

From the descriptions, it seemed that both Abbott and Ferguson had been with Parmitter at the hotel.

Loftus finished reading the final report, and put it aside.

'That seems to be that,' he said. 'Up to you now, Bruce.'

'I suppose so. I wonder if Clarissa's at the house?'

Craigie shrugged his shoulders. 'We do know that a car arrived at the house this afternoon, and that three people went inside, but that's all,' he said. 'If a postman hadn't been coming away at the time, we wouldn't know that. It's too slender a chance to build on, but we may have struck lucky.'

'We certainly need some luck,' Loftus said. 'I wish I were going with you.'

'I'll probably have to send for you,' said Hammond, cheerfully. 'There's nothing else to arrange. I'll tackle Wilkinson first, and if I've any trouble, I'll call the others in. The police won't move unless they get a summons, or anyone tries to get away.'

'That's my boy,' said Craigie. 'If it's at all possible, keep the police out of it. The first raid will be entirely off our own bat...'

'No connection with any other firm of thugs and strong-arm merchants,' murmured Loftus. 'Luck, Bruce!'

Hammond went out into the dark streets. The snow had stopped, but the roads were nearly impassable, although an army of workmen was engaged in clearing them. There was a lane down the middle of all main roads, with occasional wider patches where cars could pass one another. Just round the corner in Whitehall, a powerful car was waiting for him, and at the wheel sat Tim Kemble. The car started off slowly, its chains clanking in the roadway.

When they had reached Putney and were going slowly up the hill, sometimes afraid that even the chained wheels would not hold, Hammond told Tim that he thought Clarissa might be at Wilkinson's house.

9
PARTY

Bright lights shone from the front windows of *Hatch End*. As Hammond walked up the drive, forcing his way through the snow, glad of the rubber knee boots which he had pulled on in the car, he heard the strains of radio music and saw the shadows of two or three people against the thin blinds. The music grew louder as he drew nearer. For the first time he began to wonder whether it would be a fruitless errand.

He heard an outburst of laughter, and looked up at one window. It was open a few inches at the top, in spite of the cold. There was no wind; and above him the stars were shining like little points of burnished metal.

He climbed four or five steps to reach the porch. There were no signs that anyone had approached the house since the snow had stopped, and no attempt had been made to clear a path.

As he rang the bell, he heard another outburst of laughter.

Footsteps sounded immediately. Hammond cast one glance behind him, into a darkness brightened by the pale glow cast by the snow where the lights from the windows struck it. Just out of sight, near the top-heavy snow-capped hedge which bordered the grounds, some of the Department Z men were standing. There were fifteen of them, all inside the grounds. As many of Miller's men had flung a wider cordon. Two or three police cars and a small motor-coach were at the end of the road, for none of them had been able to come as far as the gateway of *Hatch End*.

A maid opened the door.

'Good evening.' She was a slight, young, rather pretty girl.

'Good evening,' said Hammond. 'Is Mr. Wilkinson at home?'

'I think so. Will you come in?' She stood aside to let him pass into the warm hall, and then went to a door on the right. At the door, she stopped. 'Oh, I forgot,' she said. 'What name is it?'

'Hammond,' said Hammond.

'Ta,' said she, laconically, and tapped on the door and went in. The crude harshness of a bad blues band came from the room, and there was a chatter of conversation. It was quite a party, obviously. Hammond was surprised because, as far as they knew for certain, only the Wilkinsons and their three friends were here. It was just possible that Clarissa and Lionel Marchant were taking part in these revelries.

The hall was large. An open fire burned in a brick fire-place. Heavy paintings hung on the walls, and between them were bright, colourful pictures of the Picasso school. The furniture was equally mixed, some old, one or two rococo Victorian pieces, a few ultra-modern. The carpets and the rugs were fine Persian. It was clearly the home of wealthy people, and yet it was not quite what Hammond had expected. The wide staircase led from the left of the hall, carpeted from wall to banisters. Upstairs, the landing was in darkness, and the lighting in the hall itself was subdued.

Someone shouted: 'Close that damn' door!'

The maid closed the door. The music continued, someone laughed on a high-pitched note. Hammond wondered how long it would be before the maid returned, and whether Wilkinson would recognise his name.

The door remained closed for a surprisingly long time.

Hammond glanced towards the landing.

Someone was standing there and watching him. The hall light was bright enough to cast a man's shadow on the wall behind him. It was a tall, thin shadow, but it did not indicate the stature of the man who was hidden. Hammond would not have known he was there but for the shadow itself; and after he had stared towards it for a long time, he wondered whether he was being deceived by the shadow of a vase or a piece of furniture; for the shadow did not move. Yet he had that nervy, edgy feeling of being watched.

The door opened, and the maid came tripping towards him, on absurdly high heels. Her black skirt scarcely reached her knees.

'Will you please come in, sir,' she asked, and led him to the room.

He had expected Wilkinson to come out to him.

Through a haze of smoke he saw half-a-dozen people, more men than women.

The table was littered with crackers, festoons, paper hats, and other gay trifles. A buffet meal was spread out, and wine and spirit bottles were dotted everywhere, as if to save anyone the trouble of walking across the room for a drink.

Two people were jogging about in a corner space near the radio. A man was sitting in an easy chair, with one bandaged foot up on another, and Hammond recognised the lank hair and pale, sallow face of Gregory Wilkinson. A lock of hair fell over his eyes, as if he were trying to emulate the fashion of the 'leader'. His wife Violet was talking animatedly to the lame Ferguson, and it was the sight of Ferguson which gave Hammond his first jolt, for the man's head was cropped until he looked almost bald. Had he been dark instead of fair, his resemblance to Kolsti would have been remarkable.

Mendicott, a bulky man, rather below medium height, was pouring out drinks. He looked a little unsteady as he finished and, while the maid led Hammond across the room, he handed him a glass.

'Welcome, chaps! Drink up!' He hiccuped and grinned. 'Good stuff. Best Scottish private stills. Try it.'

Because he thought it might precipitate trouble if he refused, Hammond took the glass; it was whisky and water.

'Thanks.'

'Bring friends,' chirruped Mendicott. 'New recruits to the jolly old party. Anyone else outside?'

Hammond smiled and said: 'No,' but he wondered whether Mendicott knew the house was surrounded. The feeling of disquiet deepened. He looked into the man's eyes, but Mendicott seemed quite innocent, and his eyes were rather bleary.

Wilkinson waved to a chair by his side.

'Sit down,' he said. 'I'm sorry I couldn't come out to you. Knocked my leg this afternoon—the old trouble, you know.' He had been wounded in the leg during the war, he explained, and it had not properly healed. His conversational tone was less surprising than the fact that he, as well as Mendicott, had greeted Hammond as if he were expected.

Wilkinson started to say: 'Well, how...' and then Mendicott lurched over him, with a glass in his hand. A little spilled on his trousers. 'Clumsy ass,' said Wilkinson, but he was not in any way put out.

'S'good stuff,' Mendicott assured him gravely. 'Best of the best. I say! Hope the chappie isn't a Robert. Shocking bad taste to hand a Robert unlicensed liquor, isn't it?' He peered, almost leered, at Hammond. 'Feel in danger,' he declared. 'Funny thing about me, I can scent danger.' He sniffed, exaggeratedly. 'S'gone,' he said, and, with another glass in his hand, he staggered towards the couple who were dancing. 'Coming, waiter!' he called, and then giggled. 'Sorry. Mean coming sir. Hear that, Abby—calling you sir!'

'Darling,' said the girl with Abbott, a dark-haired, rather plump but good-looking girl, 'couldn't you be a teeny-weeny bit tiddly?'

'What?' roared Mendicott. 'A *teeny-weeny* bit? Honey, I'm hopelessly drunk! Ask our new friend. He's the only one sober. I asked him if he was Robert. What a look he gave me!'

Was his talk just drunken foolishness?

'*New* friend?' asked the girl, and looked towards Hammond.

Wilkinson touched Hammond's knee.

'I'm afraid that being forced to stay indoors has rather...' he began, and then the dark girl thrust Mendicott away from her and moved across to Hammond and Wilkinson. She beamed at Hammond.

'Why, look!' she cried. 'Isn't he ducky? Do you dance nicely, ducky?'

'Take a look,' said Mendicott. 'No man with a moustache like that could possibly dance. Hic! Sorry. No offensh, old chap,' he burbled. 'Most deshidedly no offensh—intended. Any taken?'

Hammond put his head on one side, and said, 'Not much.'

Mendicott laughed on a high note.

'S'good,' he declared, happily. 'Smart answer. Perhaps he can dance. Try him, Sue.'

'Do!' urged Sue, and held out her hands.

Hammond felt quite sure that this reception was deliberate. Wilkinson seemed to be looking at him with a mocking smile, and his handsome wife, still talking to Ferguson, was also watching him with some amusement. He no longer doubted that they had been prepared for the call, but it seemed unlikely that they knew who was outside.

'I don't think...' he began.

'Be civil, Sue,' said Wilkinson mildly.

'*Me* be civil, when he's insulted me!' said Sue. She turned glowing eyes on Hammond. 'But you didn't mean to be rude, did you?' she demanded. 'Drink up. Bottoms down!' She finished off her own glass. Hammond, ready to believe that his had been doctored, sipped it slowly. 'Oh, *drink!*' she cried, and would have tipped the glass up as he held it to his lips had not Wilkinson caught her arm.

Hammond put his glass down, and stood up.

'*Will* you dance?' demanded Sue.

'I'd love to,' said Hammond. The band on the radio had burst into a frenzy. Hammond, suddenly determined to give as good as he got, seized Sue and swung her round. Wilkinson looked startled, so did his wife. Mendicott grinned foolishly, and the handsome Abbott squeezed himself between the radio and the wall, to give them more room.

The plump girl's dress had a deep plunge line, and was tight-fitting; her hair was loose and, as Hammond whirled her round, it began to fall into her eyes, came loose at the back and fell almost to her waist. At first she seemed too startled to dance freely, but soon she began to match her step to his. Round and round they went in the tiny space, Hammond dancing as vigorously as he knew how. Sue flopped up and down, caught her breath, began to lean against him, soft, yielding. Hammond was not finished. Faster and faster he whirled her round, so fast that he began to breathe in short gasps, and the girl was getting almost exhausted. Once she swept her hair out of her eyes, and stared at him in astonishment. Hammond jerked her vigorously and her teeth met together with a click.

Quicker, quicker...

The music stopped.

Hammond stood back, and bowed solemnly.

'Thank you very much,' he said, and turned and left her, sitting down by Wilkinson's side and picking up his glass. He sipped again.

Wilkinson laughed.

'Making the punishment fit the crime,' he remarked.

The words, like Mendicott's, seemed to have a double meaning. Hammond felt very hot. He wiped his forehead, and eased his collar. Sue suddenly laughed.

'I must go and spend a penny!'

She hurried out of the room, hitching up the shoulder of her dress. They were watching Hammond closely.

'Well, how *can* I help you?' Wilkinson asked.

Hammond took another sip of whisky. That must be the last, he decided; if it were doctored three sips should not do him any harm, more might do a lot.

'I came to see you about a friend of a friend of mine,' he said, 'who is also a friend of yours. This friend of mine has developed an affection for a Miss Clarissa Kaye, and he's troubled because she appears to have disappeared.'

Wilkinson laughed. At close quarters, Hammond found him quite good-looking, in a sallow fashion. His long face held a touch of drollness.

'You're doing well,' he said. '"Appears to have disappeared". Has she disappeared or hasn't she?'

Hammond said: 'The question is whether she has gone of her own accord or under coercion.'

Wilkinson raised one eyebrow.

'Abduction suspected, eh? Fergy, this ought to suit you. Our new friend says that he thinks someone has abducted Clarissa.'

Ferguson laughed. 'Abduction or seduction?'

'Well?' asked Wilkinson. 'Which?'

'Has Clarissa got a friend named Hammond?' inquired Violet Wilkinson with an innocent air. She came forward, and suddenly all of them were standing and looking down at Hammond. Violet was smiling sweetly, provocatively, Mendicott was leering, Ferguson's lips were twisted a little at one corner. The handsome Abbott, further away than any of the others, had both hands thrust into his pockets; he smirked. Wilkinson was between Hammond and the window. There was menace in their nearness.

'Well, has she?' asked Violet.

'Never heard of a Hammond,' said Abbott. 'Clarissa told me everything.' He chuckled, and the sound was not pleasant, it did not express amusement but rather a gloating triumph. 'Didn't she, Vi? I was her father confessor.'

'Hardly father,' said Wilkinson, dryly.

'Do you know, I think I've had an idea,' said Ferguson, putting his head on one side. 'Hammond, Hammond, Hammond, the name's familiar. Didn't Clarissa ring up this afternoon and say that Parmitter had been visited by an inquisitive stranger called Hammond? Copper, or something. Are *you* a policeman, Hammond?'

'If he is, he didn't announce himself as such.'

'So he must be here in his private capacity!'

'Perhaps *that* Hammond wasn't a policeman,' said Abbott.

'Anyone can have a card printed C.I.D. That wouldn't be legal, though; would it?'

Wilkinson put a hand on Hammond's knee. His long, thin fingers had a hard grip.

'What's your opinion, Hammond? Would it be legal for a man to represent himself as a policeman?' The pressure increased and Abbott, Ferguson and Mendicott closed in. They were all within a yard of Hammond, and Violet was standing just behind Ferguson.

'*Would* it?' insisted Wilkinson.

Hammond said: 'It depends why he did it. Music Hall *artistes* impersonate policemen.'

After a brief pause, the tension seemed to ease, although none of the men moved away.

'Not bad,' said Wilkinson. 'Hammond, isn't it time you told us why you came? This story about Clarissa having disappeared is all my eye. Clarissa doesn't do things like that—she's *far* too fond of Abbott. Isn't she, William?'

'Dotes on me,' claimed Abbott.

Looking at them each in turn, Hammond thought ruefully that they were dealing with him much as any Department Z men would deal with a man whom they wanted to frighten. The touch of flippancy and of facetiousness was there, but beneath it something dangerous and threatening.

He was feeling cool enough now. There was a slight draught from the window, cutting across his neck, and he put his hand to it. As he raised his hand Abbott moved sharply, but relaxed when he saw what Hammond was doing.

'You see, Clarissa wouldn't disappear,' said Wilkinson, 'unless, of course, she were spirited away by the police or someone pretending to be a policeman. Hammond, you wouldn't be so unfair as to come here and *pretend* that Clarissa's disappeared, so as to try to get information about her from her friends, would you?'

Hammond said equably, 'No, I wouldn't.'

Wilkinson squeezed Hammond's knee more tightly. 'Are you a policeman, Hammond?'

'I am not a policeman.'

'Is that really true?' Wilkinson appeared to marvel. 'But you are the man who went to see Parmitter, aren't you? Don't lie about it. We don't like people who tell us lies.'

Hammond settled back in his chair.

'I came to ask questions, not to answer them. I think...'

Wilkinson suddenly released his knee. Those steely fingers fastened about Hammond's arms, near the shoulders. It would not be easy for Hammond to pull himself free. As Wilkinson shifted his grip, Ferguson stepped forward and took out Hammond's wallet. Hammond made no effort to resist. Abbott began to go through Hammond's pockets, one at a time, while Ferguson examined the contents of the wallet. The inspection lasted for fully five minutes, and during that time neither Hammond nor Wilkinson moved. At last Ferguson finished. He had put everything back in the wallet, including the loose notes, and he tucked it into Hammond's coat pocket. When they had finished, Ferguson said:

'No police card.'

'Just a plain man,' Abbott commented.

'That's hard,' said Wilkinson. 'It's hard on you, Hammond. If you were a policeman we might be rather worried about you, but when a private citizen forces himself upon us on a night like this, he's asking for trouble. Who are you?'

Hammond smiled. 'Just a private citizen.'

Ferguson slapped him across the face. It was not a hard blow, but it took Hammond by surprise.

'I shouldn't do that again,' Hammond said.

Abbott raised his hand.

The door opened, and Sue came in. She had renewed her make-up, her hair was tidy and her dress was straight. She saw what they were doing and her eyes widened in alarm. She came hurrying across, protesting in a high-pitched voice that they must not hurt her boy friend. She stood in front of Hammond.

'Must they, ducky?' she asked.

'It wouldn't be wise.'

Wilkinson murmured: 'I don't think it would be very risky, Hammond. No one knows that you're here. There aren't many people out tonight. And you aren't a policeman—I didn't think you were when I heard that you'd visited Parmitter. I don't think the police would worry him. Not far away from here there are snow-drifts six and seven feet high. It would be just too bad if you wandered about Wimbledon Common and stumbled into a snow-drift and couldn't get put. We could hold you in the snow just long enough for you to stop breathing, but there would be no marks of violence.'

'It would be so *cold*,' Sue protested, shuddering. 'You couldn't do that.'

'Or could we?' asked Ferguson.

Abbott, who was the most serious of them all, asked in a clipped voice: 'Who are you, Hammond?'

Hammond didn't speak.

He saw Abbott lunge forward, hand upraised, and he kicked out. He caught Abbott in the stomach. The man doubled up and staggered back, making no sound. He struck a small table and sent it crashing. Glasses fell to the floor and broke. He did not fall, but straightened up and approached again, with a livid face.

'Hold it, Abby,' said Wilkinson. The pressure of his fingers was tighter now. 'Hammond, I've already warned you of your danger. We could do away with you quickly and quietly, but we don't want to—we want to know who you are and why you're interested in Clarissa Kaye and why you went to see Parmitter. Tell us, and you won't get hurt.'

Hammond was looking into Abbott's face; the last remark seemed very hard to believe.

'*Don't* make them hurt you,' murmured Sue. 'I *loved* that dance, ducky. I want you to teach us how to do it.'

'I'm not a teacher of dancing,' said Hammond. He glanced at the window, and let out a high-pitched cry. It seemed to shiver about the room.

It would be heard outside.

Abbott leapt forward, and his clenched fists battered Hammond's face. Sue pulled at him, but he shook her aside. Wilkinson relaxed for a moment, and Hammond wrenched himself free. Momentarily surprised, neither Ferguson nor Mendicott made any attempt to stop him. He pitched into Abbott, body to body, and as the man backed away he drove both fists into his face with a force which made Abbott's blows seem puny. This time Abbott fell over the table, hitting the floor amid a crash of breaking glasses. Hammond straightened up, only to find himself looking into the muzzle of an automatic held in Wilkinson's hand.

No one else moved.

'Is someone waiting outside?'

'Yes,' Hammond answered.

'How many men?'

'Enough,' said Hammond.

Abbott was getting up slowly, and he muttered in a hoarse voice: 'Shoot the swine. *Shoot* him.'

'I shouldn't,' said Hammond.

Out of the corner of his eye he saw Ferguson turn and pick up a whisky bottle from another table. Hammond tried to back away, but Ferguson moved so quickly that he had no chance. The bottle struck the back of his head. He felt himself falling forward, his senses swimming; then he lost consciousness, sprawling across the floor.

Wilkinson jumped up; his bandaged foot seemed to give him no trouble now.

'Let's move,' he said. 'Hurry!'

10
RAID

Waiting outside it was so cold that Tim Kemble could not stop his teeth from chattering. It would be difficult to move quickly even if there was no snow, though as things were it might take five minutes to reach the house. He had beaten a narrow path in the snow, going to and fro to the man nearest him, and he trudged along it again. He met Graham, who was dressed in a huge teddy bear coat, beating his arms across his chest and whistling faintly.

'Chilly,' he remarked.

'Perishing,' said Tim. 'I wish...'

The cry from Hammond came then, clear and near in the still air. Both men were pushing their way towards the house before it finished. Tim had forgotten the cold and the imagined difficulties. It was impossible to move really quickly, but he made fair speed; so did Graham and the other men who closed in upon the house. Further away Miller warned his own men, by word of mouth and radio, to be at the ready.

Tim, Graham and four others approaching the front of the house, were at the edge of the drive when the lights went out.

One moment the front of the house was bright, the light reflecting so clearly and white from the snow; the next darkness descended. Graham banged into Tim, but they kept their balance, and moved forward at a slower pace. Not far away someone exclaimed in annoyance as he was pushed over.

Torch beams shot out, criss-crossing the snow, vivid patches of light that made the outer darkness seem more intense.

'Watch the door!' a man called.

Graham, still next to Tim, muttered *sotto voce*:

'First show us the door.'

'Straight ahead,' said Tim. His torchlight shone on what looked like a heap of snow nearly waist high. It proved to be a flight of steps. He could see the glitter of the brass knocker and letter-box. He clambered up the steps, with Graham just behind, and several others were close on their heels. As Tim reached the door, Graham said:

'We're not going to waste time, are we?'

'Not a second,' said Tim. 'Hold your torch steady.' As Graham obeyed, Tim drove his gloved fist through the glass panel. Glass fell with a tinkling sound. Tim fumbled for the catch, had difficulty because of his gloves, but at last pulled it back.

The door swung open.

'Find the light,' said Graham.

'Put that torch out!' snapped Tim.

He stood on the threshold, peering ahead. The torch went out, and he felt easier; until then he had been a clear target for anyone standing in the darkness. He crept forward. Other men pressed behind Graham, and began to grope about the hall. Tim reached a wall and ran his hand over it, pushed a picture to one side, and, still groping, loosened another from its hanger.

It fell with a crash.

No one spoke; all stood quite silently, waiting. Then in a small, apologetic voice, Tim said:

'Sorry, chaps.'

He continued to grope for the light, until someone on the other side of the hall said:

'I've found a switch. Scatter.'

The agents scattered, getting behind doors and large pieces of furniture, all moving by sense of touch, able to see nothing at all. When quiet fell again, the man by the wall pressed down the switch.

A light came on at the landing.

It was bright enough to show them everything here, and cast long shadows on the doors and the walls. They peered upstairs, seeing nothing, hearing nothing. A little shame-faced, they came out of their hiding-places. As they did so they heard a thump which seemed to come from a long way off.

'That's the crowd at the back,' said Graham. 'I'll go and let them in.'

Two men went with him, each carrying a gun. They went through the passage at the end of the hall, and the rest waited until they heard sounds of the back door being opened and others of their party admitted. Then they began to search the ground floor.

Tim went into the big front room, and when he switched on the light, he exclaimed in surprise.

There was no one there, but the fallen table and the broken glasses were on the floor, and there were signs of a struggle. Whisky and gin lay in pools on the little patch of floor which had been cleared for dancing. A cigarette was burning on top of the radio, and the polish was scorched, giving off a faint, unpleasant smell. There were crackers and party caps, the colourful trifles which had so surprised Hammond.

Tim picked one up, and looked at it.

'This is not Christmas,' said one of the others, a man named Fordham. 'On with the search.'

'This isn't funny,' said Tim. 'Bruce was here.'

'*Is* here,' corrected Fordham.

They went into the dining-room, a library and a morning-room, all well-furnished. The library was piled from floor to ceiling with books, and Tim glanced at the shelves and found an impressive collection. This was the most imposing room of the house: the furniture was all old, the oak bookshelves were beautifully carved, and the whole gave an impression of learning and of comfort; it was a scholar's room.

Graham joined them with the men who had come in the back way, and a small party of agents who had broken in at a side door arrived. All had the same thing to report: there was no one on the ground floor. The domestic quarters and out-houses had all been searched, and there was no sign of any living thing, except a Scottie which had kept extraordinarily quiet during the invasion. It now mixed with the men, going from one to the other with ears and tail drooping.

Tim fondled its ears, and the dog crouched away.

'Find 'em,' Tim said. 'Show us the way, McTavish!'

The dog perked up its ears.

'Good house dog,' sniffed Fordham, sarcastically, smoothing down the thick hair. 'It's warm in here,' he added, and loosened his coat. 'Upstairs, next. Who's first for the shooting gallery?'

'If you ask me, this house is empty,' Graham said.

'It can't be,' said Tim. Yet the thought was in his mind.

With Graham and Fordham he moved towards the stairs. They walked up slowly, their guns at the ready, and reached the halfway landing, then the first floor landing. They beckoned the others, and made a thorough search of every room.

There were indications of a hurried departure. Lipstick and other make-up lay on dressing-tables in two of the bedrooms, a man's clothes were flung about, as if he had changed in a hurry before going downstairs, and no one had had time to tidy the room. In another huge bedroom where there was a four-poster bed, a cigarette was still burning in an ashtray, and on the dressing-table lay a wallet which contained nearly thirty pounds.

'Next floor,' Fordham said.

'I tell you...' began Graham.

Tim said: 'We know that there were people here less than ten minutes before we arrived. We *heard* them. And we know Bruce came here. It's crazy to think the house is empty.'

Graham said: 'Crazy or not, it is.'

There was one more floor.

In the first of the four rooms there, they found the first living person—the maid, Daisy. She was sitting on a narrow bed, smoking. She had just made up her face and was dressed for out of doors. She looked up with a pert smile when Tim and Graham went in.

'*I* haven't done anything,' she said. 'Search me.'

'We're going to,' Tim said, grimly.

She clutched her coat more tightly about her.

'Don't you get fresh,' she said. 'I can't do anything for you. All I know is that the boss told me to wait here until someone broke in, and told me they would look after me. And you'd better.' She looked at Tim's set face apprehensively.

'Do you mean Wilkinson told you that?' asked Tim.

'*Mister* Wilkinson to you, and don't you forget it. He told me he'd be back some day and I would have my job back, if I wanted it. *And* he gave me this, instead of notice.' She took a small wad of notes from her handbag and waved them in his face.

'You're lying,' Tim said roughly. 'The house was surrounded, no one could have escaped, and Wilkinson was here a quarter of an hour ago. Where has he gone?'

'I tell you I *don't* know,' she snapped, and Tim found it hard to disbelieve her.

Graham stood looking down at her.

'Did Wilkinson have a visitor earlier this evening?'

'Yes.'

'Where is the visitor?'

'*I* don't know.'

Tim touched Graham's arm.

'Leave her to me,' he said. 'Take the others and search all the rooms for a hidden door. There's probably more than one in a house like this.' A thought occurred to him, and he took the girl's arm; she jumped again, proving nervousness bravely concealed. 'Is there an old air-raid shelter?'

'*I don't know*! I've only been here three months. I've never *seen* one.'

'Is there a cellar?'

'I've never *seen* one,' she repeated, and caught her breath.

'We'll get cracking,' said Graham.

He went out, and closed the door behind him. Tim turned the key in the lock and slipped it into his pocket. Daisy watched him, her eyes now reflecting more obvious fear. For Tim's usually happy-go-lucky expression had gone, and he looked grim, sombre, determined. He took off his hat and ran his hand through his fine, fluffy hair. He was not bad-looking, but now his lips were set tightly and his eyes narrowed as he looked at the girl.

There had already been murder, committed ruthlessly; there was reason to think that Wilkinson and his friends were concerned in that. If they would kill once, as they had killed Parmitter, were they likely to hesitate to kill again? The fact that Hammond had been taken away from the house suggested that he might still be alive; but Tim knew that there had been many disappearances of men who had walked into danger, as Hammond had done, and never returned.

The only immediate source of information was this girl.

'Stand up,' he said, harshly.

She leaned back against the foot of the bed, defiantly.

He took a step towards her. 'Get up,' he repeated. When she still did not obey, he took her wrist, pulled her up and over, and brought the flat of his hand hard on her bottom.

'Don't do that!' she cried.

'You're going to answer my questions,' Tim said. 'If you lie once—just *once*, my pretty—you are going to be very sorry for yourself. Understand?'

'I'll tell you all I know,' she muttered. 'It's not much.'

She answered his questions grudgingly. A picture of the household built up in his mind. Wilkinson, Mendicott, Abbott and Ferguson had been here that evening, together with Mrs. Wilkinson and a woman named Susan Harris. Daisy said that Susan was at the house frequently and was a particular friend of Ferguson's.

After the cry which had summoned Tim and the others, Mrs. Wilkinson had hurried into the kitchen and told her to go upstairs to her room and put on her hat and coat. Wilkinson had come in, given her a bundle of notes in lieu of notice; told her that they would be back one day, and left, without locking the door, telling her that she must not leave until someone broke into the house and found her.

The only thing she knew after that was that Wilkinson had gone downstairs. His wife had called out to him to hurry, and Daisy had heard Wilkinson clattering down to join her. That had surprised Daisy, because for the last two days he had been sitting about the house with his left foot bandaged, and had hobbled everywhere on a walking stick. She was quite sure of that, but his foot seemed to have got better suddenly.

Had there been visits that afternoon?

The girl didn't know, but thought so. It had been her afternoon off, and she had spent most of the time in her room, reading and knitting. She showed Tim the book and the knitting, a vivid red bundle of wool which was going to become a pixie-hood.

What made her think that there had been visitors?

A car had driven up as far as the gate, about four o'clock, she had seen it from her window. She had not been able to see anyone get out. The car had been driven away almost at once. When she had gone downstairs, to get her own tea—Violet and Susan had got tea for the others—she had expected to find more people present, but none had been about. She thought that one of the spare rooms on the floor below had been used. Someone had made-up in there.

That was the first slight indication that Clarissa might have been at the house.

The girl was answering freely enough now.

Yes, she knew about *Warning* and she always read the News-Letter. It made her laugh, although she could not understand half of it. She was not interested in politics. She had never thought much of the Russians, but she did not care much one way or the other about them.

There had been other servants until three days before. Then Benby and his wife, the butler and housekeeper, had left. They had left during their half-day off. She did not know where they had gone, but she thought they had been told to prepare another house for the family to move into. She had no idea where the other house was. Since the other servants had gone, the two daily women had helped with the housework and she, Daisy, had done the cooking. The men had dished up the meals, and, said Daisy, 'No one could ever ask for a better employer!'

That was all Tim could get out of her.

He gave her a cigarette.

'Now you go downstairs and make some coffee,' Tim said. 'We're going to need gallons.'

When she had gone, he searched the room and other rooms on that floor. They had not been used recently. He hurried downstairs, finding two Department men on guard on the landing. No one was on the first floor, they assured him. They went into the bedrooms one after the other. There were five on this floor, all well-furnished, two in ultra modern fashion, the others more drab.

It was in one of the modern rooms that Tim found a screwed up piece of paper. He opened it out, and when he saw the first words of the note, he stiffened.

It read: *'Dear Clarissa.'*

The note was signed 'Abby' and was couched in affectionate terms. It was freshly-written, he judged, for the ink was pale. It said that 'Abby' hoped to have some time with her in the next day or two, but that there would probably be little opportunity that day. And—she was not to 'worry'.

There was no envelope; but the note had originally been folded like an old-fashioned *billet doux.*

And it was probably slipped under the door, mused Tim.

He went towards the door, still troubled about the silence from downstairs, and heard his name called:

'Tim! You there, Tim?'

'Coming!' He hurried out, for there had been a note of excitement in the call. At the foot on the stairs, a chubby young man was waiting, his eyes glistening with excitement. He put his thumb up and said cheerfully:

'Air-raid shelter, Tim. Not so very mysterious, after all. Devilish long passages, too. We haven't reached the end of them yet. Wait until you see it!'

'Who found it?'

'Fordham.'

The old air-raid shelter led from a butler's pantry. Fordham had found that the pantry, now used chiefly as a storeroom for fruit, had been recently decorated. A 'new' wall had been built, covering up the original one, and Fordham had wondered why. The rubber flooring had been taken up and, beneath it, they had found loose boards which, when lifted, led into the underground passage leading to the airraid shelter.

From below, it was possible to see that originally the shelter had been approached through the pantry, and in the original wall there had probably been a door. The steps leading down had been altered—the two top ones were comparatively new, the cement much fresher and paler than that lower down.

Electric light glowed along a narrow passage, where Department Z men were walking. Tim caught up with Fordham and Graham. The passage ran for at least a hundred yards, sloping downwards slightly all the time, and when he drew level with Fordham, Tim realised that they were probably standing beneath the next-door garden.

They had not yet reached the end of the passage.

'Have you sent a message to Miller?' Tim asked.

'Yes. He's coming. And we've had a message from him,' Graham said. 'No one's caught, I'm afraid. But they might be in the next-door house. We'll smoke 'em out.'

'Yes,' said Tim.

Was there a chance? Was Clarissa somewhere near? Would

they find Hammond? His thoughts were crystallising, and he was much more concerned with finding Hammond than Clarissa. He kept pace with Graham and Fordham, and there was just room for the three of them to walk abreast; the passage was much wider here.

They came upon a door.

It looked like wood, but when they touched it, it had the coldness of steel. They stood beneath the dim light of an electric lamp, examining it, and Graham said *sotto voce*:

'We'll probably need an oxy-acetylene burner for that.'

The door opened when he pushed.

Fordham snapped: 'Careful!'

Tim took his automatic out and, pressing against the wall on one side, kicked the door open and rushed in. He fully expected an attack; he seemed to hear the ringing of shots in his ears, but there was no sound; nothing happened, nothing moved. He went to the wall and sought for a light switch, just as he had done in the hall.

He pressed it down.

They were in a large, square room. It was well-furnished, as a sitting-room, and there were bunks at the sides, but no bed-clothes; it had obviously not been used for sleeping in for some time. The furniture was good, the distempered walls looked clean and fresh.

There were two doors.

Tim went across to one, Fordham to the other. Tim stepped inside a bathroom and lavatory combined; no one was in there. He went back into the main room, thinking that Fordham would probably have reached another passage, one leading in a different direction. As he approached the second doorway Graham was disappearing through it.

Fordham exclaimed: '*Hammond!*'

Tim hurried after him, his breathing harsh; for there had

been alarm in Fordham's voice. He pushed past Graham, and saw Fordham bending over Hammond's recumbent form. It was impossible to tell at a glance whether Hammond were alive or dead, but there was no doubt about the condition of another man who lay on the floor near Hammond, in a small book-lined room, reminiscent of the library.

He was shot through the chest.

He was a handsome man, but even in death there was a sneer on his lips; and Tim recognised Abbott, Wilkinson's aide.

Slowly he turned to Hammond.

11

POOR M. NASSI

Tim Kemble sat in an armchair opposite Craigie, and Loftus lounged against the mantelpiece, with the fire scorching the ends of his trousers. All of them looked tired, for it was after three o'clock. Tim had been back half an hour.

'Why should they kill Abbott?' he asked. 'Damn it, he was one of them. And why did they leave Bruce alive? He's had a crack over the head which broke the skin and laid him out, but there weren't any other signs of injury. At least, *I* couldn't see any. He'd been drugged. The doctor said that it was morphine. We found the puncture in his forearm, so it was injected. He was breathing evenly and he looked all right; I don't think we've anything to fear for Bruce. But Abbott—can you make any sense out of it?'

'Give us time,' pleaded Loftus.

'I suppose there must be a reasonable explanation,' Tim conceded. 'Now we know what they did, it's easy enough to understand. They went downstairs, along the passage, through the main shelter which was underneath a house on the other side of the road, and then into the grounds of that house.

Miller had his men on the wrong side of the grounds. The beggars just walked off, without anyone to question them. We found car tracks going towards London. There was a shed, nicely warmed with oil heaters, where they'd kept the car.'

'How far was the second house from *Hatch End*?' asked Loftus.

'The better part of a couple of hundred yards. Oh, I'm not blaming Miller,' Tim went on. 'It just didn't go our way, but— *why* did they kill Abbott? He was one of the gang.'

'Bruce may be able to tell us something in the morning,' said Craigie. 'You get some rest, Tim.'

Tim went out into the bitter cold night, to struggle through the snowbound streets and with his gloom.

Loftus was yawning when Craigie looked up, and then Craigie started; they both laughed.

'We'll take forty winks here,' said Craigie, and between them they opened what looked like another wide cupboard, where two single built-in beds were all ready. They pulled them down and slackened belts and collars, talking over the partial failure at *Hatch End*.

Abbott had been shot through the chest in exactly the same way as Parmitter, and with the same calibre bullets. Obviously it had not been from the same gun or by the same man.

Wilkinson's pretended lameness, Loftus thought, proved that he had wanted to make it appear that he was incapacitated. He had been forced into violence by Hammond's tactics.

'We might hear something from George, I suppose,' he said, 'but I hope he waits until morning. He's probably enjoying himself with Nassi at this moment!'

* * *

George Henry George was not exactly enjoying himself. There were two reasons for that.

In the first place, M. Nassi of San Patino had left the Haymart Hotel and, for some reason unknown to Department Z, had elected to patronise a small hotel near Reading. That night of all nights, travelling to Reading had been fraught with danger and difficulty. George had departed a little after ten o'clock, leaving his snug but anxious Polly without any hope of hearing from him until the next morning. He had with him one automatic pistol, two fresh clips of ammunition, one hypodermic syringe filled with an adrenalin solution which would induce almost immediate unconsciousness if required, and one knife. True, it was a remarkable knife, fitted with many blades; in the possession of anyone less favoured by the police it would undoubtedly have been regarded as a cracksman's tool. He had, also, some pieces of cord, a candle, a plentiful supply of matches and, a thing which worried him most, a mask which covered the top half of his face. He regarded himself as well-equipped for his venture, which was to persuade M. Nassi to explain what he had been doing with Parmitter, why he had changed his hotel on such a day—and, in short, to glean any odd piece of information.

He had with him, also, Mark Errol.

They sat side by side in George's roomy Jaguar. There were chains on all four wheels, but in places they could have done with not chains but an aeroplane to get them easily over the blocked roads. Traffic was snowbound on either side of them, even on the outskirts of London. When they reached the top of Putney Hill, quite unaware of what was happening only a mile away at *Hatch End*, a little group of policemen, A.A. and R.A.C. scouts and helpful citizens warned them that it would be folly to go on.

'But we must,' protested George.

'You haven't got a chance, sir,' said a sergeant of police. 'Not as far as Reading. You might make Kingston, but the by-pass is pretty hopeless. There's been a dozen smashes along there tonight.'

'There are by-roads,' said George.

'Try them at your own risk, sir. If I was you, I'd turn back.'

That had been the advice given to them every time they met scouts and police along the road. Four times they had been compelled to alight and help to move a car which was stuck across the road in front of them. There were plenty of stranded motorists about, sitting miserably in their cars, and cursing the weather. Only two or three drivers had got beyond Kingston since five o'clock.

They took the chance, and by sheer persistence, they reached the outskirts of Reading. There was a steep hill leading into the town, and there the Jaguar, swerving to avoid a car jutted out from the side of the road, piled into a snow-barrier.

From there, they walked.

Just after three o'clock they reached the Akers Hotel, which was a short distance from the centre of the town, on the London Road.

The journey was one reason why George was not enjoying himself. The other was the fact that there seemed no way of getting into Akers Hotel. One side was piled up with snow which reached halfway up the windows. On the other side, which had been to the leeward, the ground floor windows were barred.

George surveyed the hotel and reflected aloud:

'You know what we want to make it a real night out?'

'What's that?'

'No Nassi,' said George.

'I thought you had a sunny nature.'

That was before I had to try to climb up that wall,' George told him. 'Oh, well. Women must weep.'

He had chosen the one spot where he might be able to get to a window and force his way in. One look at the doors had convinced him that it was practically impossible to force them without making too much noise; his stiff, cold fingers were not dexterous enough. But the south side of the hotel was comparatively free from snow, and there were window ledges on which he could get a foothold.

There was one good thing; no police were likely to be patrolling the streets.

'Which window are you going to try?' asked Mark Erro.

'The middle one. It's immediately above the back door, and might be to a landing,' said George. 'Give me a leg up, will you?'

Mark bent his back.

George climbed to the first window ledge without much trouble. He was just out of Mark's reach, but Mark stood waiting to lend a hand lest he should fall. George thrust his frozen hand into his pocket and brought out a small torch. He shone it against the window and then pressed his face close to the glass, shielding it with his free hand. He swayed to and fro, his heart jumping, and suddenly lurched against the window which gave out a hollow, booming sound.

No sound came from inside the hotel, nothing appeared to have been heard. Now he could just see into the room—and it *was* a room, not a landing. On the far side was a single bed. Still swaying unsteadily, he examined the window.

The catch was not fastened.

He searched his pocket for his knife, which he had already opened—and dropped the torch. It went out as it hit the snow.

'All right,' he called softly, 'keep it out.'

It was difficult to find the bottom of the window by touch

alone, but he persisted, and thrust the knife in between the old-fashioned sash-cord window and the frame. Akers was obliging in that respect, at any rate. He pressed gently. The narrow blade was very tough and would not break easily. He kept levering, and suddenly the window squeaked up an inch.

He stopped abruptly, and listened; he heard no other sound.

Once the start was made, getting the window open wide enough to get his fingers on to the bottom was fairly easy. At last he was able to put his knife away. He blew on his fingers, protected only by thin gloves, so as to give him freedom of movement, then put them beneath the window and pulled upwards. He could only do that by leaning backwards, only his grip on the window saved him from falling.

One hand slipped.

He lurched backwards, his heart in his mouth, but managed to hold on with the other hand.

He tried again, and the window went up with a sudden spurt, groaning horribly. Having made so much noise, he might as well make a job of it, George decided, and thrust the window right up.

He put one leg inside the room, and whispered to Mark:

'I'm okay.'

Then he climbed in.

He stood for a moment by the open window, wishing that he had his torch. He could hear no breathing. Gradually he found himself able to see about the room, and he stepped towards the bed. A man was sleeping. He could just make out the pale face and the dark hair.

The man stirred in his sleep.

George took out his hypodermic syringe, and murmured: 'Sorry, old chap. Duty calls.' The man stirred again. George rubbed his hands to try to get them warmer, peering closely all the time. He could make out the shape of a bedside lamp, and wished that he dared switch it on.

Then he picked up the sheet in front of the man's face, thrust it over the mouth and nose, and pressed. The man jumped violently, and let out a muffled gasp. George felt for the man's shoulder, which was heaving up and down, then plunged the needle in. The man jumped and gasped, but the sheet smothered the sound. George maintained his pressure, using both hands because the man was struggling so violently.

It seemed an age before the struggles weakened.

At last, George withdrew his hands.

'Very sorry,' he murmured, 'but you'll only have a headache in the morning.' He put on the light, and a bright glow spread about the room. He went to the window and whispered down: 'I'll find the door and open it.'

Mark waved.

Five minutes later, George had opened the side door of the hotel, and with noiseless footsteps they walked towards the reception desk. They looked down the visitors' book, and immediately found that Nassi had registered and was in Room 17.

'Something,' whispered George. 'Mark, I *must* get warm.'

'Let's try the kitchen,' suggested Mark.

Using only the torch to light the way, they made two unsuccessful efforts to find the kitchen, then came upon it. From a small room leading off the kitchen came a blast of hot air which made their watery eyes glisten. It was the boiler-room, and the fire was glowing red through the cracks at the side of the boiler.

George took out a hip flask.

'What with this and that,' he said, 'we'll be all right. What's the time?'

'Getting on for four.'

'We've got about a couple of hours, then.' George gave Mark the flask, then took a warming sip. 'Yes, we'll be all right,' he repeated. 'Five minutes down here and we'll be as lissome as a lark.' He hummed to himself, his spirits fully restored, while Mark spread his hands about the boiler, welcoming the fierce heat. 'Careful of chilblains,' George said. 'Or do I mean chaps? Ready?'

'Righto,' said Mark.

The air in the passage and on the stairs was chill, but when they reached Room 17, he was able to handle his knife without any difficulty. The door was locked. George took one look at the lock, and chuckled softly.

'It's child's play,' he declared.

A blade went in, he twisted two or three times, and then there was a click.

He went inside.

Mark stood outside the door, on guard.

M. Edouard Nassi, who had fallen into a troubled sleep only an hour before, felt something touch his shoulder. He was awake in a flash, for he had trained himself to wake at the slightest touch—and, he fondly believed, the slightest sound. His restlessness probably explained the fact that the slight sounds which George had made entering the room and crossing to the bed had not disturbed him.

The pressure tightened.

Nassi put his hand down by the side of his leg. There, tucked inside the sheet like a warming pan, was a gun. He had become accustomed to carrying a weapon, and he liked to have it inside the bed. His fingers touched the warm steel. They tightened about it. He began to draw his arm up slowly, still feigning sleep. Whoever was there seemed intent only on waking him. It might, possibly, be a friend, but it was much better to make sure. He tensed his arm, prepared to draw it quickly from beneath the bedclothes and confront his man with the gun. Then, without a moment's warning, a pillow was thrust over his face and the bedclothes were flung back. He jerked his arm up; steel-like fingers gripped his wrist and twisted, and the gun dropped from his grasp.

He could not see, for the pillow was over his eyes, but he heard the man say:

'Naughty Nassi!'

There was a pause.

'Loaded, too. You know, that's not nice in a friendly country.' The man spoke with a North Country accent. 'Can you hear me, Nassi? Nod, if you can.'

Nassi nodded vigorously.

'Then do what you're told,' said George. 'Keep your mouth closed tightly until I tell you to open it, and make no noise of any kind. Do you understand?'

Again Nassi nodded vigorously.

George switched on the bedside lamp, then stood back from the bed, relieving pressure on the pillow. Nassi pushed it off his face cautiously. He lay blinking in the light, his hooked nose and hooded, slightly protuberant eyes giving him the look of a bewildered owl. He began to shiver. George threw a dressing-gown from the foot of the bed to the top, and Nassi sat up, slipping it round his shoulders.

'Th-th-thank you,' he whispered.

'Could light the fire,' said George.

A little, old-fashioned electric fire, all wires and burnt enamel, stood near with its snake-like coil of flex. Deliberately, he turned his back on Nassi, bent down and switched it on. Then he appeared to get his foot caught in the flex, and put down the gun.

Nassi leapt at him, flinging back the bedclothes and jumping out of bed with remarkable agility. He took only two steps to reach George. George, still kneeling, turned round. His right hand shot out and, from the whirling arms and legs, selected Nassi's left wrist. He gripped and twisted. Nassi caught his breath, making more noise than George wanted, and then an astonishing thing happened. Nassi stood where he was, with only one foot on the floor, his body twisted forward, arrested in full flight. His mouth was open and he looked horrified. There was a searing pain in his wrist. It spread from wrist to shoulder and then down his side, until it seemed like a fire which ran through his whole body.

George held him like that for some seconds, and then let him go. He collapsed in a heap.

Mark put his head round the door.

'All right?' he asked.

'Managing nicely, thanks,' said George. 'You might put him back to bed.'

'Anything to oblige.' Mark stepped forward, lifted Nassi bodily and dumped him on the bed. 'I shouldn't make too much row,' he remarked, mildly. 'They might not all be sound sleepers.' He went back to his post, quite content to stay on guard.

Nassi was breathing in short, shallow gasps.

George sat on the edge of the bed, nursing the gun in his lap.

'Listen to me, Nassi. You warned Parmitter this afternoon that someone was about to attack him. Who told you?'

Nassi squeaked: 'You are mistaken! I assure you that...'

George dug his candle out of his pocket. He flicked a lighter into flame, put the candle on the mantelpiece and lit it, and then placed beside it a knife with a cruel-looking blade. 'The candle is to burn you with and the knife to do unmentionable things,' he remarked, in a casual manner which made the words seem more menacing. 'I have a friend outside who will first gag you.'

In a queer, croaking voice, Nassi asked:

'Are you one of *them*?'

'Yes,' said George.

'Then *you* know who attacked M. Parmitter. There is no need to ask me questions.'

George glanced at the steady flame of the candle. Aloud he said: 'I shouldn't hesitate to answer, and I shouldn't show too much curiosity. Let me tell you something you already know. You left the Haymart Hotel and went to a telephone kiosk. Then you hurried back and rushed to Parmitter, to warn him— but you were too late. Whom did you telephone?'

'But you should already know,' objected Nassi.

Outwardly, he was reasonably calm. Inwardly, he was greatly frightened. This small man with the plain face and the enormous eyes seemed to be able to frighten in a few words. Was it his expression? Was it the glances he cast towards the candle and the knife? Or was it the memory of the agonising pain which had run through his whole body when he had made that ill-fated attempt to turn the tables? Nassi, who had that kind of mind, could analyse the situation even while he stared at George; and he came to the conclusion that it was a little of all three, allied to the fact that outside a much bigger man than George was waiting.

George spoke again, still mildly.

'Look,' he said. 'I have nothing up my sleeve.' He held out his right hand, palm upwards. The fingers were long and thin, the tips rounded and broad. Nassi stared at them. 'Nothing at all,' burbled George, and snapped his fingers. Then he thrust his hand forward beneath Nassi's nose.

Something sprang up from his hand. *Gas!* It bit at Nassi's eyes, mouth and nose and seemed to make them raw; tears streamed down his face and he doubled up coughing violently. The effect had been instantaneous and terrifying. Nassi had not even seen the little cloud of white vapour, certainly not the tiny rubber container in George's hand. The effect of the gas grew worse; he found it hard to get his breath. He staggered back and was unaware of the gentle grip of George's fingers on his throat, to prevent too much noise.

Nassi muttered: 'I don't believe you are...'

'This is just question and answer,' said George. 'What number did you telephone?'

'B-Bishopgate 081211,' muttered Nassi. He kept sniffing, but he felt better—rather as if he had a severe head-cold. 'B-Bishopgate 081211,' he repeated.

'Whom did you speak to?'

'*Him!*'

'Yes I know,' said George, patiently, 'but who is he?'

Nassi said: 'Wilkinson, Wilkinson! I am telling you the truth. I telephoned Mr. Wilkinson and he told me that an attack was going to be made upon M. Parmitter and I hurried back and it was too late to save him.'

So it came back to Wilkinson, who had a City office. That shouldn't surprise anyone.

'Why did you telephone him?' demanded George. 'And why did you warn Parmitter? What business were you doing with Parmitter? Chatter, little man, I don't want to hurt you again.'

And Nassi began to talk more freely.

* * *

An hour later, Mark and George left Akers and hurried down the hill to their car. Not far along the road was an A.A. box and a man was on duty near it, with a coke brazier burning with a fierce red glow. The snow around it had melted; there was a pleasant warm smell.

'No,' he said, in answer to George's eager question, 'the telephone lines aren't down yet. You'll get through to London.' He opened the box, and George put through a call to the Department, thus waking Craigie and Loftus a little before six o'clock. George was neither flippant nor careless, and told the whole story with precision and some detail. When he had finished, he said that he hoped it was of some help.

Craigie said: 'One thing helps, George, if nothing else does. Bishopgate 081211 is the telephone number of *Super-Steel's* head office.'

12

REPORT AND ACTION

A little after eight o'clock that morning, Loftus and Craigie walked across Whitehall, where two lines of traffic were now moving, and turned into Downing Street. Policemen nodded at them, and a sergeant insisted on inspecting their passes. Then they were admitted to Number 10 by a footman.

They were in a waiting room only for a few minutes before a red-haired man came in and greeted them warmly. The Prime Minister had told him that they were unlikely to have had breakfast.

'He was quite right,' Loftus said.

'Then perhaps you'll have some with him.' The red haired secretary ushered them into another room, where Hadley was sitting at a table already laid for three. He greeted them with his pleasant smile. The butler brought in bacon and sausages, tea and coffee.

Hadley listened attentively to Craigie's version of George's story. According to George, Nassi had admitted having negotiated with Parmitter for supplies of steel and manufactured armaments, to be supplied to San Patino from *Super-Steel*'s South American plant. The reason was simple: it had come to the ears of the efficient and wideawake San Patino Government that Shovia was arming heavily, but there was not yet sufficient evidence on which to base a case for the United Nations. Nassi had assured George that San Patino would be prepared to do that.

American arms had poured into the country, to equip a small but well-trained Shovian army and air force for its strong anti-Communist government. These arms were stored in almost inaccessible places up and down the country, with an ominous concentration near the frontier with San Patino.

Had that been the only thing, San Patino would have referred the matter to *Uno* and been quite happy. But, said Nassi, there was something far worse; it was rumoured that Shovia planned a revolutionary coup, with Russia backing it. For evidence, there were reports from secret service agents and the fact that the Soviet had recently withdrawn her representative from San Patino. There were other small countries, Nassi said, equally troubled by seemingly irrefutable evidence that Russia was showing disapproval of them and supporting their neighbours. When asked which other countries, Nassi had mentioned six, including all the countries whose delegates had shown no enthusiasm for Virnov's arrival.

Craigie said, 'It begins to make a pattern, doesn't it, sir?'

'Yes,' said Hadley. 'Go on.' He pushed the toast and marmalade across to Loftus.

'Nassi was authorised by his Government to get what arms he could,' said Craigie. 'And as *Super-Steel* has a big plant there, he has been negotiating with Parmitter. Parmitter made extravagant promises. According to Nassi, Parmitter told him that Marchant's apparent conversion from armaments to consumer goods is a cover for his real activities. Officially, Marchant had agreed that armaments should be internationally controlled, actually he was prepared, through subsidiary concerns of *Super-Steel*'s, to supply anything that was wanted.'

'I see,' Hadley said.

'Have you heard that Marchant is playing a double game?' Loftus asked him.

'No. I have every reason to rely on his good faith. That doesn't rule out the possibility, of course, but we shall need rather more evidence than Nassi's statement.'

Loftus chuckled. '*Rather* more is good!'

'You know what I mean. This is the first indication that *Super-Steel* might be using its subsidiary companies throughout the world for the manufacture of secret armaments, but it wouldn't be the first time that such a thing has happened. Nor is this the first indication that Russia is supporting the claims of some small States against those of others. On the other hand, Russia assures us that she is doing nothing of the kind.'

Craigie said: 'Secret diplomacy is hardly a new thing, either. How much evidence is there against Russia in this instance?'

'Little, if any. We should keep an open mind,' Hadley said. 'Certainly someone is trying to create suspicion against Russia. The attitude towards Virnov was one example, the attempt to reduce the United Nations Organisation to a talking shop for the expression of pious hopes may be another. This could be a third. None of these is conclusive.'

Loftus said, 'One thing is, sir.'

'What's that?'

'We face two possibilities,' said Loftus. 'Either Russia is

hostile to *Uno* or someone is trying to make her hostile. The first would be disastrous; the second could be.'

'Yes, I agree with you. There is no reason why I should not be frank,' went on Hadley. 'I think the second theory is the right one. I can envisage circumstances which would make Russia withdraw—if she were convinced that one of the Western powers was conniving at this.' Hadley paused, and then added in a different tone: 'I can't over-emphasise the gravity of the situation. We are nearer an understanding with Russia than we have been for fifty years. If anything goes wrong, it could drive her back to the Chinese mood of conquest by force of arms.'

There was a moment's silence, before he went on:

'What do you propose to do next?'

'We shall work on Marchant,' Craigie said.

'The story of the disagreement with Marchant's niece, Clarissa Kaye, could be false,' Loftus said. 'That would explain the fact that Clarissa escaped with the help of Lionel Marchant. We will have to call on a lot of men we had retired, Gordon.'

'Do that,' said Hadley.

'There's one puzzling anomaly,' Craigie observed. 'If Russia is supposed to be backing Shovia, why is the Shovian delegation so hostile?'

Hadley gave his deprecating smile.

'An attempt to bluff us would be in keeping, wouldn't it?'

'That may be it,' said Craigie.

'We'll tackle Pirani, too,' Loftus promised.

Hadley put up a hand, quickly: 'I think perhaps that I'd better know nothing of the details. That will make it easier for me to answer any questions that might be put in the House. And there are going to be questions.'

As they walked from Number 10 across Whitehall, where

an army of workmen was clearing snow, Craigie and Loftus carried with them the memory of Hadley's quiet, undemonstrative manner.

In the office, Loftus said.

'Well, what's first?'

'We'll raid *Super-Steel* offices,' Craigie said. 'You make arrangements for that. And give Bruce Hammond a ring and find out how he's doing.'

Before Loftus could lift the telephone, another bell rang. Craigie answered. 'Hallo, Miller.' Loftus picked up the extension telephone, and heard the Scotland Yard man say:

'I've had a report from Staines that someone who might have been Wilkinson passed through about nine o'clock last night,' said Miller. 'There is another report from Reading. The same car, a Buick—Wilkinson owns a Buick—was seen going through there on the Newbury Road. That's the same direction as Colston, Marchant's country place. There were three men and two women in the car, and another, smaller car was just behind it.'

'Have you a call out for the movements of the cars to be watched?'

'Yes. If I get another line, I'll call you again. 'Bye.'

Miller, who never wasted words, rang off, and Loftus and Craigie regarded each other, hope sparking their eyes.

'Shall I still try Bruce?' said Loftus.

'Yes.'

Bruce Hammond answered the call, and was quick to say that he had written a report on all that had happened at *Hatch End*. It was on the way to Whitehall, by special messenger. Tim Kemble was with him, and had helped to prepare the report.

'Good enough,' said Loftus. He told him of the report from Reading, then added, 'Take whatever risks you have to, Bruce.'

* * *

'Take whatever risks you have to,' Hammond echoed. He replaced the receiver and looked at Tim Kemble. 'That fit your mood?'

'Made to measure,' Tim said. 'I'm as restless as hell.'

He wasn't the only one. The agents were all prone to be affected by sudden, sharp, emotional tensions. Tim had been working at high pressure since the beginning of this affair, and the previous night's was the first reasonable sleep he had had for four days. If that wasn't enough, there was Clarissa Kaye's effect on him.

Hammond had suffered in much the same way. He had met his wife in such an affair as this. He smiled faintly, and Tim murmured:

'What's funny?'

'I was imagining Clarissa's face when I gate-crashed on Parmitter. You know her more than the rest of us. *Did* you feel that she was really trustworthy?'

Tim said, 'Yes, I did, but that's nothing to go on.'

'I rather took to her,' said Hammond. 'There's a report that she and Wilkinson have been seen. I suppose it is just possible that she's at the Marchant country home. What's the name of the place?'

'Colston,' said Tim, promptly. 'Near Reading.'

'Have you seen Mike Errol this morning?'

'No, but last night his ankle was nearly better. Will you ring him?'

Hammond did so.

Mike answered promptly that he was fighting fit. He hoped that there would be no need to disturb Mark, who was sleeping the sleep of exhaustion.

'You'll do, with Tim and one other. Whom would you like to have with you?'

'What job is it?'

'A journey into the country, and a forlorn hope.'

'I wish George could come,' Mike said, sadly. 'But he's as worn out as Mark. I think I'd like to have young Latimer. Bright lad. *And* he's good at winter sports,' added Mike, brightly. 'We'll want snow-shoes and whatnot.'

'See what you can arrange,' Hammond said. 'I'll find out what the roads are like to Reading.'

An hour and a half later Tim Kemble, Mike Errol and 'young Latimer' started out for Colston. Hammond had told Loftus what he proposed, and Loftus had agreed that it was well worth trying. Lionel Marchant and his cousin might have been able to reach Colston, and might think that they were safe there from inquiries.

The Department Z agents took two jeeps, one of which Tim Kemble drove alone, and was piled with snow-shoes, skis, sticks and ropes, all the impedimenta which might be required for heavy work in the snow.

It was half-past three before they reached the outskirts of the village of Colston.

From the High Street, between the Norman church tower and the snowy thatch of the only inn, they could see the gentle Berkshire countryside buried deep under virgin snow that glittered in the sun which, for the first time that day, began to pierce the clouds. There was little wind, and everywhere an uncanny silence. Colston must be a sleepy place at the best of times, but on that particular day it seemed desolate. They saw only two people, both women, both coming out of a post office which was half-hidden by snow.

'I'll find out where the Marchants' house is,' offered 'young Latimer', and began to plough his way towards the post office.

He was a man of medium height, not particularly broad nor powerful. A friend of the Errols, he had been vaguely aware of what they did, and had suggested that he might prove useful. He had been with the Department for some months, and, like Tim, had yet to prove himself in an emergency. He had all the qualifications for success, although he would probably be one to receive rather than to give orders. Tim Kemble, on the other hand, had been marked out—as had George Henry George—for leadership.

'Young Latimer' had corn-coloured hair, a rather thin and not unhandsome face, and large, grey, tired-looking eyes. This tiredness was deceptive; so was his slow, drawling voice.

The fat woman behind the counter of the post office looked surprised to see him.

'I didn't expect no more strangers *today*, sir,' she said. 'I wonder how you managed to get here.'

'Oh, this way and that,' drawled Latimer. 'It's a bit nippy. Still, it's worse at the North Pole.'

'It is *that*, sir! I wouldn't like to live up there.'

'Not to be an Eskimo, no,' murmured Latimer. 'I'm looking for Colston House. It's near here, isn't it?'

Little eyes in a great red face stared at him in astonishment.

'Well,' said the post-mistress, 'I never did!'

'Oh,' murmured Latimer.

'No, I certainly didn't,' said the post-mistress, leaning her elbows on the counter and thus thrusting her face closer to him. She was a mighty creature, fore and aft. '*Another* gentleman wanted to find Colston House.'

'Oh,' murmured Latimer again. 'It's a popular place.' He smiled. 'The truth is, we started out in two sections and one of us got lost. So the others arrived first—how much did they win by?'

'They came an hour ago,' she said.

'Three of them, weren't there?'

'I don't know about that,' said the post-mistress, 'I only *saw* two. *Will!*' she called, in a voice suddenly strident. '*Will!* Come in here a minute!' She stared towards a door at the back of the shop, and a tall, bedraggled-looking man came in and stood waiting. 'Will,' repeated the post-mistress, 'how many gentlemen were there in the *other* car?'

'Four,' declared Will, in a melancholy voice.

'Oh, good,' said Latimer, brightly. 'So they all got here.'

'Just lucky,' said Will. 'Passed the barn, they did, and then down it come.'

Latimer pressed more questions, and in his gruff, melancholy voice, Will told the story. The other carload of strangers had gone straight along the road to Colston House, a bad road at the best of times. It led over a small bridge which crossed the Coll River, and the river was in flood, although further up it was frozen nearly right over. Down here, at Colston, it was frozen at the edges but there was twice the normal volume of water.

Just after the other car had passed over the bridge, there had been a heavy fall of snow from an old barn near the bridge and the road. The snow had fallen across the road. Men were already working to try to clear a path, for milk- and bread-vans had to get through to outlying hamlets.

'So you can't go just yet,' said the post-mistress. 'Would you like me to make you a cup of tea, sir?'

'Nice of you,' murmured Latimer. 'The road might be clear by now.'

'Take an hour, that will,' Will declared. 'Just come from it, I have. Have a cup o' tea an' welcome, sir.'

'Perhaps the gentleman would prefer to go to *The George* and have a meal,' said the post-mistress.

Will sniffed: 'And *p'raps* they'd get one,' he said. 'Those new people...' Latimer listened to him impatiently and yet eagerly.

Ten minutes later he joined Mike and Tim, who were pacing up and down the street. The engines of the jeeps were still running, and now two or three people were peering at them from behind curtains at cottage windows.

Latimer's dreamy eyes were much brighter than when he had left them. There had been 'one lady in the party, which made five people in all'. The car looked as if it had come a long way, and the man who had inquired the way had been impatient, saying that he had an urgent appointment at Colston House.

Mike said: 'If it's Wilkinson, then Clarissa...'

Tim broke in.

'Clarissa wasn't with them, or they wouldn't have had to ask the way. You didn't ask whether the fellow had his hair cropped, did you?'

'He wore a hat all the time,' said Latimer. 'Well, what shall we do?'

'Get after them,' said Tim. 'You get the thermos flasks filled with tea, we might find it useful later on, and catch us up. We may have to wait a while by the bridge,' he added, 'it depends how deep the river is.'

'Will says it's in flood,' said Latimer. 'Okay, I'll be tea-boy. You go ahead.' He hurried off.

The snow had been cleared from the centre of the road and from the front of *The George*, too. Tim glanced at the place then drove on. The road was narrow and there was only room for one car at a time; if they met anything coming down, they would be in queer street. After a while, they came to a hill and had some difficulty in reaching the top. From the top, they looked down upon a deep valley, snow-clad, a single sheet of white; even the trees were covered so deeply that branches were hidden. Nothing showed against the virgin sheet except the thin dark line of the winding river.

They could see that it was swollen.

A little further on, they passed a copse. Beyond it, at the foot of a steep hill, men were moving about, little dark dots. As the jeep drew nearer, Tim saw that there were close on a dozen of them, and all were shovelling snow. Two vans were drawn up in front of the bridge itself, and as the jeep pulled up, Tim saw that there was a bread-van and a milk-van.

They got out and joined the crowd. A red-faced man, muffled up to the ears in a pink Balaclava helmet, grunted a welcome, and said:

'More hands, less work.' Then he pointed to two spades sticking up in the snow.

Tim and Mike put their backs into it.

A few minutes later Latimer drew up.

There was a sudden cheer from the men at the far end of the group, near the bridge; they were through. A man hurried from the crowd and climbed into the bread-van, which was at the head of the little convoy. He raced the engine, then moved, the wheels chain-wrapped and clanking. The men stood back by the side of the path. The van slithered a little, but suddenly its front wheels touched the edge of the bridge.

There was a ragged cheer. Someone laughed. Someone else said, 'What we could do with now is some *beer*.'

'What a hope,' said the man with the pink Balaclava. 'Now last year...'

Tim and the others heard that exchange as they got into the jeeps. Tim let in the clutch of his and started off. The milk-van had reached the bridge, the bread-van was on the other side and crawling up the hill on the south of the valley. The jeep was crunching steadily through the snow, and Tim was thinking that the strangers ahead had only an hour and a half's start.

Next moment, the bridge blew up!

13

HIGH EXPLOSIVE

Until then, the only sound inside the jeep was the roar of the engine. The end of the bridge was ten feet away, and Tim had accelerated. He saw the blinding flash, but had no time to think about it or to wonder what it was. A vivid red and yellow, it was followed by a great roar and then a blast which swung the jeep round and sent it skidding into the shallow ramparts of the bridge. Mike lurched against Tim as they skidded round. The roar of the explosion still deafened them, they could see and hear nothing else.

Then Tim saw the edge of the bridge.

He tried to clutch the brakes; he could not reach them. Mike was sprawling over the front of the jeep. They crashed into the rampart, and their stomachs seemed to hit their throats.

The jeep overhung the broken rampart. Tim could see clearly enough now.

The racing, swirling waters below seemed to be leaping out to clutch at them. That was all he needed to see: just the water which looked like dark molten metal, flowing so swiftly;

and he could feel the jeep swaying slightly downwards towards the water.

He heard voices.

He thought: They're going to try to hold us.

Then, with a lurch, the jeep fell.

The fall was not far; one moment they had been hanging over the bridge, the next they were beneath the icy water, and the jeep was on top of them. Tim banged his head against the windscreen. For a dreadful moment he was afraid that he was going to lose consciousness.

The water closed over him. Biting cold, rushing like a torrent and dragging at him, it forced him against Mike and the far side of the jeep. He could not breathe, there was an awful pressure at his chest. He dared not struggle. He got a hand to the door of the jeep and tried to open it, but the pressure of the water against the door was too great.

He bobbed up, into the air!

The cold seemed to slash his face, but it *was* the air and he could open the door. He was still sitting in water; he would go under again any moment.

The door opened, and he eased himself out.

He did not know what happened to Mike, but kicked and struck out. He *must* have a chance. The water was running very fast, buffeting him right and left. Once it flung him upwards, next moment it sucked him down again. At the last moment he took in a great gulp of air; then the pressure at his chest was back again, like a great vice, crushing him, forcing him to let the breath out, and to draw in water.

He bobbed up again and felt something clutch at his shoulders. Thank God, thank God. He reached the surface, and the tugging grew stronger; he was being pulled against the current to the side of the river. Not until he reached it did he realise that Latimer and several men from the working party were pulling him. He could not see clearly, but he looked about desperately for Mike Errol.

Someone said: 'Make him run.'

He found himself being dragged up the bank of the riven. The snow was a foot deep or more, he and the others could only move slowly. Then other people dragged him to the road. He could hardly move, he was so stiff; water freezing on his face was painful in spite of his numbness, his skin seemed to be cracking.

'Run,' a man bellowed into his ear. 'Run, *run!*' He tried to, but his feet slipped, and but for their hold he would have fallen. But soon he *was* running mechanically, blindly, and he felt warmth creeping back into him.

At last he managed to gasp, 'The other—man.'

'Never mind him—*run!*'

Tim kept running. He seemed to be on the go for a long time, pounding through that white sheet, his feet slipping this way and that. Now he was really warming up, the blood was throbbing in his ears. *Thump-thump-thump-thump-thump.* It was getting painful, he must have a rest, he must...

He heard a car engine.

At last they let him rest. He turned round and saw the jeep, with Latimer at the wheel. As it drew up he saw Mike Errol sitting at the back, his head lolling forward.

'Hurry,' said Latimer, and he was not drawling then.

Two men helped Tim into the back of the jeep. One climbed in by Latimer's side, and soon they were moving rapidly towards the village. The man who had joined Latimer was a policeman; underneath his mackintosh Tim saw the bright buttons of his uniform. The policeman started to pummel Mike's chest and stomach.

The jeep turned into the village, and outside *The George*,

the rear wheels skidded. They swung round and struck the post which carried the inn sign. A flurry of snow fell from it.

The door of the inn opened as Latimer and the policeman helped Tim from the car. He staggered to the door while the others lifted Mike out. A burly man stood with his arms akimbo, as if to deny them entrance. Tim saw his expression, one of acute distaste, almost of alarm, when Mike was carried towards the door.

'We want a bedroom, quick,' said the policeman, and there was a note of truculence in his voice.

'I haven't got...'

'*Quick*, I said!'

The burly man gave way, with ill-grace. He walked to the stairs, without offering to lend a hand. There was an awkward turn halfway up, and Mick's head struck the banisters. The landlord led the way into a large, double room with twin beds. He pulled off a bedspread and turned down the blankets. The policeman dumped Mike on to the bed, and Tim saw the landlord's lips tighten as he stood looking on. Any normal man would be eager to offer help.

'Now telephone for Dr. Arden,' said the policeman.

The landlord went out of the room.

'And bring the gentlemen a spot of whisky!' called the policeman.

The landlord went heavily down the stairs. The policeman seemed to know what he was doing. While he knelt astride the bed, and pressed firmly on Mike's ribs, Latimer began to pull off Mike's fur-lined knee boots. It was like a farce, thought Tim. If only Mike were not in such a bad way...

Latimer looked round. 'Take the other one, Tim.' He tapped the policeman on the shoulder. 'I'll have a turn.'

Ten minutes passed before the landlord returned with a

tray, whisky and a syphon. The policeman had taken over again.

The landlord put the tray down, and did not offer Tim a drink. As Latimer went over and poured one out, the landlord watched him almost suspiciously.

'Doctor coming?' asked Latimer.

'Ten minutes,' he said.

As the whisky warmed him, Tim began to feel much more himself. The meaning of the explosion was all too clear. A deliberate effort had been made to prevent anyone from reaching Colston House: a time-fuse had been set to a high-explosive.

Soon the doctor came into the room. There seemed no change in Mike's pallor, nothing to indicate that he was alive.

After a quick examination, the doctor said:

'We'll have those clothes off him, get him some hot blankets and a hot bath as soon as he's round. Some coffee, too,' he added. 'As sweet as you can make it, landlord.'

The surly man nodded, and went out.

Tim went to the door and watched him. The man glanced at the door of the room opposite, which Tim noticed was ajar. Why had the landlord looked at it so intently? Who was in there?

He stepped into the passage; further along, another door closed with a snap.

Tim was conscious of being watched, and that and the landlord's behaviour increased his disquiet. But he forgot all that when he saw Mike's face twitch.

The doctor said cheerfully:

'We'll have him all right in a jiffy!'

Mike was already stripped. The doctor put a blanket over him and Latimer started the artificial respiration again. Tim went into the passage, and as he did so he saw the landlord creeping up the stairs, glancing over his shoulder as if he too were afraid of being watched.

Tim slipped back out of sight.

The landlord went into another room, closed the door behind him, and then began to talk. Tim could hear his voice but nothing of what he said. He was tempted to go close to the door, but the landlord came out again, and closed it sharply.

'Get a hot bath ready,' called the doctor.

The landlord went into a bathroom, and water began to run.

A maid came upstairs, with coffee.

It was a quarter of an hour before the policeman, Latimer and the doctor took Mike into the bathroom. He was conscious and fully aware of what had happened. Tim, still curious, and in need of a change of clothes, sought out the landlord.

He found him in a small office, poring over a book. He jumped up when Tim coughed.

Tim beamed. 'We're making an awful nuisance of ourselves, but—could I borrow a dressing-gown? Or a spare suit? Any old clothes will do.'

The landlord got up without a word, and led the way upstairs. Ten minutes later Tim was pulling on an old serge suit over rough woollen underwear. Throughout the procedure of selecting the clothes, the landlord had not once spoken; he seemed more surly all the time.

Tim beamed at him.

'Thanks very much,' he said. 'My friend will have to stay the night, I'm afraid.'

The landlord drew in a deep breath.

'Only fools would travel in weather like this. We haven't got any room here.'

'Are you often so full?'

'Any law against it?' demanded the landlord, and moved off.

Latimer came out of the big bedroom, where Mike had been taken again. He was smoking a cigarette and smiling ruefully.

'Odd show,' he said. 'Landlord very mysterious, officer of the law very uppish, generally we aren't welcome. What have you been prowling about for?'

'Doors will open and close,' Tim told him. He lit a cigarette. 'You know, we've still got to get out to Colston House tonight. I wonder what the other routes are like?'

'Non-existent, probably,' said Latimer. 'And this is not the home of the Bailey Bridge. The villains got ahead of us. Lucky thing you and Mike weren't twenty yards further on.'

'Yes,' said Tim. 'I...'

Then he heard a door open, and looked along the passage. A girl came from a room and walked towards them, smiling as if at some secret joke. She was plump, dark-haired, and rather merry-looking. She glanced at them seductively as she passed, and hummed to herself.

Latimer said, 'Buxom wench.'

'See where she's going,' said Tim.

Latimer widened his eyes, but hurried to the head of the stairs, leaving Tim alone in the passage. He turned to go into Mike's room, but as he did so another door opened, and he looked along the passage. Another girl stepped into view.

'I thought it was you,' said Clarissa Kaye. 'You're a very persistent reporter, aren't you? The *Gazette* is to be congratulated.'

There was no malice, only good humour, in the words.

* * *

It was not a good moment for Tim.

His ducking and the anxiety which had followed it had taken the vitality out of him. His mind was working only at half-pressure. He realised that vaguely; he realised also that he should not be so astonished to see Clarissa here, and yet he was. So he was angry with himself because he stood gaping while she regarded him without the slightest embarrassment.

'Or aren't you a reporter?' she asked.

Tim began to recover. 'I'm qualifying,' he said.

'And qualifying well, I imagine,' said Clarissa. 'Can you spare me a few minutes?' She turned and led him into a small bedroom. It was pleasantly furnished and pleasantly warm. No one else was there.

'Well?' said Tim, almost accusingly.

She pointed to a chair.

'Do sit down,' she invited. 'You must be tired. I'm very glad you came off so lightly. We were afraid they would do something to the bridge, that's why my...' she paused, and then added deliberately: 'my friends have gone a long way round. With luck, they'll be at Colston House by now.'

'And who are your friends?' asked Tim.

'Wilkinson, Mendicott and Ferguson,' said Clarissa. 'My cousin Lionel has gone with them. That is why the hotel is so full, they have reserved all the rooms. But it isn't likely that they'll be back, and if they are I've no doubt the men will gladly double up, so you can have at least one room. Will that help?'

'Yes,' said Tim. 'But you're playing with fire, Miss Kaye.'

'I know,' she said freely. 'And I know that fire burns!' She watched Tim narrowly for a while, and then went on: 'Who *are* you? Ferguson thinks that you're from the police.'

'Wrong,' said Tim.

'That's a pity. I was hoping that you were. Surely you *can't* be with those cropped-headed, dark-faced men.'

'I am not,' agreed Tim, heavily.

'Then if you're not with them and not with the police and not with *us*, who are you? Can Gregory be right? He suggested Secret Service.'

'This Gregory Wilkinson is obviously a man with a fine flight of imagination,' Tim said, drily.

He could not make sense of this conversation, he could not understand what Clarissa was driving at, and yet one thing seemed to stand out: she was opposed to the men with cropped heads. He watched her closely, his thoughts running much more freely and wondering what his next move should be. Before he decided, the door opened and Latimer's 'buxom wench' came in, followed closely by Latimer, who looked bewildered.

Susan Harris gurgled:

'Clarissa, isn't he *lovely*? He's really sweet—followed me all over the hotel.' She treated Latimer to a luscious smile, and patted his arm. 'I won't run away from you any more, ducky. Have you told the reporter all about it, Clarissa?'

'No,' said Clarissa. 'I thought I'd wait...'

As she spoke, the door opened again.

No one had heard a sound. No one was looking towards the door. Tim had reassured himself, and was looking forward to hearing a story. Then he saw Clarissa's expression change; one of alarm replaced mild amusement. He swung round.

A little man stood in the doorway pointing a gun towards him. Another, also carrying a gun, sidled into the room. They were dark and thin-faced; at a quick glance both might have been taken for Kolsti. Their cropped heads were like little black bullets—and their guns looked deadly. It had happened so suddenly that Tim could not move.

Latimer could. He cried:

'Oh no, you don't!' and jumped forward.

Two reports were deafening in the small room. Two bullets struck Latimer in the chest. Latimer staggered forward, his hand at his side as if he were trying to get at his gun. Then he pitched downwards, while the little man who had fired slewed his gun round to cover Tim.

He waved his free hand.

Tim realised that he was telling Clarissa to go to the door. Tim said hoarsely: 'Don't! Miss Kaye, don't...'

The gun was jerked towards him, menacingly, and the man at the door came in. He took Clarissa's arm, and led her into the passage. There was not another sound in the inn. The echo of the shots seemed to linger in that room; but there was nothing else.

The man covering Tim backed to the door. Clarissa had disappeared. Susan was standing quite still, staring at the gun, mesmerised. Tim could see Latimer out of the corner of his eye, and he remembered Parmitter's death.

The little man took the key out of the inside of the door, slipped outside very quickly and, as Tim rushed at it, locked the door. Tim crashed into it. The impact shook the room, but made no impression on the door. Tim drew back, shaken. Susan went down on her knees beside Latimer, and tried to lift him. Tim forced himself to examine the door. It opened inwards; there was little chance of breaking it down.

Tim turned, stepped over Latimer, and reached the window. All he could see was a snow-covered yard. He opened the window and climbed out. It was not far from the ground, and the snow would break his fall. He dropped, lost his footing, and then picked himself up, wet through for the second time that afternoon.

Dusk had fallen, and the sun was lost in a purple haze. Tim

went towards the road. No one was in sight; there were lights in the windows of two cottages; the only signs of life.

He raised his voice and shouted: '*Police!*' but it seemed a pointless thing to do out here.

He was near the corner when he heard the snort of an engine. As he reached the corner, he saw the jeep moving along the road towards Reading and away from Colston House. Sitting in the back with one of the men was Clarissa, without a coat; Clarissa, peering behind her. Two other little men were in the front of the jeep, two more clung to the sides. It was making good speed along the treacherous road.

Outside *The George* was the doctor's car.

Tim rushed towards it. No one came from the inn, no one had responded to his call. Where was the policeman? For that matter, where were the doctor, the landlord and Mike?

He reached the car, started the engine and turned in the wake of the jeep. There was a hopeless feeling deep inside him. He had no weapons here; one jeep was at the bottom of the river, the other was a quarter of a mile away, out of sight but clearly audible; and the men in it were armed. The best he could do was to keep it in sight and hope to find out where it was going.

He reached the crest of a hill; and he had to make the attempt, slim though the chances were, and...

He stopped abruptly.

The jeep was travelling towards some cross-roads, and Tim could see what the men in the jeep could not—a big army truck was racing towards the corner. Unless one or the other stopped, a smash was inevitable.

14

ROUT OF LITTLE MEN

Tim thrust his thumb on the horn and kept it there. He was two hundred yards behind the jeep and there seemed little chance that his warning would be heeded. Both vehicles tore towards the cross-roads at a speed suicidal on that surface. Tim could see Clarissa's fair hair blowing in the wind, and the little men hanging on to the jeep, in danger enough without the new threat lumbering towards them.

The high-pitched note of the car horn wailed through the air. Tim thought the army truck slowed down. Then, when he went downhill, the whole scene was hidden from him and he waited in sickening suspense for the crash. They could not avoid it. He set his teeth and waited.

It came.

Not so loud, not so deafening, as Tim had expected. He heard the sudden racing of one engine, then silence as it cut out. He put on an extra burst of speed, and came in sight of the cross-roads. He could not see the jeep, but could see the top of the truck, which had not overturned.

He slowed down.

Why was there no sound? He could hear no voices, and their sound should travel far on such a clear, cold evening. It was much darker now, but if anyone moved from the scene of the crash he would be able to see them clearly enough.

He edged the car forward until the radiator nosed beyond the cross-roads. Then for the first time he saw the jeep, thrown to one side after it had crashed into the side of the truck. He saw Clarissa standing quite still by the side of the truck, and the little dark men standing about, all of them motionless and staring towards the driver of the truck. It made no sense; at least, it made none until he saw the driver clearly.

It was Bruce Hammond!

In Hammond's hand was a sub-machine gun.

It flashed upon Tim Kemble that this made the complete circle. The affair had started with a machine-gun in the hands of one of these men—Kolsti. Now Kolsti's associates were helpless because one was pointing towards them.

So little time had passed since the crash, there had been scarcely time to move. Now the men began to stir. Not only did the little dark men with one accord rush towards the fields, but men spilled from the back of the covered truck. Tim recognised George Henry George and Mark Errol, Fordham, Graham and several other Department men.

'*Yip-yip-yee!* yelled George, and he came running forward.

Tim saw one of the little men turn.

A gun was pointed towards Clarissa.

The man had reached a clump of trees, and none of the men from the truck could see him. The other little men were racing across the snow, with surprising agility.

Tim flung open the door and bellowed:

'Look out, Clarissa!'

Clarissa turned as the little man fired. At the same time

George reached the trees, and two shots were fired almost simultaneously. Clarissa stumbled. Tim jumped out of the car and raced toward her, but young Graham was helping her up. She was not hurt, but was blue with cold and her teeth were chattering. When she saw Tim she gave a twisted, distorted smile.

George was running after the little man who had fired, and the other Department Z men were now hot-foot after their quarry. Tim saw that Graham, still with Clarissa, wore snow-shoes; that explained the ease with which the Department men moved. Quickly though the little men ran, they had no chance against Hammond's party. Tim saw that two Depart-ment Z men followed the trail of each dark-faced man, and saw two overpowered before turning to Clarissa, Graham and Hammond, who had climbed down from the driving seat.

Tim said: 'Hallo. Joined the army?'

Hammond smiled. 'It looks like it. The quicker you get Miss Kaye indoors somewhere the better. Where did you find your car?'

'From the local sawbones,' said Tim. The question reminded him of the unnatural silence at *The George* before he had left. 'Odd thing,' he went on. 'The village is full of mystery, but I know one place where Clarissa will get a warm welcome. Coming with me?'

'I'll follow,' said Hammond. 'Explanation later.'

'Right,' said Tim. 'You might tell Mark that Mike's had a nasty turn, but he's on the mend now.'

Graham, who had hurried to the back of the truck, came out with a thick rug and wrapped it about Clarissa. She was too cold to speak coherently or to move freely. She sat in the back of the car, and Tim set off for the village, puzzled by the sudden arrival of the Department in such strength, but satis-fied that things would move very quickly now.

He pulled up outside the post office. A lamp was burning near the window, spreading a yellow glow on to the snow. He helped Clarissa out, and half-carried her into the post office. The fat post-mistress uttered the inevitable: *'Well I never!'* and in the same breath she called 'Will!'

Tim left Clarissa sitting in front of a blazing log fire in the kitchen, with the fat woman's assurance that she would get the young lady something hot immediately.

The truck was not yet in sight.

Tim hurried across the road to *The George*. The front door was wide open. He called out when he stepped into the hall, but no one answered. He hurried upstairs, more than a little afraid of what he might find. There was a ruthlessness about the little men which...

Suddenly, vividly, he remembered Latimer, who had been shot in the chest. On the road and at the cross-roads he had forgotten him. His heart was beating fast as he hurried up the stairs.

Susan was coming out of the bathroom, carrying a towel. She looked at him quickly, suddenly tense, but when she recognised him she relaxed.

'How is he?' asked Tim.

'I don't think he'll live,' said Susan. 'If only I could get the doctor. I can't get him on the telephone.'

'He's already here, I've seen his car. How did you escape?'

'There was a key in my bag,' she said.

He hesitated outside the door of the big double room, then turned the handle. The door was locked. He put his shoulder to it, and the door gave way just as he heard the engine of the truck in the street outside. He staggered into the room, with Susan just behind him.

The doctor, the policeman, the landlord and Mike Errol were all there; all were sitting down; all seemed to be asleep.

For one fearful moment Tim thought they were dead; and then he saw that Mike was breathing heavily, and he quickly found that they were all only unconscious.

Footsteps sounded in the hall downstairs.

'Who's this?' Susan demanded, urgently.

'Friends,' said Tim. 'Don't worry. There's been a rout of the sallow little swine.' He smoothed down his hair, and then went with her into the small bedroom, knowing that it would be some time before the doctor came round.

Latimer died very soon afterwards.

When Tim helped to search the prisoners, he found it difficult not to break their necks. There was just one cause for satisfaction, however—each prisoner had a red, diamond-shaped card in his pocket, each with a different number.

No one looking into the big lounge of *The George* that early evening would have suspected that a close friend of the men present had been killed only an hour or so before. There were ten men in all, and they lounged in the chairs and settees, all taking the respite offered them with eager alacrity. On the small tables there was beer; for, without consulting either the landlord or the policeman, Fordham had gone to the bar and found there a small barrel. The barrel was now resting on a stool near the window, and Fordham and Graham were sitting by it, ready to replenish the glasses. They were kept busy.

Now and again, every one of them glanced towards the door. Hammond and Tim had been out for some time, their ostensible purpose to question the landlord and the two girls; and every man here, in spite of his apparent nonchalance, was eager to be at work again. They would have pushed on before this but for the blown bridge.

George and another Department Z agent had managed to leap across the gap in the bridge and were on their way to Colston House. They would be waiting further along the road when the others followed. In a cold garage, the four prisoners lay bound hand and foot. Hammond had questioned them, but they were no more prepared to talk than Kolsti had been.

The party in the lounge had heard Tim's story.

They had heard, too, an explanation from the policeman, who had been satisfied by Hammond's credentials and left them in possession of *The George*, which was due to open to the villagers half an hour later. With the exception of one man, the staff of the inn had been sent out that afternoon. All of them lived locally. The policeman had discovered only the previous day that the landlord, whose name was Parker, had a police record.

Parker was now upstairs in a box room waiting to be questioned. Hammond and Tim were with Clarissa, who had arrived, wrapped in a tweed coat borrowed from the postmistress. Susan was also with them, listening with intense interest to the questions and answers.

Clarissa's story was only partly satisfactory.

She admitted that she was a friend of Wilkinson, and that she had taken part in the anti-Soviet activities of *Warning*. Also she had known that her cousin Lionel was in the downstairs room at the Haymart Hotel and that, to escape police questioning, she had joined him and gone to Wimbledon. According to her story, she had left Wimbledon with Lionel Marchant and his wife before Hammond had arrived at *Hatch End*. They had intended to go on to Colston House the previous night, but had put up at *The George*. Before morning, Wilkinson and his party had arrived, and it had been agreed that the men should go on to Colston House, leaving Clarissa and Susan behind. Only Lionel Marchant's wife had gone with them.

Hammond waited until Clarissa had finished, before asking:

'Why have they gone to Colston House?'

'Because they knew the sallow-faced men were trying to get there,' answered Clarissa.

'How did they know?'

'Gregory Wilkinson has a way of learning these things.'

'That's hardly an answer,' said Hammond.

'It's all I can tell you,' retorted Clarissa.

Hammond said sharply: 'You mean that it's all you're prepared to tell us.'

'Even if we could,' Clarissa shrugged, 'why should we tell *you*? You're not policemen. Mr. Kemble evaded the issue when I asked him whether you were from the Secret Service. I have worked far too hard and taken far too many risks to take chances.'

Hammond took a card from his pocket, and handed it to her. It carried the signature of the Home Secretary and the Assistant Commissioner at Scotland Yard, and requested all citizens and civil and military authorities to afford the holder every facility; and all the lettering was superimposed upon a faint grey Z. When Tim saw the card he wondered whether Hammond was wise to use it.

Clarissa studied it intently, then looked up, obviously relaxed, and glanced at Tim.

'So Gregory was right,' she said. 'He felt sure he was. That's why *you* are still alive, Mr. Hammond.'

'Is it also why Abbott was killed?' Hammond demanded.

Clarissa said: 'I can't tell you why Abbott was killed, but I can tell you that had he had his way, you would have been shot.'

'It's quite true,' Susan said quickly. 'I'd gone on ahead, and we were going to leave you behind, but Abbott slipped back with some paltry excuse, and Gregory went after him. I heard the shots. Just what happened I don't know, but Gregory said that Abbott was dead.'

Hammond said slowly: 'That fully satisfied you, did it?'

'*Every*thing Gregory says is all right with me,' said Susan.

'I see. Where is his wife?'

'She hurt her foot when she was getting into the car at Wimbledon, and she went to stay with some friends. That was rough justice, really. Greggy had been pretending that his foot was bothering him, in case anyone thought that he had left *Hatch End* when, of course, he had been there all the time, and poor Vi—*wasn't* it a shame?'

Hammond looked at her thoughtfully.

He believed that she knew more than she had told him; and that Clarissa did, too. But they volunteered no further information, in spite of the card.

'Did the landlord make you welcome last night?' asked Tim.

'Greggy has a way with him,' Susan said. 'He didn't want to admit us, but Greggy used some influence, so we stayed. I won't pretend we've enjoyed it. There was something wrong all the time. The beastly little dark men, of course.' She shivered, and it was not affectation. 'Until they appeared this evening, I'd no idea they were here.'

That part of the story had already been told.

Two of the men with cropped heads had gone into the big bedroom and, while one had covered the occupants of the room with a gun, the other had injected a narcotic drug. None of them was likely to suffer more than a hangover next morning, but none except the policeman would be of much use that night. The policeman appeared to have received a much smaller dose than the others.

'We'd better see the landlord,' Tim said.

'Bring him, will you?' asked Hammond. When Tim had gone, Hammond looked from Clarissa Kaye to Susan, and spoke very gently. 'I don't want to be rough with either of you, but I must know why Wilkinson brought you here, and what you've been doing with Wilkinson. Abbott was murdered. You are both accessories to that crime. You may think it a trifling affair compared with the issues at stake, but it might be enough to hang you both.'

Clarissa said: 'I don't think that frightens me very much. How can I be sure that your card really belongs to you?'

'If the telephone lines weren't down, you could call Scotland Yard. As it is you'd better take my word for it.' He took a cigarette out and lit it, without offering his case to them. 'Why did Wilkinson want to get to Colston House?'

'I've told you—because the little dark men were known to be going there.'

'What did they want?'

Clarissa shrugged her shoulders. 'I don't know. I don't think Gregory knows, but wherever they go, he or one of his friends goes. One of them was watching Oslam House the other day, that's how he came to know about the attack on "Virnov". As Virnov was at *Uno* at the same time as the attack, it was easy to guess what trick had been played.'

'Why was the story sent to the Press?'

'Abbott did that, without orders,' said Clarissa, and added: 'There is nothing else I can tell you.'

15

COLSTON HOUSE

It was never pleasant to get tough with a woman, but he would have to, Hammond told himself. Susan would give way first, he would have to start on her. While he was making up his mind there were footsteps outside, and Tim brought in the landlord.

The man was terrified. His hands were clenching and unclenching, and he could not meet their eyes.

Tim said cheerfully:

'There isn't much in it, Bruce. Parker's made a packet on horse doping, and betting on certainties. He retired and came out here. Our dark-faced men discovered what he'd been up to, and forced him to let them stay. Wilkinson also knew what he'd been up to, and used similar pressure. The local Robert seems to have winkled out his black past, too. Not a happy retirement, but I think you'll find that's all there is to it.'

Hammond said: 'Is that so, Parker?'

'Yes,' muttered Parker, 'I'm glad to get it off my chest, I haven't had a minute's peace since I came here. It's been—it's been *terrible*.'

'How did the little men get in touch with you?' he demanded.

'One of them came to see me. I couldn't argue with him, he had me where he wanted me! There wasn't anything I could do, I tell you! He said he would be sending visitors from time to time and I was to look after them. He told me I wasn't to accept anyone else, I was always to say that we was full up. No one but his friends have stayed here since I came, until—until last night.'

'You see how wonderful Gregory is,' murmured Susan.

'How many visitors have you had?' demanded Hammond.

'Six,' replied the inn-keeper. 'Just *six*. It's cost me a fortune, I could have been full up most nights. I haven't had much custom downstairs, either, the villagers wouldn't come. I was ordered not to be friendly with them. It's ruined me,' he muttered.

'Who are the people who have stayed with you?' Hammond asked.

Parker drew a sharp breath. 'They've all called themselves Smith or Brown. Most of them—all but one—were little tykes like you've got locked up in the garage, the other was a big overbearing Englishman. He went up to the house sometimes.' In Colston, 'the house' obviously meant Colston House. 'I can tell you his name, too,' he added. 'Parmitter. I saw it on a letter he dropped out of his pocket.' Parker drew in his breath when he saw Hammond's expression. 'I tell you he was Parmitter!'

'No one's called you a liar.' Tim cocked an eyebrow at Hammond. 'More mystery about Parmitter. But we can't get much more here, can we?'

Hammond looked at Clarissa. 'We'll get all we need before we've finished. Parker, what are the attics like?'

'They're clean enough,' muttered Parker.

'Take me up to them, will you?'

Parker led the way upstairs, climbing a narrow flight of steps which creaked on every tread. The attics were lit by small-powered lamps; obviously they had once been used for servants' quarters. Single beds, all of them neatly made, were in each of the three small rooms. The windows were too small for anyone to climb out. There were electric fires, all switched off, and the rooms struck bitterly cold.

'Take the fires and the bed-clothes away,' Hammond said. 'I'm going to leave the two women up here. You won't bring them food or drink, clothing or blankets. Is that clear?'

Parker gaped. 'On a night like *this*?'

'On a night like this,' said Hammond. 'I shall leave some men here to make sure that you do as you're told. Don't try to slip anything upstairs to them. You'll only make your own position worse.' He paused. 'Get the rooms cleared in five minutes. I want the two end rooms.'

He went downstairs for Clarissa and Susan.

Ten minutes later they were standing on the tiny landing, and Hammond said in a relentless voice:

'You will be in separate rooms. There will be no heating, no food, no bedding. As soon as you decide to talk, you may come downstairs. Do you understand?'

Clarissa went into one of the rooms. Susan hesitated, then shrugged her shoulders and flounced into the other. From the door, she said brightly:

'Come up and dance with me sometime, Hammy dear. It'll warm *you* up!'

Hammond locked the doors on them.

Downstairs, he told Tim what he had done. Tim made no comment, but as they went down to the crowded lounge, where the ten waiting men were singing in what they fondly thought was harmony, he asked:

'You're not going to wait for them to talk before we move, are you?'

'No. Half a dozen of us will try to get to Colston House tonight.'

A burst of singing came from the lounge as Hammond touched the handle of the door.

'Just a moment,' said Tim. 'What *did* bring you here?'

Hammond smiled. 'The reliable Miller. He had a call put out through the whole of the Home Counties. There were one or two reports, on the strength of which I asked you to come here. Then he picked up a message from Reading about the four little men. One of them had his hat off in the car they used, and his cropped head caught the eyes of a watchful policeman. There are times when we'd be lost without the police.'

'Don't I know it!' exclaimed Tim. He stepped into the room, where Graham was now sitting on the barrel and 'conducting' the choir. The men draped about the room in a variety of inelegant poses glanced towards the door and then back at the conductor. Every face was set and serious, every man appeared to be putting his level best into the round song.

The tempo was quickening:

> *Three green bottles, hanging from a wall,*
> *Three green—bottles!—hanging from a wall,*
> *If one—green—bottle*
> *Should acc-i-dent'ly fall!*
> *There'll be two—green—bottles*
> *Hanging from the wall!*

Tim caught Hammond's arm. 'Something's just struck me,' he said. 'The police saw the cropped hair...'

Hammond leaned towards him.

'Sorry—can't hear!'

'What?' asked Tim, bellowing.

'Can't hear!'

> *Two green bottles, hanging from a wall,*
> *Two green bottles...*

Tim dragged Hammond into the passage and closed the door.

'Now what?' asked Hammond.

'If the police saw a carload of the little beggars in Reading, where are they?' asked Tim.

'I don't follow.'

'Parker says these men have been here for two days, so the carload was *not* the men whom we've locked in the garage,' said Tim. 'Sorry if I'm mixed, that damned tune is going through my head.' The truth, thought Hammond, was that Tim was thinking of Clarissa Kaye, upstairs, shivering. 'But you see what I'm driving at. There's no car at *The George*, the garage was empty. Where's the carload of men gone? Confound it!' he roared. 'The post-mistress told Latimer of a carload which had got over the bridge. We've been telling ourselves that we've caught the devils, but they're on the way to Colston House—Wilkinson and his brood *and* four of the suicide squad.'

Hammond said grimly: 'Tim, go and try to scare something out of the men in the garage. Handle them as you like. I'll get the chaps ready for the next stage of the journey.'

Hammond opened the door as the last line of the refrain of the round song quivered through the room. As it finished there was a solemn brandishing of tankards and glasses, and Graham began to pour out again.

Hammond raised his voice.

'Last round,' he said. 'Then most of us will be moving. Graham, choose one...' he paused, and then added: 'No, make it two, to stay with you until Clarissa Kaye and Susan have decided to talk.' He explained, and apart from a murmur that it was a 'bit hard' no one commented. 'As soon as you've got something put a call through to Craigie.'

'Right,' said Graham, cheerfully.

'Where's Tim?' asked Fordham.

'Going to interview the cropped heads,' said Hammond. 'I'll see how he's getting on.' He hurried out of the room and into the yard. It was so cold that he started shivering. He thought of the two women upstairs, and set his lips. It was their own fault; whatever secret they held must be told, it was impossible to take chances with them or to be lenient. Yet he could not get it out of his head that Clarissa and Susan were doing what they believed to be right.

The garage door was open and he could see Tim standing just inside. Tim Kemble seemed to be standing very still, and he was not speaking. Hammond called out, and Tim glanced over his shoulder. In the single light which shone over the doorway, Hammond saw his tense, pale face. Alarm seared through Hammond as he hurried to the garage.

Inside were four dead men.

The prisoners had been put in the garage because it was empty of tools, there was nothing in there with which they could injure themselves; the lesson of Kolsti and Parmitter's murderer had not been neglected. Everything which the men might have used as weapons had been taken away, yet there they lay, dead. A stink of bitter almonds reached Hammond's nostrils.

Tim said in a hushed voice:

'Cyanide. They must have had it in their mouths.' He turned quickly away into the clear frosty night. Standing there, with one hand in his pocket and the other at his mouth, he added in a thick voice: 'There's something about it that frightens me.' He still looked pale. 'This utter ruthlessness, even with themselves—how far *will* they go? What are they trying to do?'

Hammond said: 'Break Up *Uno.*'

'If they're as ruthless as they seem to be...'

'They've got a chance to succeed,' Hammond said. 'That's why we're here. That's why Clarissa and Susan are freezing upstairs.' He looked round, and saw the Colston policeman wading through the snow towards them.

He told the man what had happened, and the policeman insisted on looking into the garage. After one glance he turned away. He recovered and promised that he would see that everything was looked after.

'Good,' said Hammond. 'Now, I'd like a guide to Colston House. Is there anyone in the village who knows how we can get there across country?'

'You *can't* get there, the bridge is down,' said the policeman.

'We're going on foot. We can supply snow-shoes,' Hammond told him, 'and we must cross the river somehow.'

'Well, Sam Oakes *might* guide you,' said the policeman. 'He's just gone into the inn. He used to work for Sir Hugh Marchant on the estate, but they caught him poaching pheasant.' The policeman said that with remarkable *sang froid.* 'What will it be worth to him?'

'What will he want?'

'He won't do it for less than five pounds,' said the policeman.

'Offer him ten,' said Hammond, 'and tell him we're in a hurry.'

Half an hour afterwards, Hammond, Tim, Fordham and four other Department Z agents started out with Sam Oakes, a little wizened man who had little to say for himself and who carried a swinging lantern, for Colston House. They carried their snow-shoes.

From the top of the hill Tim glanced back at the village and *The George*. Yellow gleams of light showed clearly; he recognised the lights of the inn. One was the highest there was in the village; it might be Clarissa Kaye's room.

Why hadn't she talked?

He forced himself not to think of her. There was the inescapable fact that somewhere between the river and Colston House were four of the 'suicide squad' and Wilkinson's party. It was possible that all of them had reached the house, although Sam had assured them that cars could only have got through with the greatest difficulty. The house was in the least accessible part of the country. They would have to climb the far side of the valley, then go down and up another, before they could see it.

At last they reached the river.

The bridge had been blown only in the centre. Torches shone on the gap, which was two yards wide. But for the snow on the far side, none of them would have hesitated to jump.

Sam went forward, calling over his shoulder:

'If we had two or three planks from the barn, we could make it.'

Hammond said: 'We'll get them.'

It was a quarter of an hour before they were able to break boards from the barn walls, and push them into position. The bridge swayed perilously when more than two men walked on it. Once there was a sickening crack as it lurched forward.

Sam, in the lead, grabbed at the broken rampart and just saved himself from falling. Beneath them the wild roar of the river was like near thunder: it sounded menacing and seemed to draw them down towards it. Above, the stars lit up the sky, and the pale silver of the moon was dropping towards the horizon; it would not be up much longer, soon full darkness would be about them.

Sam called out: 'Okay, now.'

Tim crossed the river first, the planks bending in the middle. His heart leapt to his mouth, and he seemed to feel the water closing about him again, but he reached the far side safely. He put on his snow-shoes, as the others came over safely.

Within five minutes, Sam began to lead them across the fields. Even with their snow-shoes, it was heavy going. At the top, Sam paused for breath, and decided that he would experiment with snow-shoes. They lit cigarettes and waited while he put them on. From here they could see no light anywhere.

'Ready!' said Sam. 'Single file, now.'

The country was broken by bushes, great mounds in the snow, and the ground beneath the snow was more uneven. Now and again they found they were walking over small trees and bushes and gorse. They passed several thickets, and once there was a sudden, whirring noise, making every man thrust his hand to his pocket, to his gun.

'Partridges,' said Sam, with a sniff. 'You'll soon be able to see the house.'

Hammond, just behind him, grunted a reply. They went plodding uphill again. When they reached the top of the next hill they could look down into the valley.

On the far side, halfway up the slope which they could see in the pale afterglow of the moon, was Colston House.

The house was a beacon against the semi-darkness. Light

shone in all directions, not only from the windows but from cars which stood outside, their great beams of headlights shining on to the snow. It was like a distant fairyland, and had a beauty which made all of them stand and stare; it did not seem reasonable that whoever was inside should try to attract so much attention.

Then, loud and clear across the stillness, came the crack of a shot. None of them saw the flash of flame which preceded it, but they watched more intently. Just before the sound of another shot came floating towards them, they saw a tiny yellow flash.

'So someone's attacking the place,' Tim said, in a low-pitched voice.

The stutter of a machine-gun cut across his words; and that too was being fired from the outside.

16

GREGORY WILKINSON

Hammond touched Sam's arm.

'You've finished your part of the job,' he said. 'Go back, tell my men at *The George* what is happening, and tell the policeman to try to get a call through to the nearest town and police station.'

Sam said: 'They can try.'

'Then that's all we can hope for,' said Hammond. 'Off with you.' Sam turned and sped across the snow. Now that he had not to lead them, he moved more freely, but they did not see him; they watched the house. The stutter of the machine-gun had stopped now, and there was no more shooting. They were near enough to be able to see if men moved against the light. There were no silhouettes.

'Good idea to have the lights on,' said Fordham, coming up and stamping his feet. 'No one can approach without being seen. Are we going to split up?'

'Not yet,' said Hammond. 'They won't see us for a long time. Single file again.'

Out of the darkness two more men materialised, George

and the other Department Z scout. The shooting had been spasmodic for the last five minutes, George reported. He did not know who was in the house, for he and his companion had lost their way and only arrived a quarter of an hour earlier.

The going was easy enough at first, being downhill. Hammond watched the house for a further outburst of shooting. If there were only four men in the attacking party round' the house, it meant only one at every corner; and he had enough men with him to overcome them without any difficulty. The attackers would not expect anyone to come from the village. This battle was being fought in the isolated grounds of Colston House; the people there doubtless believed that it was a fight to death.

Tim's question hovered about his mind: *who* was attacking?

The suicide squad had gone first, by road; Wilkinson and his men, presumably, had followed. So the likelihood was that Wilkinson was attacking. Hammond did not want to go too fast; when they drew near to the house, they wanted to be able to breathe silently.

Another shot came from the far corner of the house, then, almost simultaneously, more shots came from the two other corners that were in sight.

The Department Z agents reached the foot of the shallow valley, with the house only three hundred yards in front of them. They could not see the attackers until suddenly one man ran from the cover of a tree towards the house. Immediately there was a burst of fire from the house. The man stopped, taking cover behind a bush. Next moment another man moved from another point. Hammond realised what was being attempted. The attackers were approaching cunningly, a few yards at a time, and drawing fire. Now he realised that the spasmodic bursts of shooting were cover for the men as they made the attack. The nearest man was only ten yards from the front door of the house, only three from the front of a car which stood with headlights blazing.

Two shots came swiftly, and the headlights went out.

For a moment the drive seemed dark, but he could see shadowy figures rush forward. Hammond held his breath. Was this the final attack? Would the men outside get in too soon for him to approach them from behind? He saw two men running; then there was a burst of machine-gun fire again from the house. The attackers flung themselves down behind the car, which hid them both from Hammond and from the people in the house. The shooting stopped.

Hammond stood still, and the others gathered about him.

'Two men to every spot where there's shooting,' Hammond said. 'Fordham, you and I will take the drive.'

'Righto.'

'You take the side where the garage is, Tim,' Hammond ordered.

They separated and began to walk in twos towards the attackers. Most of these men could be seen from behind now, because of the light. All were crouching behind bushes or stone work, and there was a lull, as if they were waiting for the men by the car to recover and to make another burst.

Hammond and red-haired Fordham reached the drive.

The men by the car straightened up; so they had not been injured badly. They were both small men, and one had lost his hat. He groped for it. Against the bright light shining from a ground floor window the round, bullet-like head was visible.

Fordham whispered: 'So Wilkinson's inside.'

The man found his hat, and crawled back through the snow, away from the car. There was a mutter of voices, not five yards away from Hammond. He was hidden from the talking men by a low brick wall. The men were talking in a language which he did not understand.

'It might be Burmese,' Fordham said.

They watched the point where the two little men had taken cover. Hammond was thinking that the attackers would probably launch another attack any moment, and that he and Fordham must start shooting, aiming low.

The talking stopped. There came an outburst of shooting from one of the corners, and more answering fire from the house—not a machine-gun this time. The burst of firing lasted longer than any of the earlier ones, and it was still going on when three little men leapt forward in front of Hammond and Fordham. They did not shoot but rushed towards the front door. There was something in their intensity which told Hammond that they were now making their final rush.

Hammond fired, and Fordham's gun flashed; the shots sounded loud. Their frozen fingers were stiff upon the triggers, but they were at too short a range to miss. One after another the little men fell, one pitching backwards, the others falling on their faces. Not a single shot came from the house itself.

Suddenly a shadow appeared in the doorway.

'*Who's there?*' That was Wilkinson's voice.

'*Hammond!*' called Hammond clearly.

'Better run for it,' Wilkinson called. 'We'll hold our fire.'

There was shooting at the corner of the house. Hammond could see the flashes as the shots were fired. He hesitated for a moment before straightening up and running towards the porch. There was one fear in his mind; that Wilkinson intended to shoot him and Fordham as soon as they drew near.

He reached the porch, with Fordham just behind him. A shot was fired from the side, but struck the brickwork.

Wilkinson appeared by the side of the open door, and Hammond ran past him. Fordham followed close behind. They dodged to one side, near Wilkinson, who was standing with a submachine gun pointing towards the doorway. His long, lantern face was set in a sardonic smile, his dark hair was brushed carelessly from his forehead.

'This time you *are* welcome,' he said.

'I hope so,' grunted Hammond.

'Anyone else with you?'

'Several men,' said Hammond.

'I always did believe in miracles,' Wilkinson said. 'How does it feel to be a miracle?'

In spite of himself, Hammond laughed.

From one of the rooms a man called out:

'Whom are you talking to, Greg?' It was Ferguson.

'Sue's Hammy,' Wilkinson called back. 'You see how right I was.' He raised the gun as another outburst of shooting came, but no one appeared on the drive.

'Watch the drive, will you?' he asked. 'I'll go and tell the others.' He turned and hurried off, his tall figure a little rounded at the shoulders. Just before he disappeared along a passage, he glanced round, and there was a sparkle in his eyes.

They heard him talking...

There came the sound of footsteps in the house, someone cried out, and Wilkinson's voice was raised:

'Don't shoot!'

Tim's voice could just be heard:

'Thanks, Greg!'

Wilkinson laughed. 'Hammond is here,' he said. 'He's welcome, too. I'll go and warn the others.' He came hurrying into sight again, winked at Hammond and Fordham, and disappeared along another passage. He was gone for ten minutes. There was no more shooting, but the silence outside might be deceptive. It was impossible to judge how many of the little men had taken part in the attack, and equally impossible to know whether they had concentrated their main forces on the front door or elsewhere.

Wilkinson came back with a fair-haired man whom Hammond had never seen before, but who was so remarkably like a young Sir Hugh Marchant that he had no doubt as to his identity.

'We might try and finish the job off,' Wilkinson said. 'I think we've got most of them. There were seven. Three at the front, two at the side entrance and your friend has dealt with them, and a couple of singles, just to keep us busy. There might...'

He broke off abruptly. There were two shots, which came swiftly upon each other, followed by a cry of pain; Hammond realised that it was the first such cry he had heard, the men whom he had shot had fallen silently. Three of them were there in the snow, within sight.

After a moment's silence, Hammond recognised the voice of one of his men, the unmistakable voice of George Henry George. 'That's that, I think. Nasty little brutes, aren't they?' He raised his voice. 'You inside, Bruce?'

'Yes,' called Hammond.

Wilkinson said: 'I'd better go and make sure that everything *is* all right.' He hurried off, and after a few seconds there came another plaintive cry from George Henry George.

'But my dear chap, I've got *nothing* up my sleeve.'

Hammond began to laugh.

Half an hour later, a thorough search of the grounds near the house was finished, and every one of the little dark men accounted for. Three had been killed in the fighting and three others were badly wounded. The only one not seriously hurt was sitting in an easy chair, with a bandage on his forehead. Wilkinson said that these men preferred death to capture; he said he had caught one when the man had broken into *Hatch End*. Suicide might be because they were frightened of what would happen to them if they lived, Wilkinson added.

Only a patch of the prisoner's cropped hair showed. His dark eyes glittered.

Wilkinson and Ferguson were in the room with Hammond and the rest of the Department Z contingent. George Henry George was sitting by a blazing log fire in the drawing room, amusing himself with playing cards. The room was luxuriously furnished, with plenty of easy chairs and settees. Fordham was sitting at a grand piano, playing a note now and again, looking up towards the ceiling with his eyes half-closed. Tim, in his borrowed serge, was the only one badly-dressed. He sat near George, who kept on complaining that the cards would not come right.

Trolley wheels rattled on the floor outside.

'Ah,' said Wilkinson. 'Soup.'

The door was opened by a middle-aged woman who helped an elderly man to guide in a dinner-waggon. On it were two great steaming tureens of soup, piles of bread cut into squares and, on the second shelf, a huge piece of cheese and a tin of biscuits. Cutlery glittered beneath the two chandeliers as the waggon was wheeled round.

'Couldn't hope to get a quick dinner for everyone,' Wilkinson said. 'I thought this would do for a start.'

'Just right,' said Hammond.

'Happy thought,' called George. 'I knew there was something the matter with me. Starvation.' He watched the servants ladling out the soup into generous-sized dishes. Small tables were brought in.

'I hope you're not wondering whether it's poisoned,' said Wilkinson suddenly.

Hammond said: 'No, I'm not. Wilkinson, does Clarissa Kaye and the woman Susan know what you've been doing?'

'Most of it,' said Wilkinson. 'Why?'

'They refused to talk freely.'

'They're very loyal,' said Wilkinson. 'They needn't be stubborn any longer. They're still at *The George*, I hope.'

Hammond said: 'Yes. In the attic, without food, fire or blankets. They were too stubborn. I can't take risks, Wilkinson. I've got to know what all this is about.'

Wilkinson's expression altered. For the first time since Hammond's party had arrived he looked angry. But he considered his words, although there was a hostile glow in his eyes when at last he said:

'Sadism is your middle name, I gather?'

Hammond said: 'The sooner you talk the quicker I can send a man to release them.'

'You can send one now.'

'Not until I've heard your story,' said Hammond. 'I've told you what I'm doing. Now I'll tell you that evasions, half-truths, trickery of any kind will only lead to more trouble, for all concerned. The quicker you talk...'

He broke off as the woman handed him a bowl of soup.

Wilkinson also took a bowl. His gaze did not leave Hammond's face, but now a faint smile played about his lips.

'All right,' he said. 'I like men tough. For the last four years I've suspected the existence of an organisation planning to break up the United Nations. The chief target of the attack is Russia, because Russia can do the damage if she thinks *Uno* merely a talking shop.' It was odd to hear this tall, dark man echoing Hadley's words. 'I didn't like the idea.'

Hammond said: 'Don't forget that I know all about *Warning*.'

'You don't,' Wilkinson told him. 'You only know what I've allowed the world—and that includes the police—to know. It would take a long time to tell you all about *Warning*. Just now I want to satisfy you enough to get those girls free. I knew of this organisation. I didn't know enough of it to be able to report to the Government or to any authority. Whispers—rumours—an occasional paragraph in a newspaper—the anti-Russian campaign, which meant the anti-*Uno* campaign, was spreading pretty fast. But you know that.'

'Yes,' said Hammond.

Every man there, except the butler, was looking at the two as they stood facing each other. Spoons clicked on china and then moved up to ready lips, but no one watched what they were doing.

Wilkinson put his bowl down.

'I got most of my early information from Parmitter. Being in steel, which so often means armaments, he was approached from many quarters for supplies. Some smaller nations who thought—and had been made to believe—that Russia was hostile towards them, were very anxious to have arms. Parmitter booked many orders, and kept his ear very close to the ground. He discovered that the agents of this organisation—and of its size and importance there was no doubt at all—were all very much alike. You know what they're like, now.'

Hammond nodded.

'We couldn't find out where they came from, who employed them or where they lived,' said Wilkinson. 'Most of this campaign took part outside Great Britain. We weren't officially concerned. But I had an idea. I always felt sure that if

Uno did break up it would be because Russia was driven to withdraw. I thought the best way of getting in touch with the organisation was to start *Warning*. Virulent anti-Soviet propaganda would make a lot of people angry, but that didn't matter. What mattered was that the people behind the trouble should look for sympathisers in England. There are one or two rather furtive groups about, most of them ex-18B people. Someone who would boast about being anti-Russian, be picked up by the Press and held up to scorn and ridicule; that was what was wanted. Mendicott, Ferguson and I all had a pretty rough time during the Korean war. We all saw this thing in much the same way. Clarissa—whom we'd met through Parmitter—joined us. As she lived here with Marchant, she was in a good position to find out what kind of goods were being sold and asked for—that was most important—where *Super-Steel* was concerned. None of us was violently anti-anything, but we all agreed that we wanted to wipe out this organisation. That was a worthy enough purpose, wasn't it?' The sardonic smile was back on his face.

Hammond nodded.

'Thanks,' said Wilkinson drily. 'We four, my wife and Susan Harris were all in this. We kept getting small bites. We kept ourselves rather exclusive, because we were afraid that we might enlist someone who couldn't be trusted. It wasn't easy to keep the pretence up. It got Clarissa into trouble with her uncle, for one thing. But I'm going too slowly. Those girls...'

Hammond turned to the rest of his men, and asked:

'Who'll volunteer to go back to the village?'

There was no immediate response; the transition from Wilkinson's story to Hammond's abrupt question was too sharp.

George Henry George put up his hand.

'Please, teacher.'

'And me,' Tim volunteered.

'Two will be enough,' said Hammond.

They went out, George a little reluctantly, Tim eagerly. He had waited only because he had not wanted to be the first to volunteer. Wilkinson saw them to the front door, and then returned to the big room, where the servants were making another round with the waggon.

Wilkinson said: 'Thanks, Hammond. There isn't a great deal more of the general theme, although there's a lot of detail. You've probably guessed by now that the organisation we were trying to find *did* plant a man in our midst. Abbott. We'd suspected him for some time, chiefly because he'd made much love to Clarissa, and, at times, his questions were a little pressing—as if he were trying to find out how much we knew. And he gave the newspapers that story. The night before last we were on the way from *Hatch End*, after we'd left you asleep, and Abbott said he'd dropped something, and went back. I followed him. He was about to shoot you. I didn't waste much time,' Wilkinson finished drily.

'Thanks,' Hammond said.

'Pleasure. I didn't know who you were for certain at *Hatch End*—I couldn't be sure you hadn't visited Parmitter on behalf of the enemy, who might have suspected Parmitter's loyalty. That's by the way. You want to know just what I've found out. Well, this organisation exists. Its most active agents—these little dark men—are Shovian. I think that they get their orders from Shovia and, more recently, through Pirani, the chief Shovian delegate to *Uno*. I think they discovered that Parmitter was double-crossing them, and shot him. A servant here saw one about the grounds and told Lionel, who told me. I don't know how it came about...'

Hammond said: 'We were told that you were telephoned by Nassi at *Super-Steel* offices, that you warned Nassi, who told

177

Parmitter.'

That's not true,' Wilkinson said. 'Marchant and I are not on speaking terms, and I never go near Headquarters. But I don't know that the minor mysteries count much. I'm worried about what they're trying to do in England. I came down here because I heard they had set out for this place, and I thought I might learn more about their immediate plans. I think I have. One of them has talked quite freely.'

There was an absolute hush among the men when he stopped.

'I think they plan to destroy *Uno* during the London conference. One powerful charge of explosive would be enough, wouldn't it?'

1 7

REPORT

Someone dropped a spoon.

It struck the kerb of the fireplace and clattered noisily. There was no other sound. The two servants stood at the side of the room, looking on disinterestedly. All the Department Z men were watching Wilkinson. Ferguson and Mendicott, the one resting his maimed leg on a pouffe, the other with his hands thrust into his pockets, were the only two who seemed prepared for the bomb-shell.

At last Hammond said:

'Yes, one would be enough. Getting one inside the hall wouldn't be easy.'

Wilkinson shrugged his shoulders.

'It would be almost as easy as losing an umbrella in a train. No one knows *all* the delegates. Any one of them might lose his admission card, or a card could be forged. There are Press, public and official staff, any one of whom might be impersonated, and as the only objective would be to leave a small packet under a seat or behind a curtain, the job could be done in ten minutes.' Wilkinson's sardonic smile had an edge of sombreness. 'The man who did it would not necessarily try to escape. He might well be one of the suicide squad. He would probably feel that it was well worth while selling his life for that.' Wilkinson turned to the little man with the bandaged head, and murmured, 'Wouldn't you?'

After a moment's silence, the man opened his lips and said: 'Yes.'

He did not give the word any particular emphasis, but he meant it; there was no doubt of that. It was the first time that any one of the little dark men had answered a question. He succeeded in heightening the tension which was already febrile from Wilkinson's lucidly developed story.

Hammond spoke into the silence.

'Is an attempt to blow up the Session being planned?'

The man stared at him blankly.

Wilkinson turned and approached the man.

'*Is it?*'

The man spread out his hands.

'I do not know what is planned. I just obey my orders. I have never failed before.'

'Where do you get the orders from?' asked Hammond.

'I have nothing more to say,' said the little man.

Wilkinson said, 'We'll see about that.' A quick glance at Hammond seemed to say: 'That's enough velvet glove.' Hammond nodded. Wilkinson raised a hand towards Mendicott, who stepped across the room and suddenly dragged the little man from his chair. He hoisted him over his shoulder, and walked out of the room.

Fordham followed him.

Wilkinson beckoned to the manservant for more soup. The tension relaxed a little, but in the minds of most of the men was the thought: *One powerful charge of explosive would be enough.*

Into Hammond's mind's eye there had sprung the scene at *Uno* when Virnov had been speaking. He remembered his deep feeling of satisfaction because they had saved the Russian from the attack, but none of them had seriously thought that it was an isolated incident.

'Well, what next?' asked Wilkinson.

Hammond said, 'I think you and I will go and sort this thing out.' He led the way. Graham and a Department Z man went out after them. Hammond had said nothing much, but in that moment he had established his ascendancy over Wilkinson. He had made it clear that Wilkinson must talk much more freely than he had done.

The first thing Hammond wanted to know was the real reason why he had come here, to Sir Hugh Marchant's house.

Loftus and Craigie each had a copy of Hammond's report.

They had not been able to get through to Reading or Colston House by telephone, but at half-past eight the morning after the battle of the house, George Henry George and Fordham arrived at the office. They had driven through the night from the village, where Hammond had sent the report. Everything was well at Colston House. One little dark man had withstood a lot of pressure but eventually had talked. Clarissa and Susan had been little the worse for their incarceration in the attics; and Wilkinson, in spite of what he had done, seemed useful.

'Almost,' George had said, 'like one of us.'

These and the other obvious things had been passed on by word of mouth. Hammond dealt with the general theme of Wilkinson's story.

'Wilkinson tells me,' he wrote, 'that the dark men first

showed an interest in Colston House two weeks ago, when there was an attempted burglary. He says he does not know what they were after. When we drove them out of *Hatch End* they made contact with Lionel Marchant, who had gone on ahead of them. Marchant had been approached by one of the dark men and threatened with violence unless he produced the key to the vaults at Colston House. From this, Wilkinson judged that something in the vaults was urgently wanted. He decided to try to get there first. The weather helped him.

'From the explosives in possession of the dark men, it seems clear that they intended to force a passage into the vaults. At the moment no one can enter them except Marchant and his private secretary, Carfax. I have made no effort to force the doors, thinking it better for you to arrange for Marchant to come down here and open them.

'We have established that the little dark men blew the bridge; that they coerced the landlord, Parker, into allowing them to use the attics of the inn; that they are natives of Northern Shovia; that there are probably another fifty somewhere in the country and—this goes without saying—that they are prepared to go to any lengths to attain their objectives. They receive orders regularly, and although the man from whom we hoped to get information has been stubborn, one of the other wounded men has talked a little. There is a Council of Three, the identity of whose members he does not know, which directs the operations. None of the active agents appear to know what they are to do until the moment when they receive their instructions. There seems little doubt of their hostility towards both Russia and *Uno*. Their headquarters seem to be somewhere in London.

'They showed equal hostility towards Nassi. Certainly they have no love for him. Wilkinson has stated that Nassi did not get the warning about Parmitter from him. You may have checked this story by now. Abbott and Ferguson were the men with Parmitter in his room.

'From what I have been able to judge of the personality of Wilkinson and his friends, including Clarissa Kaye and Lionel Marchant and his wife, I would say that they are reliable. They feel a bitter resentment at the conduct of international affairs recently, and are rebellious against the present Government in this country. Their contention is that certain powerful arma-ments manufacturers in this country and abroad are too strong for our own and foreign Governments, and that only disinterested people could hope to get results.

'They have no particular affection for Russia, but do not believe that the Soviet Government wants war—or even a quarrel.

'Their anti-Soviet activities, they claim, have been a blind intended to attract genuine anti-Soviet factions, and so get on the inside of the movement which they call The League of Dark Men. In this they appear to have succeeded hardly at all.

'They insist that Parmitter was working with them but that Marchant was unaware of this. They knew that Marchant would have little patience with an organisation such as theirs, and, had he known about it, would immediately have reported to the authorities.

'Lionel Marchant and his wife were persuaded by Clarissa to assist them.

'The young Marchants went to the Haymart to discuss the matter with Clarissa and Parmitter. Clarissa Kaye felt that it would be disastrous if the police did discover what they were doing, and therefore escaped through the window to avoid questioning. Lionel Marchant has been quietly getting infor-mation for Wilkinson.

'Wilkinson knew that it was possible that the police would make inquiries at *Hatch End* but stayed there, throwing the party as a red-herring, in order to try to find out whether I was, in fact, a member of the Secret Service or the police.

'Clarissa Kaye and all the others were sworn to silence and I think it unlikely that they would have talked freely without Wilkinson's permission. All of them, including Mendicott and Ferguson, hero-worship Wilkinson, who has exceptional intellect and stature. They appear to regard him as the Leader. He says he fostered that illusion in order to make *Warning* appear to be just another Fascist organisation.

'Wilkinson says that he has no evidence but thinks Abbott worked for the dark men. He quotes the newspaper story as an indication. He does not know whether Pirani is concerned but thinks it likely. He is sure that the delegate at *Uno* is Pirani, and not an impersonator.

'He has offered all the help that he can give us and pledges the loyalty of himself and his friends.'

Craigie finished reading, and began to make notes on a fresh writing pad. Loftus ran through the report, and then turned over the things which George and Fordham had told him.

'It will want a lot of checking,' he said. 'But we've got the Shovian angle proved, I think.'

'We'll soon find out for certain,' Craigie said. 'I think we'd better tackle Pirani at once.'

'Openly?'

'No, not yet.'

'When is this show of magic being put on for him?' asked Loftus. 'Tonight, isn't it?' When Craigie nodded, Loftus said: 'I think we might let George have a few hours' sleep, then send him along to replace one of the Massinos. There's one other thing we ought to do right away.'

'Find out about this man named Wilkinson at *Super-Steel*,' Craigie said. 'When we've done that, tackle Marchant again.

He ought to have a load off his mind when he knows what Clarissa has been up to.'

'Is *Uno* meeting today?' Loftus asked.

'Yes.'

'We might get someone to gate-crash, and find out whether it can be done,' he said. 'It's a job we can give to one of the youngsters, and if he fails, try with someone more experienced.' He shivered. 'One small charge of explosive. It's a crazy business!'

'You go and find out what you can at *Super-Steel*,' said Craigie. 'I'll fix the rest.'

Loftus took a photograph of Wilkinson with him when he left the office.

It was a little after ten-thirty when he reached *Super-Steel's* headquarters. He did not see Carfax or Marchant at first, but an under-secretary who had been told to put everything at his disposal. Loftus set to work among the commissionaires and the girls at the reception desk downstairs. None of them could remember ever seeing Wilkinson at the offices. Two recognised his photograph and were sure that they would have known had he ever visited Sir Hugh or any of the other directors. Then Loftus went to the switchboard. It was a big private branch exchange, with eight operators. Before getting to the real point of his questions, he inquired about the extent of the telephone system. Every office had a separate line, there were outside lines to every branch office in England to the main offices in Europe, and there was teletype contact with the American and Far Eastern plants. There was always two operators on duty who knew five foreign languages.

With every additional item of information, Loftus was more and more impressed.

He asked the dark-haired, efficient-looking supervisor if there was a Mr. Wilkinson on the staff.

'We receive calls for a Mr. Wilkinson sometimes,' she answered, and he thought she looked a little uneasy.

'Who takes them?'

'They always go to Mr. Carfax's office.'

'Do you know when the last call was put through to him for Mr. Wilkinson?' Loftus asked.

'I think I can find out, sir.' The woman went away and spoke to a fair-haired, peroxided slip of a girl sitting at a switchboard. There was a whispered colloquy, and then the supervisor came back.

'It was Monday afternoon, sir, in the middle of the afternoon. The speaker was somewhat excited. He spoke in both English and French, and the operator who took the call believes that it was a M. Nassi, of San Patino. He has telephoned Mr. Parmitter on several occasions, and his voice was easily recognised.'

'Did he speak to Mr. Carfax?'

'Well, the call went through to Mr. Carfax's office.'

'Can you find out whether he did speak to Mr. Carfax himself?'

'Only by asking him or his secretary, sir.'

'I'll go and see him,' said Loftus.

'I'm not sure that he's in,' said the girl. 'Several calls have been put through to his office this morning and none of them has been answered. Usually his secretary is on duty at nine-thirty, it is most unusual.'

'I'll go and see,' said Loftus.

None of the three commissionaires had seen Carfax come in that morning, but one of them had seen his secretary, a Mr. Naylor. There was nothing surprising in not seeing Carfax, it appeared; there was a small private entrance which he sometimes used, especially if he came in with Sir Hugh.

'Is Sir Hugh here this morning?' asked Loftus.

'Oh yes, sir, I've seen him upstairs.'

Loftus went up in the lift, intending to go into Marchant's office without being announced, but an army of secretaries and underlings prevented that. Marchant did not keep him waiting long, however.

'Well, Mr. Loftus, what progress are you making?'

'Just a little,' said Loftus. 'Just now I've another worry, and need Mr. Carfax's help badly. Do you know whether he is in?'

'Oh yes. He came in with me.' Marchant pressed the switch of the talking box and waited. But the cultured voice of the secretary did not answer. Marchant frowned and turned another switch; there was still no answer. 'That's unusual,' said Marchant. 'Most unusual. Either Carfax or Naylor is always there.' He went to the door and opened it, calling: 'Carfax, are you...'

He stopped abruptly.

Loftus strode after him, his stick thumping on the floor. Marchant was standing quite still and staring into the large office beyond. Loftus looked over his shoulder.

Carfax was sprawled on the floor by the side of his desk. Through a further door, which stood open, Loftus could see another man sitting back in a chair, his eyes closed and his face deathly pale.

He needed only a moment to find out that Carfax was dead; Naylor, the secretary, had been drugged, and would probably recover before the day was out.

Marchant was completely shocked by the discovery. He seemed to go to pieces. Loftus watched his handsome face set in the agony of grief. He did not question Marchant immediately, but handled the formalities. A doctor was sent for, and

Miller arrived in person. Nothing was said outside the office until the doctor had confirmed Loftus's opinion.

Carfax had been stabbed to the heart. Naylor had been drugged by an injection of morphine. There was no trace of a weapon.

'It's odd that they used two different methods,' Loftus said to Craigie.

'They may not have been able to get hold of a powerful enough drug to kill Carfax quickly,' said Craigie.

'The little dark men at Colston village poisoned themselves,' Loftus pointed out. 'I can't make it out. No one was seen to enter Naylor's office this morning. Naylor himself fetches the mail for Carfax and for Marchant. It's true that the offices are really a self-contained suite, with a separate entrance, but Marchant himself was in his office from the time Carfax arrived until Carfax's body was found. He says that he heard nothing.'

'It sounds like a job for Miller,' Craigie said.

'He's already here. Anything else turned up?'

'No,' said Craigie. 'You haven't told Marchant what we've learned, I suppose?'

'I'm just going to,' said Loftus. 'I'll ring through again if I'm going to be long.'

He replaced the receiver, and looked at Marchant, who was staring out of the window. The sun shone through one corner of the window. Outside the brightness of the morning was a welcome relief from the leaden skies of the past few days. There was some improvement in the road conditions, but the frost was severe.

Emotion had faded from Marchant's face, now, except from his eyes. He smiled grimly.

'I am afraid that shocked me badly, Mr. Loftus.'

'I can understand that,' Loftus said. 'Has Carfax ever told you that he was afraid of anything like this?'

'No, there was no inkling of such a thing.' He smoothed down his wavy hair, and lit a cigarette. 'I am very worried because of what it might mean. Carfax was in my full confidence.' His voice hardened. 'Have you any reason to believe that he might have been disloyal?'

Loftus told him what he knew.

He went through the whole story, putting in details which seemed to have no immediate bearing on Carfax's death—or the apparent fact that Carfax had talked to Nassi as 'Mr. Wilkinson'. To the story of Clarissa, his son and Wilkinson, Marchant made little response, but he seized on the telephone call from Nassi.

'Do you say this "Wilkinson" is supposed to have warned Parmitter that there was to be an attack on him?'

'Yes.'

'Then Carfax, if he did that, acted for the best,' said Marchant slowly. 'He tried to save Parmitter.'

'That seems likely,' agreed Loftus. 'And Parmitter was working with Wilkinson, with this ludicrous idea that it was possible for a small group of private individuals to deal with the matter. Possibly Parmitter took Carfax into his confidence.'

Marchant said: 'That appears to be irrefutable. And yet...' he broke off, and shrugged his shoulders. 'I will not pretend to be able to understand it, Mr. Loftus. I sympathise with the enormity of your task.'

Loftus asked: 'Would it be easy to get a small quantity of explosive, small enough to escape notice, yet powerful enough to wreck the whole building?'

'Quite easy,' said Marchant.

'I know it exists, but it isn't easy to get,' Loftus said. 'There are plenty of such explosives, but most of them are in the experimental stage and all of them are closely guarded. Have you any samples here, Sir Hugh?'

Marchant said: 'I do not keep experimental or dangerous explosives in London. They are kept in the laboratories up and down the country.' He frowned, and looked at Loftus with a sudden gleam of alarm. 'There is a little at Colston,' he declared. 'It is kept in the vaults.'

Loftus exclaimed, '*Now* we know what the dark men were after!'

'But they didn't get it,' said Marchant, slowly, and added, 'Does that mean they will try again?'

18

A JOB FOR GEORGE

W hile Loftus and Marchant were talking in the City, a mild-mannered man named Jackson, recently enlisted in the Department's service, meandered as if aimlessly about the streets of Westminster. About ten o'clock, he reached the street wherein there was the Great Hall. The Hall, beflagged enough to shame Oslam House, had an imposing domed centre, and looked massive and indestructible.

Jackson, who did not know why he had been given this task, certainly did not ponder over the effect of a highly powerful charge of explosive inside the Hall as he watched the delegates going in. They arrived by taxi, on foot and by private car. A surprising number alighted from buses at the end of the road and hurried importantly to the flight of steps which led up to the Hall. Most of them seemed in a hurry. Men of all shapes and sizes, and one woman to perhaps every twenty men, walked up the steps, showed their passes to the attendant police, then went inside.

The hubbub in the outer hall, which Jackson saw from the steps, was like Bedlam; literally like Bedlam. At the sides were the advisory bureaux and on one wall was a huge map of London and its environs. For the convenience of the delegates, places of interest were clearly marked in red, and included theatres, museums, assembly halls, the parks and the railway termini.

Beneath the map was a mob—the right word was mob, mused Jackson—chattering and milling in all directions at once. Only a thin trickle moved towards the assembly hall, for that morning's main session did not begin until eleven o'clock.

Jackson had a forged card.

He showed it casually. A policeman checked it, and let him through.

Mixing with the throng, now and again Jackson heard a word or two and a few sentences which he could understand, but foreign tongues predominated. Everyone appeared to be talking at once. He wandered about until he reached the doorway of the assembly hall. Glancing inside, he saw what Craigie had told him to look for: the Shovian delegation was already in its place, with Pirani sitting aloof from the others. Pirani looked a sick man.

Talking to one of the other members of the delegation was a well-known British statesman, and, not far away, darting occasional hostile glances, was little Nassi, with two other members of the San Patino delegation.

Jackson wandered into the assembly hall, walked round it, nodded here and there and received casual greetings in a dozen tongues. No one took any particular interest in him.

At five minutes to eleven, the hall was full.

When the session started, Jackson, who had no right at all to be there except the authority of the forged pass, was sitting at the back. It would not be true to say that he was the only one who looked bored. A delegate from an obscure European state was addressing the meeting as if desperately anxious to be finished with his task, and sentence by sentence his words were translated into French and English.

Hakka, the Secretary-General, was tapping his desk with a gold pencil which glinted in the electric light immediately above him. Another light shone on the design of palm leaves on the great curtain hanging behind the chairman. The symbol of peace, mused Jackson...

At one o'clock, the session was adjourned for lunch.

At half-past one, Jackson had reported to Craigie that gaining entry was as simple as shelling peas.

Craigie went into consultation first with Hadley and then with Miller, and for the afternoon meeting fifty plainclothes men, in addition to those who were always on duty, packed the hall and the side-rooms of the Great Hall. Just before three o'clock, when the final rush for the afternoon session began, another, more experienced agent of the Department presented his forged card. He reported later that he felt that every movement he made was watched, but provided a man had no objection to dying with the rest, it would be quite easy to take in a small packet; after all, the delegates could hardly be searched one by one, could they?

Craigie had to admit that they could not.

By the middle of the afternoon it was established that the explosive which Marchant had stored in the vaults of Colston House was untouched. By then, too, Marchant had seen his son and Clarissa, who had returned to London. He made it abundantly clear that he was shocked by their decision to work without consulting the authorities, but beyond that bore them no hard feeling.

No trace of the little dark men still at large was found.

Nassi, Pirani, the delegates of the other suspect States, Virnov—for his own sake—and others were closely watched, but no one approached them. Since the murder of Carfax, a veil appeared to have been drawn over the affair. The fact that only twelve hours had passed since that murder, yet the lull already seemed unbearable, was a measure of the tension suffered by all who knew that something was amiss.

All Carfax's secretary had been able to say was that a man had entered his outer office when he had started off for the post, and pricked him with a needle. The man had clapped a hand over his mouth, to prevent him from shouting. The next he knew he had been in the sick-room at *Super-Steel*, with a nurse and the Special Branch man who had been stationed with him to take his story on his recovery. His assailant had not been a little, dark man, but a stranger dressed in ordinary clothes.

The only detailed information which Wilkinson had been able to give them was the names of Parmitter's would-be customers. But a list of those had already been found among Parmitter's papers; all were from the States which were already under suspicion.

Loftus, Craigie, Tim Kemble, Hammond and George Henry George were gathered in Craigie's office a little after five o'clock that evening. George, who had come in last, looked round and remarked breezily: 'Just the brains of the party, eh?'

'And nothing up our sleeves,' said Tim, who looked much brighter than for some days past.

'What's on?' asked George.

'Nothing,' said Craigie. 'You'll have your chance with Pirani tonight, George.'

George rubbed his hands. '*Abracadabra* and *Open Sesame*, I've had a chat with Massino, and he's given me one or two hints. When we have a dinner I'll give you a free show. But seriously—is it much use tackling Pirani now?'

'What makes you ask that?' asked Craigie.

George said: 'Just a tickle in the cerebrum. I mean, isn't it too obvious? Shovia for the Shovians might be a battle cry, but if Shovia is really behind this business, would they use Shovians who can be picked out a mile off? Wasn't there some talk of making sure that Wilkinson was right about their nationality?' he added.

'He is right,' Craigie said.

'Little dark men all Shovians except Kolsti,' burbled George. 'The thing is, would Shovia use such obvious people? Or wouldn't someone else be more likely to get hold of a few Shovians who have no love for their fatherland, and use them? I mean, there are different sects and factions in Shovia, aren't there? Which particular part do the dark men belong to?'

'They come from a northern province,' Craigie told him.

'Another disgruntled minority, perhaps.'

'These are native Shovians, not naturalised Europeans or men of European descent,' Craigie pointed out. 'There's no known movement for autonomy among them. Kolsti's family is Shovian, too. There aren't more than two hundred thousand left of the real natives in the country, which has a population of seven millions. From all reports, they're keenly nationalistic.'

'But there's something in what George said,' remarked Loftus. 'It points a finger almost too obviously at Shovia.'

'But when we analyse what we know of these people, we've got to admit that they don't behave as if they were being paid for the job,' Craigie said. 'It's a cause to them, or suicides wouldn't be so frequent. The most likely cause to appeal to a Shovian is Shovia. There might be a faction there hostile to the ruling Government, although we know of none. I've spent the afternoon with the Shovian consul,' he added. He tapped his meerschaum against the side of the fireplace, then filled it carefully. 'He assures me that the country is quite united, that the native population has full rights of citizenship and is completely satisfied. Shovia is worried by San Patino and one or two other states, thinking that they might have the backing of one of the big powers. There are the usual rumours of concentrations of arms and men along certain parts of the frontier, but he doesn't seem seriously perturbed. He knows of no direct threat to Shovia, and the country is quite prepared to accept any *Uno* decision on all matters concerning its foreign relations. That's the official opinion; and that's also Pirani's instructions from Shovia. It looks so innocent; almost too innocent. Anyhow, George, find out what you can tonight. You'll have the freedom of Pirani's suite, it will be a chance in a thousand. Shovian diplomatic language is French, and you're good enough with it to get through.'

'A last chance,' murmured George. 'Leave it to the magician!' He took a match from Craigie's ear, solemnly struck it on his thumb-nail and applied the light to Craigie's pipe.

M. Antonio Massino was a tall, dark, slender man, with fiery black eyes and a pale skin. George had met him that afternoon, and been astonished to find that in private life M. Massino spoke with a fruity Cockney accent. It was particularly fortunate, said Massino, that he had been asked to find a place for George Henry George, because his brother was ill with influenza.

George went to Massino's Chelsea house at about half-past six, and was received with open arms both by Massino and his wife and dresser, a surprisingly young buxom woman, who bubbled over with good humour.

'You're in good time, mister,' said Massino, who seemed to take pleasure in his accent when he was not performing.

'Royalty and all that,' murmured George.

'Royalty!' sniffed Massino. 'I *'ave* performed before Roy-'Cripes, wot a night! I wouldn't turn aht for many people tonight, I don't mind telling you.'

'Royalty, but I don't call a man like Pirani Royalty.'

'Well, diplomacy's the next best thing.'

'Is it?' asked Massino. 'I'll tell you wot *I'd* do wiv diplomats.'

'Go on, tell me,' urged George, curiously.

'Drahn 'em,' announced Massino. 'Look wot a mess they always make of fings. Look at *Uno*, nah. A lot'f cackling ole women, that's wot they are.' His dark eyes, not smouldering now, turned to George with a merry twinkle in them. 'But don't mind me. Before the Common Market I had a big French business. Spent most of our time in the South o' France, eh, Lil?' He appealed to his wife. 'Proper spoiled *my* living. Nah, let's run through your tricks agine.'

George's sleight of hand was enough to bring an approving gleam to Massino's eyes, although when he had finished Massino said grudgingly:

'You'll just abaht make it, George.'

'High praise,' murmured George. 'You don't know who will be at this show, do you?'

'Ticket only,' said Massino. '*You* oughta know, being a dick.'

'You know what diplomats are,' murmured George.

They left in good time. It was still bitterly cold, but transport was moving freely, and soon afterwards Massino's car pulled up outside the brilliantly lighted consulate which, George saw with jaundiced eye, was beflagged.

The Shovian Consulate had once been a small hotel. It still

looked like one. Structural alterations, partly due to air-raid damage, had been made so that Pirani's private suite was in one corner, and extraordinarily difficult of access. It was on the floor above the big reception hall, which was to be used that night.

Massino had been given precise instructions on where to go and what to do, and a Special Branch man had for some days been on the domestic staff. Thus, George knew that no one was to have access to Pirani's suite except through the reception room and the small ante-room which would be used by 'The Massinos'.

George's task was to search the suite while Massino held the audience.

At the door a policeman asked for their invitation cards. While his was being scrutinised, George looked about him. He saw Graham and Fordham walk past. He caught a glimpse of Hammond in the foyer of the consulate, and there were several other Department men present. That cheered him. He was also cheered by the reception accorded to him and Massino. Bepowdered and bewigged flunkeys, who looked as if they had stepped out of an earlier century, met them.

George passed the big hall where the official reception was taking place, and the first surprise of the evening came then.

Clarissa Kaye was there.

George went into the room set aside for the Massinos, wondering whether Wilkinson had also been invited. He changed into tails. Nothing could make George imposing, but he looked neat in his dress clothes, and his heavily made-up face was likely to spread cheerfulness everywhere. Massino looked sombre. Since he had reached the consulate he had said very little; and when he had spoken it was in a booming voice very different from the Cockney drawl which he used in an aside to George.

They set up their tables in an ante-room, and, at a quarter to nine, were ready for the performance, which was to begin at nine o'clock. If they were lucky, said Massino, it wouldn't be surprising if they were kept waiting for an hour. Promptly at nine o'clock, a steward came into the ante-room.

'His Excellency would like to have you announced now. Are you ready, gentlemen?'

'Massino is *always* ready,' boomed Massino.

Three minutes later, George was with him in the reception room.

There were over two hundred people present, with the bearded Pirani, a picture of dignity, sitting with a slim, golden-looking young woman in the centre of the front row. A small platform had been erected for the performers, and from that eminence Gorge could see everyone there. He felt reasonably secure behind his make-up, but he wished Clarissa were not there.

He saw Wilkinson, Susan and Ferguson.

It was not surprising that they should stare at him, for he was to perform first and then leave the stage to Massino. The polite murmur of applause made him grin; he saw that Wilkinson and his party joined in it, and seemed to be interested in him no more than in the others. Pirani, looking tired, was sitting back in his chair.

Massino was declaiming resonantly:

'You are now about to see, Excellency, ladies and gentlemen, you are now about to see a performance of magic from the great, the *greatest* performer in the world. I do not make that claim lightly. *Watch*! Try all you can to see what he does, to discover the secret of his mastery. I ask only for one thing; during the performance, the actual performance—*silence*, please.'

Massino bowed portentously.

George beamed about him, and pushed back his cuffs in time-honoured fashion. He picked up a pack of cards, went through a few elementary tricks, and then saw that Pirani was looking at him with narrowed eyes and an expression of impatience. Cards were not good enough for Pirani! George beamed still more broadly, and called for a volunteer to assist him.

Wilkinson was up in a flash!

'Oh, well,' murmured George.

'Okay?' whispered Massino.

'I'll take him,' said George.

Had Wilkinson come because he suspected the truth? Was this a challenge? If it were simple chance, would his disguise be foolproof at such close quarters? That was unlikely. He gave Wilkinson a hand up to the stage. There was a polite round of applause. Wilkinson smiled sardonically, and George felt sure that the truth was out.

He produced an egg from Wilkinson's ear.

Pirani, obviously a simple soul in his amusements, sat up.

George began to perspire as he worked. Wilkinson also perspired. Massino stood just out of sight, and now and again George thought that he was whispering caustic comments. Wilkinson seemed too bewildered by the speed of the tricks to pay much attention to George, who quickly dismissed him and called for a helper from the fair sex. Neither Clarissa nor Susan came up. He went on for twenty minutes, and a stream of oddments were tossed to the floor, all manner of things which brought gasps of astonishment from the audience. No, thought George, he wasn't bad, but Massino...

The applause was thunderous when he went off.

Massino patted his shoulder.

'Not bad,' he said, patronisingly. 'Now watch *me*.'

'Not my job,' said George. 'You hold 'em.'

'I'll hold them all right,' promised Massino. He went forward, booming forth, and George cooled off under the blandishments of Madame Massino and a beer.

The rooms of Pirani's suite were deserted. With police and his personal servants outside the suite, there appeared no need to watch it. George knew that police also watched the windows, there was no chance of anyone breaking in, and the only way into the private rooms was from the big room or from the ante-room where he had changed.

George set to work in a small room obviously used as a study.

He had no keys, but none of the locks was difficult. He looked through paper after paper, seeing that they were of no importance, the ordinary routine of the delegation's work. There was a mass of cables from Shovia and documents signed by the President of Shovia, but all of them simply indicated the attitude which Pirani was to adopt at *Uno*. Soon there remained only one small, locked brief case, which he had not examined. There was only one way to open it—by cutting the lock from the leather. He found the leather tough and hard to cut. He broke the blade of his knife, scowled, and started to work again. He really needed a chisel, he decided; it would take him twenty minutes. As he had to damage the thing, it might be as well to take it away with him and finish the job outside.

But he persisted.

He heard a sudden outburst of applause from the big room, and hoped that did not mean that Massino had finished. There was no sound of movement, and Massino's voice boomed out, as if he were announcing another trick. George turned to the case again.

In five minutes, he had it open.

Inside were several papers and a small box. He took out the

box. It was made of blue plastic, and had a small lock. He looked at it carefully for a few moments. In such a box as this an explosive might be carried. He wondered if Pirani always carried this brief case with him to *Uno*.

Then he heard a movement.

He dropped his hand to his pocket, where he carried a small gun. He heard a whisper; it was Wilkinson, and then a giggle which might have been Susan's. Then he saw the door opening gently.

He did not get a clear view of them before the explosion-came from downstairs. The floor seemed to heave and the walls to close in upon him. He heard a gasp from the woman outside, and then found himself flung against the wall, with plaster falling on him and pictures thudding to the floor.

Throughout it all, he clutched the little box.

19

LITTLE BLUE BOX

The rumbling of the explosion died down. The floor still seemed to be swaying when George got to his feet. He staggered to a chair which had been flung on its side, righted it, and sat down. Something had struck him on the head, and he felt dizzy and dazed. There was a heavy drumming in his ears; his heart was beating fast. He took in great gulps of air.

Then he remembered hearing Wilkinson's voice.

He got up, and crept to the door. By some freak of the explosion it had jammed, and would not open.

He could hear cries outside. Someone was screaming. There was a word which he could not catch being shouted time and time again.

He thrust the little blue box into his pocket, then put both hands to the door handle and tugged. It did not budge. He heard a noise which sounded like falling water; it was not water; it was a crowd on the move—stampeding! The cries were louder now, a dozen people seemed to be screaming at the same time. He heard the thud of running feet, and again one cry repeated, nearer and louder; and this time George distinguished the word.

Fire!

There was no window in this little room.

George wiped the perspiration from his forehead and, while he was getting ready for another assault on the door, looked about the room. It was a shambles. The lamp had crashed from the centre of the ceiling; that was probably what had hit him on the head. He felt his head gingerly; there was a nasty bruise, and when he looked at his fingers they had blood on them.

'Oh well,' he said, and pulled at the door again.

Nothing he could do would shift it.

There was no sound of movement on this floor now, but he could still hear the screeching, the one word was being repeated time and time again. *Fire, fire, fire, fire!* George felt hot, and thought absurdly that it might be because the fire was getting near.

He picked up a heavy chair, and crashed it against the door. The chair broke, but the outer door was hardly scratched.

George took out his automatic, wishing that it were a service revolver. He fired at the lock, but the lock itself was not holding the door, it was jammed far too tightly.

He wiped the perspiration off his forehead again. It *was* hotter than it had been a few minutes before. He could smell smoke, too. The noise of running people had stopped. Perhaps they had got out of the big room. That was, if anyone *in* the room had been able to move after the explosion. George remembered the crowded room, the people sitting shoulder to shoulder; and he recalled the rapt expressions on those faces. The golden-haired girl who had been sitting next to Pirani; was she all right? Was Pirani alive?

He picked up another chair and crashed it against the door,

but it broke in his hands. He looked round, but needed no reminder that the room was windowless. There was just this door; the room had been selected, undoubtedly, for Pirani to work in absolute security.

The smell of smoke was becoming more pungent.

He thought he heard the roar of flames.

He called out, making his voice as deep as possible, but there was no sound in response. Everyone had flown; *and only Massino knew that he was in this room.* As Massino had been in the big room, there was little chance that he was in a fit condition to send help.

What was he thinking about? Wilkinson, Susan and possibly others of Wilkinson's party had been outside the room. *And they had gone, knowing he was inside.* He went to the wall by the desk and felt it; it was hot to the touch. When he turned round again, he saw that a few wisps of smoke were creeping beneath the door. So the fire had reached the passage. The door was not hot.

He took off his collar.

He could think of no way out. No one heard his shouts, no one was likely to be in the upper part of the building. There was, perhaps, one hope; that Hammond or some of the others would try to get in when he did not show up. He thought again of the location of this room. It could *only* be approached through Pirani's suite, and if the fire had started in the big room, after the explosion, no one could get through there. On the other hand, they could get into the suite through the windows.

He heard footsteps in the room beyond. A man came hurrying towards the door.

George shouted, 'Get it open!'

'Coming!'

The voice was distorted and he did not recognise it, but he

did not think it was Hammond's or any one of the Department men's; he would recognise them soon enough. He heard a thud on the door, but no sound of breaking. It was getting unbearably hot. He pulled at the handle, straining every muscle. The door was quivering under the onslaught from the other side, but it did not give way. The thuds were coming repeatedly, but why was there only one man?

There was a pause, and into it the man said in that distorted voice:

'Get away from the door.'

George hesitated, then backed to a corner. Smoke was creeping about the room everywhere, and he started to cough. He wondered why he was to get away; probably his would-be rescuer was going to shoot at the lock.

Something crashed against the door, with a louder thud than anything before; *and the door sagged open.*

Smoke billowed in as George went towards it. A fit of coughing shook him, but he forced himself to stagger on. He saw a large armchair just outside the door; the man had lifted it and brought it crashing down; the weight had been enough. He heard the man coughing between his own spasms. Still coughing, he climbed over the chair. He could see only vaguely. A tall man in a dress suit was standing near him, beckoning. A hand touched George's arm. He felt himself dragged towards the next door, which led to the passage.

Now he could hear the roar of the flames.

They reached the passage where he saw a red glow in one direction; and in the other there was only a blank wall.

'We'll have to chance it,' said his companion, after a bout of coughing.

Only then did George recognise Wilkinson.

Wilkinson said hoarsely, 'This way.'

He led the way into a small bedroom. George realised why

a moment later, for Wilkinson went to a hand-basin and turned on both taps, then thrust two towels into the bowl. As he did so, he remarked:

'The place is a death trap.'

'Yes,' said George. 'Thanks.'

Wilkinson grinned. 'It's a pleasure,' he said. 'Where are your friends?'

'Busy, I imagine.'

Wilkinson tossed a soaked towel to George, and took the other. All the time the roar of the fire was in their ears and there was a sickly smell, rather sweet and yet nauseating. George recognised it; and he thought again of the people in the room.

'Now for it,' Wilkinson said.

Keeping close together, they approached the flames. The walls of the short passage were blackened and crumbling. They heard a rending, crashing sound, as if a roof had fallen in; it occurred to George that it was probably the staircase. He put the towel over his face, and steeled himself to go forward.

Wilkinson went first. George gave him less than ten seconds' start, then he lifted the towel to draw in a deep breath, and plunged forward.

The floor held.

The heat closed about him as if he were in an oven. He felt a sharp pain at his hands as the flames scorched them. He rushed on blindly, not seriously thinking that he had a chance. He could not take count of time, he felt the burning at his hands and his ankles. Then a floorboard gave way. He was still surrounded by flames, but knew that the staircase was ahead of him. It might have collapsed, but all he could do was to run.

Suddenly the floor gave way beneath him.

* * *

The first Hammond knew of the explosion was the roar; and then came the crashing of windows. Glass blew out all along the front of the buildings where he was standing and talking to Tim Kemble, Fordham and several Department men. Until then, the evening had been quiet and uneventful. They knew that Wilkinson, Clarissa, Susan and Ferguson were inside, but had made no attempt to interfere with them. George would be sure to see them. It was certain that the attendants inside would allow no one except the artistes to use the ante-room for dressing. That had all been carefully arranged, and Hammond did not see how anything could go seriously wrong.

Then came the disaster.

Hammond kept his feet, but Tim and Fordham were flung into the road. They came up against a bank of frozen snow. The fall shook them, but they were quickly on their feet again and soon inside the consulate. Alarmed attendants were already rushing towards the big room.

The crash of falling walls and ceilings thundered about them. After that there was an odd, unnatural silence, broken only by a rumbling sound which seemed a long way off. Suddenly people began to scream.

As Hammond raced up the stairs, with the thought of George uppermost in his mind, he was met by a solid phalanx of people rushing from the reception room. There was no question of women first; men and women, many of them bleeding from open wounds, many screaming—men as well as women—poured out like a torrent. Above the sound of the stampede came the screams and cries of helpless people behind.

Suddenly, there was a cry of '*Fire!*'

Hammond and the Department Z men had been swept back into the foyer, fighting desperately to keep their balance.

Fordham was carried into the street. There was a crush in the doorway, and Hammond, pushed against the reception desk, began to shout for order, to try to stop the panic; but his voice was scarcely audible.

Tim managed to fight his way across the hall to join him.

'We must get up,' he shouted.

Hammond glanced up at the teeming staircase. A dozen people had already lost their footing and others were falling, put the landing itself was clear. The cries and groans from the big room seemed to grow louder; and now they could see the ugly tongues of fire shooting out in all directions.

Above them were the banisters which bordered the landing. Immediately beneath was a large chair. Hammond climbed up on it, stretched up his hands and touched the banisters. He pulled himself up. A wave of heat struck at him, and he started to cough.

Tim came up.

They forced their way over fallen bodies towards the main door and stood there, hardly able to think, unable to close their eyes against the horror. The fire had started on the far ide of the room. From there, apparently, the explosion had some. No one was near it. The explosion had blown the people way, but there were other things to see....

Hammond sought for the doorway.

It was out of sight; which meant that it was hidden by the ames. He hurried across the room, treading on dead or unconscious people. Once he slipped. He looked down and saw Pirani. The Shovian delegate was dead, and his beard was badly burned. Next to him was a golden-haired girl, her face set in a grotesque, unnatural smile. Probably they had been killed instantaneously by the blast.

The flames were getting fiercer.

Then Tim exclaimed, 'Look!'

Near the door leading to the landing, trying to get up, hair dishevelled, dress torn and bare shoulders poking through, was Clarissa Kaye. She managed to get to her feet, and then began to look about her as if searching for someone. Then she moved towards the door, but stumbled and fell.

Hammond said, 'Look after her.'

He took it for granted that Tim would do so, but Tim stayed by his side as he went towards the wall of flame.

Without warning, part of the ceiling fell in front of them.

One moment Hammond was stepping towards the door, just able to see the outline, and the next something struck him heavily on the head. The same piece of plaster caught Tim a glancing blow, but did not put him out.

Hammond had lost consciousness.

The roar of the flames grew louder.

Tim bent down and lifted Hammond, then staggered back with him towards the door. More pieces were falling from the ceiling. He reached the doorway, and as he did so Fordham and several others of the Department men, with police men and S.B. men, came hurrying up the stairs.

It was impossible to get into the other rooms of the suite all they could do was to save as much life as they could there. As Tim carried Clarissa Kaye downstairs, he wondered what had happened to Wilkinson, Susan and Ferguson; but none of them loomed so large in his mind as George Henry George.

A quarter of an hour later, a man crashed down from the burning banisters into the hall; quickly after him came and other. Their clothes were blazing, they had towels over their faces, and they lay still where they had fallen. Police hurried forward to drag them away from the landing, which way likely to collapse at any moment, as the stairs had already done.

They were the last people to be taken out of the consultation.

* * *

There was no hope of keeping the story of the fire from the newspapers.

Over a hundred people escaped from the reception room, some of them only slightly injured. Reporters were there at the time of the fire, and the story spread first from mouth to mouth, then from headline to headline. In the early morning news, the B.B.C. solemnly announced that it was understood that the disastrous fire at the Shovian Consulate was preceded by an explosion.

Loftus was listening to the news.

His lips twisted wryly at that statement. He listened to the grim story of the casualties: it was feared that over a hundred people had lost their lives. The cause of the explosion was unknown. It was suggested in some quarters that a small H.E. bomb had sunk beneath the Consulate during the war; there had been several heavy raids in that part of London.

Finally: 'Although eleven delegates to the United Nations Conference at the Great Hall were killed in the explosion, the sitting of the Emergency Session will continue this morning, when M. Virnov, Soviet Deputy-Commissar for Foreign Affairs, is expected to address the Conference.'

Loftus switched off.

He was alone in the office, for Craigie had been summoned early to Downing Street. He had before him a list of the Department Z casualties; mercifully, they were few. George Henry George was not so badly burned as had at first been feared. He and Wilkinson were in hospital. Hammond was recovering from the effects of his second blow over the head. He had medical orders not to get up for at least two days.

George and Hammond could be counted out for the next few days, George probably for weeks.

Fordham had also become a casualty; in escaping from the fire and the explosion, he had broken his leg.

Graham and Tim were fit, and, of course, there were recently re-enlisted agents and those who had not been on duty near the Consulate.

Loftus needed no telling that the view taken of this disaster at Downing Street would be such that the whole of the C.I.D. as well as the Special Branch would be called upon. It was possible that the Department would be given the task of directing operations, but equally possible that authority would be handed over to Scotland Yard. Because, thought Loftus, bitterly, the Department had not exactly shone. It was no consolation that no one else had made any progress, either.

Ferguson had died in the fire; so had Susan Harris. The only member of *Warning* to escape fairly lightly was Clarissa Kaye, and Loftus was expecting a call from the nursing home where she had been taken. He would visit her immediately she was in a fit condition to talk.

Two agents were with George Henry George, in the hope that when he came round he would be able to tell his story. Until then, none knew what Wilkinson had been doing at the consulate. Craigie had agreed with Loftus that there was at least a chance that Wilkinson was responsible for the explosion. It was difficult to reconcile that with the fact that two of his friends had been killed and Clarissa Kaye injured but it was possible that the leader of *Warning* had told a story to evade suspicion, and equally possible that its members were inspired by the same suicidal fervour as the little dark men.

Massino and his wife had died in the disaster, but the biggest blow was the death of Pirani. If Pirani *had* been concerned with the League of Dark Men, it was fantastic to think that they had been responsible for the disaster.

The telephone rang, and Loftus limped across to his desk- and picked up the receiver.

'This is the Westminster Hospital,' said a girl. 'Hold on please.' Loftus held on, hopefully; this was probably word from George.

Young Jackson came on the line almost immediately;

'N-O-S...' he began.

'All right, Jacker,' said Loftus. 'How's George?'

'Well, not exactly at the top of his form,' answered Jackson. 'But he's come round and he's very anxious to see you.'

'I'll be there in two shakes,' Loftus promised.

George was lying flat on his back. His face and head were unburned, but his hands were in great white bandages and there was a cage over his legs, suggesting that his legs were also burnt. Plump Polly George got up from a chair by the side of the bed as Loftus entered. Polly looked the type to burst into tears at such a thing as this, but instead she was cheerful; Polly kept her tears for lonely moments.

'Bill, you *must* tell him that he's to have a month's complete rest,' she said, 'or else he will want to get up the day after tomorrow and play silly tricks.'

George looked at her with a smile that tried to be cheerful.

'I'll spend the month teaching *you* some tricks,' he said. He watched her until she had gone out of the room before he looked at Loftus. 'Hallo, Bill. Sorry about this. We can use able-bodied men just now.'

'We'll manage without our jester for a month or two,' Loftus said. 'But talk, George.'

The story took half an hour to tell. Twice during that time a nurse looked in and expressed herself forcibly. The third time she looked in, Loftus got up with alacrity.

'All ready, nurse!'

'So I should think,' said the nurse. Ostentatiously she took

George's temperature; and it was true that George was flushed and his eyes were more feverishly bright than when Loftus had entered.

'Don't forget that box,' said George, as Loftus reached the door. 'It should be in my pocket.'

'I'll find it,' said Loftus.

He hurried out of the room, told Polly that George would have as much leave as he needed, and then went to see the matron. Soon he was going through George's clothes. When he saw their condition he marvelled that George had come through alive. His legs must be in a very bad way; his shoes were burned through so that only a little of the uppers was left.

Loftus pulled at the pockets. The burned cloth crumpled in his hands. On instructions, nothing had been touched, and he took out George's wallet, which was scorched but in fair condition, and the other oddments. Among them was the little blue box. He slipped it into his pocket, took George's identification card and passes from the wallet, and then asked the matron to see that his wife had everything else.

'Better not let her see the clothes,' he added.

Then he learned that Wilkinson was also able to talk.

Wilkinson had not escaped facial burns; the skin had been burnt from his chin, and he was heavily bandaged there. But his head and eyes were unaffected, and he could just manage to speak.

'I'll save you asking questions,' he said. 'We managed to get invitations to the show through Parmitter, last week. We'd not met Pirani, but were very interested in him so we went along to hold a watching brief. Silly of us perhaps, but you people haven't exactly sparkled. I know we were followed, but...' he broke off, and there was a smile in his eyes. 'No one could follow us into the suite. You had guarded it too closely, but we were able to slip up. Susan and I went, after I'd recognised George and wanted to find out what he wanted. Also, I was looking for a little blue box which I thought Pirani had. Have you found such a box?'

Loftus looked blank. 'Blue box?' he asked. 'No. What's it like?'

'Not much bigger than twenty cigarettes,' said Wilkinson. 'If you do find it, be careful. It's dynamite!' He even managed a ghost of a laugh, and added: 'Well, not dynamite, a lot more powerful. I wish you'd found it.'

20

'DYNAMITE'

L oftus did not get back to the office until after eleven
o'clock, for he had gone to see Clarissa after talking
with Wilkinson. All the time he carried the little blue box in
his pocket, and he was conscious of it at every movement.
Wilkinson had told him that the box contained some samples
of a high explosive on which *Super-Steel* had been working. It
had been entrusted to Lionel Marchant who had passed it on
to Wilkinson, from whom it had been stolen.

When Loftus reached the Department Z office in Whitehall, he placed the box in front of Craigie with great care.

'Wilkinson and Susan were sitting near the door,' Loftus
said. 'According to Wilkinson, Massino had the rest of the
audience enthralled with a trick which included a manifesta-
tion of ectoplasm—or smoke!' added Loftus. 'One corner of
the room was temporarily hidden in smoke, and Wilkinson
and Susan took their chance then.'

'There was a smoke trick,' Craigie said. 'I've been told
about it from several sources. Most of the people I've spoken

to seem to think that Massino was responsible for the explosion.'

'Is that worth checking, I wonder?' asked Loftus.

'Miller's doing what he can on it. We've taken Massino and his friends for granted. I don't think there's much chance that they played a different kind of trick, but it's as well to be sure. But the smoke certainly explains how Wilkinson and Susan got into the suite.'

'Yes,' said Loftus. He looked at the box. 'Well, the only thing of real importance seems to be that little pretty.' He picked the box up gingerly and inspected the tiny lock. 'It's secure enough. Notice anything odd about it?'

'There's no effect from the fire,' said Craigie.

'Yes—fireproof, fire-resisting. That's probably just as well. We'd better find out if Lionel Marchant or the great Sir Hugh know how to open it.' He paused. 'They might also be able to tell us precisely what's in it. It's time I looked Marchant up again.'

Lionel Marchant had corroborated Wilkinson's story, and it was evident that he had been easily swayed by Wilkinson's stronger personality. Although like his father in appearance, Lionel lacked strength of will. Both Loftus and Craigie were uneasy about him. He had access to so many secrets of vital importance, although it was some time since he had left the firm to control the Colston Estate.

This was a good opportunity to see him again, and the interview should at least solve the mystery of the box.

'Where were Lionel Marchant and his wife last night?' Loftus asked, suddenly.

'At Sir Hugh's London flat,' said Craigie. 'So was Violet Wilkinson—apparently there's been a complete *rapprochement*. They had no visitors, according to the reports. Take Tim along to see them, will you,' he added. 'Tim will have to take over outside for the next few days.'

Loftus telephoned Tim Kemble and arranged to meet him at the *Super-Steel* offices, made the appointment with Marchant and his son, and reached the *Super-Steel* Headquarters at noon. Nothing had changed in that throbbing, seething seat of power. As he went upstairs, Loftus reflected a little sententiously that it was remarkable that one man could have created such an organisation; that Marchant was the real power here everyone knew.

Lionel Marchant was in the big office with Sir Hugh.

The resemblance between them was marked; except that Lionel was much younger, he looked a copy of his father; his hair waved in exactly the same way. He smiled affably enough at Loftus, and Sir Hugh shook hands.

'I hear that Mr. Hammond was hurt last night,' he said. 'My son and his wife were invited, but were unable to go.' He spoke with feeling. 'How is Hammond?'

'Not badly hurt,' Loftus told him.

'Now, how can I help you?' asked Marchant.

Loftus took out the little blue box.

He expected to see a change of expression on Lionel Marchant's face. He expected the older man to exclaim. So he placed the box carefully on the great flat-topped desk while looking at the two men.

Both looked blank.

'What's that?' asked Lionel Marchant.

Loftus said, 'Haven't you seen it before?'

'No,' said Marchant. He picked it up. 'Fireproof plastic,' he said. 'It's a neat little container, but it doesn't mean anything to me. What did you expect...'

He broke off, startled, for Loftus swung round and snatched up the telephone.

'Tim, go to the hospital, make sure that Wilkinson's still there!' He waited impatiently until an operator answered him and then said: 'Get me the Westminster Hospital, and Scotland Yard. Hold the Yard on for me until I've finished with the first call.' He held on, looking at the Marchants intently. 'Don't take any chances,' he called to Tim, who was already at the door, and then looked grimly at Marchant and asked, 'May I use the telephone?'

Marchant said, 'What the devil's got into you?'

'Wilkinson told me he got this box from your son,' said Loftus. 'I—hallo...' he heard the hospital operator. 'Casualty Ward, please,' he said, and in a few seconds he was talking to Jackson. 'Have you seen Wilkinson lately?'

'No.'

'See if he's still there,' said Loftus.

As he waited, for Jackson did not pause to ask whether he had taken leave of his senses, but went off immediately, he saw father and son exchanging glances. Was there a gleam of suspicion in the older man's eyes, he wondered? Neither of them moved, and Jackson quickly came back to the telephone.

'Yes. He's fast asleep.'

'Make sure he is asleep and not dead,' Loftus said. The Marchants started, while Jackson was startled to protest.

'I say, old chap...'

'He might conceivably have killed himself or someone else might have managed to poison him,' Loftus said. 'Miller will be sending some men over in a few minutes. Stay in Wilkinson's room until they arrive.'

'Right.'

Loftus replaced the receiver, but the bell rang immediately, Superintendent Miller agreed to see that the hospital was watched.

Loftus replaced the receiver and wiped his forehead.

'I'm afraid Wilkinson has put something across us.' There was bitter note in his voice. 'That is, unless you have, Mr. Marchant!' He was looking at Lionel. 'You didn't give him that box, did you?'

'Of course I didn't,' said Lionel, indignantly.

Sir Hugh asked: 'What is supposed to be in it?'

'A small amount of a powerful explosive,' said Loftus.

Sir Hugh picked it up, and said thoughtfully:

'We can easily make sure of that. We can take it downstairs to the engineer's shop and get it opened. Would you care to?'

'I certainly would,' said Loftus.

They went downstairs together. Only once did Lionel speak, to assure Loftus that he had never seen the box in his life before. It would be necessary soon to put Lionel Marchant through a stiff interrogation.

A little, sharp-nosed man in the engineer's shop looked at the box, sniffed, looked at his bench and sniffed, and said that it shouldn't take long.

'Handle it carefully,' warned Loftus.

The little man sniffed again. 'I know how careful I've got to be.'

Loftus smiled faintly. The man picked up a tiny saw. He put the box in a vice, without gripping it too tightly, and set to work. All of them watched him with close interest. He worked round the lock, getting the point of the saw in first and then making a neat cut. Soon the lock fell out. He took the box from the vice and handed it to Sir Hugh.

Marchant handed it to Loftus in turn.

Inside the box were several sheets of folded paper, but nothing remotely like an explosive.

Loftus supposed that Lionel ought to be forgiven the bleating laugh with which he greeted the discovery.

* * *

There was nothing written on the three folded sheets of paper, as far as Loftus could see. He took them to Craigie who immediately sent them to the Scotland Yard laboratory for examination. Probably something was written in invisible ink; and all known processes of bringing that to light would be tried within the next hour.

Loftus went to see Wilkinson again. The medical staff were difficult, saying that the sick man should not be disturbed, but Loftus insisted, although he had an uncomfortable feeling that he would achieve nothing, that the opposing forces were too strong and too cunning. The feeling of helplessness which that engendered weighed heavily on him.

Wilkinson woke out of a heavy sleep. He could not struggle up in the bed, but came to very quickly. Loftus wondered if he had expected this second call.

'Not more trouble,' he muttered.

'That little blue box,' said Loftus. 'Who really told you about it?'

'Lionel Marchant,' asserted Wilkinson, promptly. 'I've told you that once.'

'He denies it,' said Loftus.

He could not understand the expression in the other's eyes. Something happened to Wilkinson, something in Loftus's brief statement caused it. He was silent for a long time. Then he spoke in his low-pitched, uneasy voice:

'All the same, he gave it to me. He's lying, not I. And if he would lie to you about this, he lied to me!'

Wilkinson half rose from his pillow, and the nurse came hurrying across the room and pressed him back gently. She said something which Loftus could not catch, but Loftus was interested only in what Wilkinson said. 'He lied to me!' There was a load of hatred in Wilkinson's voice. Into Loftus's mind there sprang the earlier story: *Warning* had been founded in order to attract the real enemies of Russia in this country. Abbott had been one of them; now Wilkinson believed that *Lionel Marchant* was another.

Wilkinson said: 'Get him before it's too late, Loftus!'

'He's being closely watched,' said Loftus, slowly. 'I'll get him all right.'

He hurried out of the room to Tim Kemble and Jackson, and he took them with him. From downstairs he telephoned Marchant, who said that his son was now in the next office. As they hurried downstairs and got into his car, many facts were racing through his mind. Lionel Marchant had been on both sides of the fence, his father's and Wilkinson's. He had been in a perfect position to judge the progress which each was making. He had not gone to Pirani's reception, although he had a ticket for himself and his wife; possibly he had known what was going to happen, and had deliberately stayed away.

Loftus closed his eyes as Tim drove as swiftly as he could towards the *Super-Steel* offices.

Outside the offices were Special Branch men and one or two Department Z agents on guard, as they had been for days. Neither of the Marchants had left the building. Loftus and Tim hurried up to the first floor, while Jackson waited in the big hall. Loftus pushed the secretaries and their underlings aside and entered the great man's sanctum without a by-your-leave.

Marchant looked up.

'Now what's the trouble?' he asked.

Loftus said: 'I'd like to see your son again.'

'He assures me that he knows nothing at all about the box, and I think I would know if he was lying. You don't seriously suspect...'

Loftus said: 'I think he lied to me, Sir Hugh.'

Slowly, Marchant rose from his desk.

'I suppose it is possible,' he acknowledged. 'But you don't know my son. He is quite incapable of taking any part in such an affair as this. He is not even qualified to work here. I found that estate management was much more suitable for...'

He seemed to be talking for the sake of talking, and continued as Loftus went to the door of Carfax's room. Loftus felt the heavy weight of depression upon him. Marchant was frightened. That seemed the only explanation of his manner, the nervous twisting of his hands, the way his voice rose. He might now have reason to suspect that he had misjudged his son's quality.

Loftus opened the door.

Lionel Marchant was sitting at Carfax's desk, slumped across the chair. In his right hand was a hypodermic syringe. When Loftus touched him, he fell forward.

In front of him was a sheet of writing-paper, covered with sprawling handwriting. Loftus motioned to the door and Tim went to watch Sir Hugh, while he read the note.

'I can't go on,' Lionel had written. 'It's too much for me. Loftus and Wilkinson between them will find the truth sooner or later, from now on I shall be in constant danger.

'Le me outline briefly why I have worked as I have done. I have never agreed with my father that armaments are a thing of the past. I believe in them. I believe that the difference between nations can only be settled by war. I believe that power should be to the strong and that the weak should fall. I have been—ever since I was able to think—afraid of what would happen if the power of Great Britain should be seriously challenged by other states. I have watched the growth of the U.S.S.R. with increasing foreboding. I have watched the way in which it has taken more and more control of *Uno*. I believe that eventually there should be a clash between Great Britain and Russia. I want to avoid active war for a long time to come, so that we can become *really* strong. For that reason, only for that reason, I believe that *Uno* is a danger to this nation and, in the long run, a danger to the world.

'Therefore, I would have it broken.

'I thought that if Virnov were killed, that would be enough. Since then I have come to realise that Russia is eager to help the consolidation of *Uno*. I believe that the only way it can be destroyed is *physically*. I am not alone in this belief. I am but one of the Council of Three. They will finish what I have begun. And they will finish it *soon*.'

Loftus read the letter twice, measuring its inconsistencies, the haphazard phraseology, the confusion of ideas. It was just such a letter as might be expected from a man on the point of suicide, a man weak in himself but envious of power. There was undoubtedly some truth in the explanation; although not in the premises. It was easy to imagine that Lionel Marchant had been used as a tool by others, his weakness forged into their strength because of his opportunities for evil-doing.

'*I am but one of a Council of Three.*'

That sentence seemed to glow in front of Loftus's eyes as he turned away from the dead man and went into Marchant's room.

Tim had told the steel magnate.

Loftus said: 'Did you know what he was going to do?'

Marchant said: 'I was afraid of it.'

'And you let him do it.'

'He was my son,' Marchant said, in a voice which was hardly audible. 'He was my son.'

Loftus's voice was harsh.

'You were afraid that he would commit suicide. You allowed him to have the opportunity, although I telephoned to warn you. That was equal to *helping* him in his work.' The industrialist's eyes were narrowed and seemed to be filled with anguish, but he did not speak. 'You know the issues at stake. You know what happened last night. You know of the threat to world unity, and yet you helped him to do it.'

'He was—my son.'

Loftus said: 'May it be ever on your conscience.'

He turned and left the room.

Tim followed him, and closed the door. Naylor was approaching, and looked at them curiously. Loftus waited until he had gone into his own room, and then said:

'Go and get Jackson, Tim. I want Marchant watched.'

Soon Jackson came hurrying along with Tim.

'Stay with Marchant every minute,' Loftus told him in a low voice. 'Don't let him out of your sight.'

He opened the door, and saw Marchant looking at some papers on his desk. When he glanced up, there was a listless expression on his face. Hope had poured into Loftus but seemed to have drained out of Marchant.

'What is it?' he asked.

'I am asking one of my men to see that you are safe until this is finally over,' Loftus said.

'I'm safe enough,' Marchant told him.

'As safe as your son?' Loftus asked bitterly.

He went out and closed the door.

Tim walked with him to the landing and then down the stairs. Everyone who passed seemed to stare at Loftus, and it was not because of his ungainly bulk or the stiffness of his walk. Tim was still acutely conscious of the change in the big man. What *had* happened? How had the situation been worsened?

They drove in silence to the office, and found Hadley with Craigie. Hadley's smile vanished at the sight of Loftus's expression. Craigie started, and his meerschaum slipped from his mouth.

Loftus limped to the fireplace and sat down, then looked up at them. Tim was standing near the door, still puzzled, hardly noticing Hadley's presence.

No one spoke.

Then Loftus took out his cigarette case and tapped a cigarette on it with slow, deliberate movements. When he had finished he began to speak.

'It's worse than we feared, Gordon. It goes deeper than we'd feared. And I don't see any way to stop it. They mean to get *Uno*. They'll get *Uno* unless we can work a miracle. There is to be a session this afternoon, isn't there?' he asked bleakly.

Hadley said: 'Yes.'

Loftus went on: 'Lionel Marchant is dead and appears to have made some kind of "confession". The truth is that he was murdered and the confession written for him. Carfax was killed in the same office, in a different way but in that same office. It's next door to Marchant's.' He drew a deep breath. 'Marchant killed them both,' he said, abruptly. 'I haven't told Marchant that I'm sure. Our one chance is to watch and follow him. He will almost certainly give the signal for the big attempt.'

After a long pause, Hadley asked:

'Are you quite sure of this, Loftus?'

'If you ask for proof I can only give you circumstantial evidence. But have a look at it. Parmitter worked for Marchant, and discovered part of the truth. He told Wilkinson, who persuaded him to work as a spy in *Super-Steel*. Parmitter's belief in armaments as the only way to security was a pose. Carfax also learned the truth about Marchant. Carfax took calls as "Wilkinson" to keep Parmitter in touch with events. Parmitter didn't fully trust anyone. But he wanted to get in touch with Carfax and sent Nassi to telephone. Carfax had learned that Parmitter was to be shot that day. He warned Nassi. But Carfax was no fool. He knew quite well that his word was only hearsay and he could offer no proof. Proof was essential before he made any move. He relied on Marchant's trust in him. Marchant learned the truth, and killed him, sending someone in to attack Naylor so that the murder appeared to come from outside. You remember the two different ways of attack—a knife, which we never found, and the hypodermic syringe. An unknown man drugged the secretary, but Marchant killed Carfax. And Marchant could only have known of the real objects of Carfax and Parmitter if someone working for Wilkinson told him. That spy might have been Abbott, or else Lionel Marchant.'

He paused, and tossed the cigarette into the glowing fireplace. No one spoke. He prodded the mantelpiece with his walking-stick before he went on:

'Doesn't it add up?'

Craigie said: 'It adds up, Bill.'

'Here are some more figures for the column. Marchant discovered that Wilkinson was working against him, not knowing who he was; and also that Wilkinson had first won Clarissa's loyalty, then his son's. Wilkinson undoubtedly suspected that Marchant was behind the League of Dark Men, behind the whole foul scheme. Who would benefit more? Who would be a more likely man than the virtual owner of the biggest steel corporation in Great Britain, with plants throughout the world? Who could want *Uno* to fail more than Marchant does? It's so obvious.'

For the first time a bleak smile crossed Loftus's face.

'Of course, we don't want to believe it,' he went on. '*You* don't want to believe it, you can see the terrible possibilities lurking in the background. But before we come to them, let me finish. You'll say that Wilkinson accused Lionel of lying when he said that he knew nothing about the blue box. The truth is that in the end Marchant and his son were working together, but Lionel was weak and his father strong. Lionel might have cracked under questioning; Marchant will not. So Marchant killed him. All the time he offered us every facility, he even opened the box for us, he behaved irreproachably; and from time to time he killed, in order to make sure that nothing could be traced to him.'

'Now—what?'

'Now we know that Marchant is chiefly responsible we can see the full horror of it. If you want any telling, go to *Super-Steel's* offices. Get a first-hand picture of the complex organisation which *spreads throughout the world*. North, South, East and West there are *Super-Steel* plants. There are hundreds of subsidiary and associated companies, the power of that organisation is so vast that it can hardly be conceived. There isn't anywhere not affected. *Super-Steel* is wealthier by far than many small countries and it can still play on the passions of nations like Shovia, like San Patino. It can set one against the other, and it can also sow more than the seeds of discord among the big nations. It can help to create distrust.'

After another pause, he added abruptly:

'The one hope is that Marchant hasn't yet given his instructions for the final act.'

Hadley said sharply:

'The Hall must be cleared at once, the next sitting postponed.'

'Oh, yes,' said Loftus. 'That's one way of doing it. But it's after one o'clock. You can stop them all going back this afternoon. You can stop them meeting again tomorrow and the next day. I don't mean that there's no hope of preventing complete disaster in the building. But supposing you *do* stop them from going back? What will happen? The world will know simply that the *Uno* Conference broke up. Isn't that exactly what Marchant wants? Officially we can give the reason, but isn't it too fantastic to expect the world to believe? Remember, it can only be done on *our* initiative. We can stop the session, but if we do we shall destroy *Uno* more effectively than a high explosive would. *We* know the danger; can we convince the other delegates? Can we convince Russia and the United States that we've been forced to do it? I don't think we can. I think they—the great masses of their peoples as well as many of their statesmen—will believe that we have acted because we don't want *Uno* to succeed. Questions affecting us are being thrashed out; it is a remarkably convenient time for us to stop the session. Our delegates have made wonderful speeches, we've built up a reputation for wanting not only world peace but a form of World Government, but won't the others be only too ready to believe that we have been putting out a smoke-screen to hide our real intentions?' He brushed his hand across his hair, and added harshly: 'Isn't that right? Or have I gone crazy?'

Hadley moved quietly towards the door.

'I'm afraid you're right,' he said. 'You've forgotten only one thing.'

'What's that?'

'I can get in touch with the major Embassies and tell them the truth now. I can summon an emergency session of the Big Five and *they* can make the decision to postpone the next sitting. It will have to be a stop-gap decision. Their hands will be forced, but—well, it's got to be attempted,' went on Hadley, and he went out as Craigie pressed the button and the door slid open.

He did not look back.

Tim spoke as the door closed.

'Surely we can force the truth out of Marchant? There's a Council of Three, you say. Lionel's gone. If we get his father, there'll only be one left. Marchant must talk.'

Craigie spoke mildly.

'There is a chance that you're wrong about Marchant, Bill. It's a slender one, but it's possible. You know that if you tackle Marchant and he is innocent, there's absolutely nothing that anyone can do to help you from the consequences, don't you?'

'I'll chance it,' Loftus said.

Tim said in a low-pitched voice: 'It's just possible that Clarissa can help us in some way or other. And it's even possible that Wilkinson...'

'You can cut out Wilkinson now,' said Loftus. 'Oh, we can tackle his wife and we can tackle Lionel Marchant's wife. We won't get anything from them. It's just possible that Clarissa knows more than we realise. I don't know whether you're the right man to tackle her.'

Tim said: 'May I see her, Gordon?'

Craigie nodded, then pressed the control button and the door opened for them to go out.

21

FINAL ACT

Tim Kemble watched Loftus drive off, and then turned to his own car, which was parked near the entrance to the Department's office. Two or three agents were in sight, walking up and down because of the cold, making sure that no attempt was made to raid the Department. Tim could have taken any one of them with him, but he preferred to go alone.

As he drove towards Clarissa's nursing home, he thought 'My first big show.' He was only just beginning to realise the enormity of it. Loftus had seen that so quickly, Hadley and Craigie had picked it up at once. Tim remembered Loftus's expression on the way from *Super-Steel* and he remembered the effect of the big man's entry into the office. He seemed to see Hadley's face, and Craigie's, as the full truth dawned upon them. *Uno* must meet or die. There was the issue, in simple enough terms. Lives could be saved; but if they were, in the dim, bleak future there hovered the threat of disaster greater by far than anything that had happened before. Unless there was unity there must be disunity.

Uno must meet.

Tim's mind was as blank as Loftus's had been about what could be done to find the final, damning proof against Marchant, to remove both dangers. If the assembly were once postponed...

The car pulled up outside the nursing home.

Tim hurried up the steps, which had been cleared of snow, and was admitted by a trim maid.

'I think Miss Kaye's left, sir,' she said, when he asked for Clarissa. 'She wasn't badly hurt, and I think she went half an hour ago.'

'Make sure, will you?' asked Tim.

The maid went off, to return very quickly with the matron. Yes, Miss Kaye had left at half-past twelve. A car had come for her, and she appeared to have been expecting it.

Clarissa had a small flat in Mayfair, a *pied à terre* near Wilkinson's West End flat. It was only a few minutes' drive away. Tim pulled up, and saw the familiar face of a Department Z agent who was walking up and down the street. He was annoyed with himself; of course Clarissa had been watched, but he had not noticed that no one from the Department had been outside the nursing home.

The agent came up.

'Is she inside?'

'Well, she was,' said the agent. 'Tommy's at the back, and he would have reported if she'd gone out that way.' He frowned at Tim's expression. 'Not more trouble, I hope?'

Tim said: 'Trouble enough. Thanks.'

A maid opened the door, and took him into Clarissa's room. It was small and charming. Clarissa was sitting in front of a coal fire. She was dressed as Tim first remembered her at the Haymart, in a simple frock of navy blue. Her hair was singed a little, but she had escaped the worst of the flames after the explosion, and although her right hand was bandaged, she got up promptly enough and smiled a greeting.

'Hallo, reporter!'

'Hallo,' said Tim. 'How are you?'

'Counting my blessings,' said Clarissa, and her eyes grew shadowed. 'How's Gregory?'

'Who? Oh, Wilkinson. He'll pull through.'

'And your friend—George, wasn't it?'

'He'll be all right, too.'

Tim found it surprisingly difficult to talk. Perhaps Loftus had been right, and this job was not for him. It would not be easy to tell *any* girl that her uncle was suspected of such a plot as this, that among his crimes was the murder of his son. And, at the back of Tim's mind, there was the little demon of doubt, the bare possibility that Loftus was wrong.

'You look sombre,' said Clarissa. 'What else has happened?'

Tim told her, quietly. He told of Lionel's death and the virtual certainty that his father had killed him. Of Carfax; of the consequences if *Uno* failed to meet. Words came out clear and precise. Clarissa listened intently, making no comment, showing no particular sign of shock or horror. At last he spread his hands out before the fire, and finished:

'So you see, anything you can remember, any trivial thing about Sir Hugh, might help us.'

She did not speak for some time, but took a cigarette from a box, forgetting to offer him one. And then she said a strange thing:

'Was it Loftus who first thought of this?'

'Yes.'

'I should never have thought him capable of it,' said Clarissa. She looked at him again with a curious expression in her eyes, and then she said: 'I wish you hadn't come, Tim. There is so little I can do.'

It was the first time she had used his Christian name, yet he hardly noticed it.

'I don't understand you,' he said.

She leaned forward. 'Well, what *can* I do? It's shocked me more than you realise. I just can't think.' She stood up, restlessly. 'I've been working with Gregory and the others to find out the truth. We've so often been near the truth. We learned about Kolsti's attempt just too late to do anything about it. Sometimes I've been almost afraid that it would turn out like this, but I've never let myself believe it, I've always...'

She broke off, for there was a tap at the door.

'What is it?' she called out.

The maid said: 'There's a gentleman to see you, Miss.'

'He must wait,' said Clarissa, and added in a low tone: 'I can't see anyone now.'

'He says it is urgent. He wants...'

'I suppose I'll have to see him,' said Clarissa.

She touched Tim's arm and hurried to the door, moving with that supple grace which had attracted him from the first. From the door, she glanced over her shoulder with a smile which was too bright, too radiant; it did not fit in with her words. Her manner was so different from her words in every way. She was not as shocked as she pretended. She could not even successfully pretend to be.

Tim got up.

He heard a murmur of voices and stepped to the door. Who had come to see Clarissa, who had been able to make her get up like that? He opened the door. He saw a man standing in the small hall, putting something back into his pocket. Tim caught a glimpse of something red—a red card. Into his mind there flashed a picture of the little red cards with the numerals on them, that had been carried by the little dark men. This man was not small or dark, but he was obviously a foreigner. Tim thought he had seen him before, but could not be sure.

A door opened in the flat.

Tim stepped into the hall. The man looked up with a start of surprise.

Tim said: 'Let me see that card.'

'I—I do not understand you, sir.' The man spoke in halting English, but he looked more than startled. 'My card?' He took a white visiting card out of his pocket. 'That...'

Tim held out his hand.

'Not that one.' He took the man's wrist and twisted it. The man staggered helplessly against him. Tim slipped his hand into the waistcoat pocket where the red card had disappeared. He felt it, and pulled it out.

It was one of the diamond-shaped cards, and the number on it was 5.

The man had shown this card to Clarissa.

He drove his clenched fist into the man's jaw, an uppercut delivered with all his strength. He heard the man's teeth snap together, then let him fall. The blow had hurt his wrist and forearm, he rubbed them as he turned towards the room into which Clarissa had gone. He dropped his hand to his pocket, took out his gun and transferred it to his left hand. Then he stepped towards the door.

Clarissa was bending over a cabinet, and pushing it towards the wall. On the top of the cabinet was a little blue box, a replica of the one which George had obtained from Pirani's room.

Tim covered her with the gun as she finished with the cabinet and took the box. She turned at last. When she saw him, she backed so violently that she knocked against a chair and sat down in it involuntarily. The box nearly fell. She clutched it again, but it slipped to the side of the chair.

'Don't touch it,' Tim said, in a voice which he hardly recognised as his own. 'Don't touch it.'

'*Tim!*'

In the fingers of his tender right hand he held the little red card.

'Recognise it?' he asked.

'Tim, I—Tim! You don't think...'

'I *know*,' said Tim. 'It's all over, Clarissa.' He hesitated, he found words so difficult to utter. 'A family affair, wasn't it? The Council of Three. Get up, and leave that box where it is.'

She sat staring at him. There was no other sound in the room. He could just see the edge of the little box against her skirt. She put her hands on the arms of the chair, as if to steady herself.

'I shall shoot you if you don't do what you're told,' he said, and still he found it difficult to recognise his own voice. 'Don't make any mistake, Clarissa.'

Slowly, she got up.

The blue box, lodged against her thigh, fell flat on the chair behind her. She stood in front of it. He motioned her to one side. She obeyed without argument. There was the box, just a little square thing of blue, so innocent-looking.

He took a step towards it.

'Tim,' she breathed, 'don't interfere. Let me send it away, let us finish with it. Tim, you don't understand!'

'I understand that you're in this awful business with your uncle.'

'But you don't know why! Tim, we're not evil, we know this is the right thing to do. It must be done. All this talk of unity and peace, all this talk of disarmament again and of a world Council, it can't really work, we must stop it before it gets too powerful. *Great Britain* must hold the power, we can't trust others, we *daren't* trust others.'

'We're not going to trust you,' Tim said.

'You don't know what you're doing!' She backed away as he approached and stretched down his hand for the box. 'Be careful!' she cried. 'Don't bang it!'

'So that's the one with the explosive in, is it?' asked Tim. 'And your boy friend outside was going to take it to *Uno* this afternoon. He won't. I think I've broken his neck.'

'Tim, you *must* listen to me...'

'I'm going to,' said Tim. 'So are the others.' He slipped the box into his pocket. It rested against his side and dragged the lining of the pocket, for it was much heavier than he had expected. 'You can start now, Clarissa. You can pick up the telephone and dial Whitehall 1212 and tell Superintendent Miller to ask Craigie to send his men here.'

'Tim!'

'All right, I'll do it,' he said.

She had backed towards the telephone. For the first time he wondered if she had been talking just to take him off his guard, whether she was trying to prevent him from reaching the telephone.

'Stand aside,' he said.

'You mustn't do it,' she breathed. 'You must let...'

And then she picked up the telephone and flung it at him, *aiming at his side.*

He knew that she had tried to fling it at the box. He dodged. The telephone went past him, reached the end of the flex and crashed on the floor. As it did so, she flung herself at him. He pushed her back, but she struck at the gun and it slipped from his hand. Next moment she was upon him again, scratching, biting, kicking. He backed away, but she held on. All the time the box tapped gently against his side.

Then he got his left hand about her throat, and squeezed; he had to squeeze hard. She scratched at his face and he could feel the blood oozing up, but he maintained the pressure until she relaxed. At last he released her. She dropped to the floor in front of him, gasping for breath, only just conscious. Tim turned and picked up the telephone. He held it to his ear, and found that it was working. He dialled Craigie's number, and told Craigie what had happened.

'I'll have men there in twenty minutes,' Craigie promised.

Tim put the receiver down, and stepped to the cabinet. There were bottles inside it, dozens of bottles and dozens of glasses. The glasses and the bottles clinked against each other as he drew out a whisky bottle and then a glass. He spilled a little whisky over the edge of the glass, but there was enough left for him to take a deep drink. He put the glass down, and stood quite still, looking at Clarissa. Her colour was better. She was trying to get up. He waited until she was sitting in the chair, clutching at her swollen throat. She did not once look at him.

Ten minutes had passed since he had telephoned Craigie, and there was no more danger now.

At last she spoke in a hoarse voice which only just reached him.

'Why don't you shoot me?'

'You have a lot to talk about yet,' said Tim.

She took one hand from her throat and held it out appealingly.

'If I tell you everything will—will you shoot me? Tim, you won't make me go through the trial, you won't make me suffer like that. You won't let them *hang* me!'

Tim said nothing.

'I'll tell you everything if you'll only shoot me. If you don't promise, I won't talk, no one will ever talk! Promise, Tim!'

He drew a deep breath. He hated promising her anything

knowing that he would not keep it, but he had to make her talk.

He said, 'All right, Clarissa.'

'You—you mean it?'

'I'll shoot you,' Tim said.

And then she began to talk...

Ten minutes later, when Craigie arrived in person with his men, she had told Tim all that he needed to know and she screamed to him to carry out his promise. But he took her arm and forced it up into her back and made her go ahead of him, to open the door.

Hadley entered the Whitehall office at half-past five that afternoon, and with him were Virnov, Kellaby of the United States delegation, Matutin of France and Soo of China, Craigie and Loftus were there to greet them. Tim, after making his report, had gone. No one knew where. Craigie and Loftus had decided that it was best to let him go, for they knew that he would return.

Marchant was at Cannon Row Police Station. Miller and his men were now searching Marchant's home and private office and Clarissa's flat. He had twice reported that the necessary evidence was there. They had found the addresses of the little dark men, who were being rounded up by the dozen.

Hadley and his companions had just come from the Great Hall.

Solemnly, he presented the others. Craigie found his hand tender after he had finished shaking hands, and Loftus was flexing his fingers. It was an odd little scene, and the outburst of talking which followed was equally affecting. Virnov took the lead; when he had finished, Loftus laughed a little with embarrassment.

'Don't thank me,' he said. 'Kemble...'

'Where is this Kemble?' asked Virnov.

'He'll soon be back,' said Craigie. 'I have the full report of Clarissa Kaye's confession here. You will not want to be worried with the details.'

'Please!' exclaimed Virnov. 'I would like to be worried, if that is the word, with *everything*.'

So Craigie talked.

He told them what they had discovered up to that day, and of Loftus's conclusion after he had left Marchant; and then he filled in the details with Clarissa's story.

Clarissa had told how she had first joined Wilkinson because of the obvious activities of *Warning*, how he had trusted her and how she had told Marchant. That was when she had joined in the great conspiracy. The one purpose was to bring disaster to *Uno*. How it was achieved had not greatly mattered.

Marchant had thought of using the northern Shovians, all of whom had been recruited from a subsidiary plant which he secretly owned in Shovia. Pirani had been selected as the victim of the plot; he was, eventually, to be found guilty of the conspiracy, after his death. He had been frightened by threats on his life, coming anonymously; that explained his unusual manner at the Emergency Assembly. Suspicion had been directed towards him in San Patino and other small countries. The scheme had been cleverly planned to make it look as if Shovia were genuinely afraid of Russia, and suspicion had been planted in the minds of the San Patino Government suggesting that they had the support of Russia.

Loftus had been right in his general analysis of Marchant's motivation and actions. Clarissa had admitted that first

Wilkinson and later the Department had worried them and forced them to act too quickly and too carelessly. The attack on Colston had been arranged because Marchant was afraid that the Department was getting too close to the truth. An attack on his residence would suggest that he was a victim. The little blue box with the explosive was to be stolen. Then the replica, containing papers, was to be planted on Pirani—as it had been done, simply to mislead anyone who found it, for Parmitter had known of it. Lionel had 'told' Wilkinson to impress the man with his sincerity. Marchant had done everything he could to discredit Parmitter before killing him. He had sent Kolsti to see him before the day of the attempt on Virnov; if Kolsti were caught, Parmitter would be blamed for a part in the conspiracy. Marchant had hoped that Parmitter's death would make the police ease off their inquiries. Then Wilkinson had been told by Lionel that he thought Pirani had stolen the blue box. That explained Wilkinson's move on the night of the performance. Clarissa should have received a message from Marchant not to attend Pirani's reception. She had told Tim that this message had been sent, but had gone astray.

Loftus thought it probable that Marchant had deliberately let her go, in case she should not be strong enough to withstand interrogation.

The explosion at Pirani's had a double motive. First, to suggest that Pirani had the explosive in his possession and, afterwards, for Shovia to stand convicted. Second, to kill Wilkinson and the others of *Warning* as it was known that they would be present.

Faced with Wilkinson's accusation, Lionel had done the thing any weak man might have done: he had lied. From there the danger to the Marchants had increased in tempo. The explosive itself was to have been planted that afternoon by a man—the man Tim had seen—with forged papers. He had to leave the box, and get away.

Marchant had always arranged that Clarissa or Lionel should negotiate with the dark men. Craigie thought that Marchant had always intended first to try to blame his son and then, if necessary, his niece. At every step, he had planned to protect himself.

'How much was sincere; how much was vanity; and how much was evil,' said Loftus, 'no one was ever likely to know. The trial of Marchant and of Clarissa Kaye might answer some of those questions. Certainly it would focus the attention of the world on the desperate need for *Uno*.'

Virnov took off his *pince nez*, and nodded gently.

'Yes, my friend,' he said. 'It has been absorbing. And it is a great tribute to you, Mr. Prime Minister.' He smiled gravely at Hadley. 'Such a department as this Z, now—almost it is worthy of a different country!'

The Prime Minister presided at a dinner party, held four months afterwards, a few days after the trials. At Hadley's request, Tim Kemble sat on his left. Wilkinson and Mendicott were also there. It was a gay gathering; for once Polly George and Christine Loftus and the wives of other agents were present at an official Department Z gathering.

Tim proposed the toast of Virnov.

George put on an act...

Hadley proposed, with quiet eloquence, the health of Department Z.

ABOUT THE AUTHOR

John Creasey, born in 1908, was a paramount English crime and science fiction writer who used myriad pseudonyms for more than six hundred novels. He founded the UK Crime Writers' Association in 1953. In 1962, his book *Gideon's Fire* received the Edgar Award for Best Novel from the Mystery Writers of America. Many of the characters featured in Creasey's titles became popular, including George Gideon of Scotland Yard, who was the basis for a subsequent television series and film. Creasey died in Salisbury, UK, in 1973.

DEPARTMENT Z

FROM OPEN ROAD MEDIA

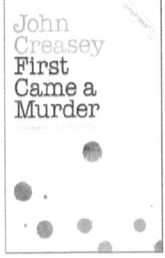

OPEN ROAD
INTEGRATED MEDIA

OPEN ROAD

INTEGRATED MEDIA

Find a full list of our authors and
titles at www.openroadmedia.com

FOLLOW US
@OpenRoadMedia